Firefly Season

a novel

✳✳✳

by Melanie Lageschulte

LARGE PRINT EDITION

Firefly Season: a novel
© 2021
by Melanie Lageschulte
Fremont Creek Press

Kindle: 978-1-952066-18-4
Paperback: 978-1-952066-19-1
Hardcover: 978-1-952066-20-7
Large-Print Paperback: 978-1-952066-21-4

Cover illustration by Melanie Lageschulte
House image: tokar/Shutterstock.com
Background image: robynleigh/iStock.com

Web: fremontcreekpress.com

ALSO BY MELANIE LAGESCHULTE

The Growing Season series
Growing Season
Harvest Season
The Peaceful Season
Waiting Season
Songbird Season
The Bright Season
Turning Season
The Blessed Season
Daffodil Season
Firefly Season

Short fiction
A Tin Train Christmas

1

The hostas were only two dollars each, and Melinda couldn't say no. Her only question was: How many would it take to span the north foundation of her farmhouse?

"I have several with stripes of white, they really stand out." The plants' proud owner pointed to a row on the end of her table, which had a prime spot right in front of Prosper's water tower.

"And some with yellow variations in the leaves, too. Of course, the elephant-ear varieties will cover a lot of ground. How much space are you trying to fill?"

"Too much." Melinda sighed and adjusted the brim of her floppy straw hat. It wasn't even noon, and only early May, but the sun was already bright and hot over the city's small-and-only park. "Someone planted a huge bed with ferns decades ago. But they're dying out, no matter what I try."

"Well, time for a change, then. Just let me know when you've decided." The older woman moved away and began to rearrange the transplants she'd brought to Prosper's first plant swap. Almost twenty tables were set up in the park, with green thumbs from all around the area offering slips of perennials, early-start annuals, and young vegetable plants. While many vendors asked for small fees for their wares, a few were happy to give away the excess they'd started indoors.

Finally, Melinda pointed out six hostas from the middle of the pack, then three more from the right. And four from the left.

They were all so lush and healthy, and she could imagine just how wonderful they would look once they got into the ground and were able to stretch their roots. She'd want to plant them as soon as possible, but that wasn't going to be a problem. Melinda had two sets of helping hands that day.

When the woman reached for the stack of cardboard flats resting under the table, Melinda gently waved her off.

"I have several plastic totes in the car," she explained. "I came prepared to buy in bulk." Then another variety caught her eye. "Oh, I can't help it. I'll take five of those, too. All of them do well under trees, right?"

"Sure do. You get that bed full, you'll find somewhere to put the rest of them, I'm sure. And of course, hostas are hard to kill."

Melinda grimaced as she thought of her dear Hobo, who was one of the sweetest dogs in the world. Except when he raced around her northern-Iowa acreage, hot on the trail of squirrels. Or coated himself with mud down at the creek, then flopped in whatever patch of shade was most convenient. Her barn cats, Sunny and Stormy, also planted themselves wherever they pleased. Which always seemed to be smack-dab in the middle of whichever flower bed was currently showing off its best blooms. But the hostas should have a fighting chance, as long as the sheep didn't get out and trample them. And if the rabbits left them alone ...

"Hard to kill, huh?" Melinda reached for her wallet. "Load me up. I'll find somewhere to put them. Oh, one other thing: How do they react to paint?"

"Paint?" The woman laughed.

"I'm having my house painted sometime this summer. I suspect they'll get splattered."

"I'm guessing you're going with latex, right? Should wash off in the next rain. Or, worst-case scenario, they'll just have a few more speckles on their leaves."

As Melinda handed over the cash, she reminded herself that splurging on a few extra plants wouldn't make one bit of difference to her renovation budget. Her charming farmhouse looked its best from a distance, as it needed a serious sprucing up. Getting the exterior painted, and redoing the roof, were going to take up a serious chunk of time, as well as money, in the next few months.

In the end, it would all be worthwhile. She couldn't wait until it was finished, until Horace could see his family's home receive the updates he and his brother hadn't been able to afford. Or maybe, two elderly bachelor farmers simply hadn't cared how the house looked. More likely, they'd been unwilling to spend the cash to spruce it up.

Thinking of Horace drew Melinda's thoughts to the peony beds on the south side of the house. They were planted by Anna, his mother, decades ago, and were due to bloom in about a month. Which Melinda calculated would be just about the time a painting crew might roll up her gravel drive and plant their scaffolding in place.

"It's a good thing that peonies are just as tough as hostas," she told the woman. "They're going to be underfoot, too."

"Just tell the guys to watch where they're stepping with those heavy boots, and everything will be fine." The woman paused. "I guess I'm assuming it'll be a bunch of men doing the work."

"That's just it. I don't know for sure who's going to do it." Melinda rolled her eyes. "If you know of any female house painters, I'm all ears. Somehow, I think they'd be more careful with the flowers than the men. But beggars can't be choosers. I haven't had time to get any estimates yet."

"My neighbor was pleased with the crew that did his place last summer. Let's see. Oh, yes, I know the name."

Melinda was glad the seller's adult daughter and husband were there to help other customers, as this conversation was netting her far more than a sweet deal on hostas. The woman reached into her apron for a scrap of paper and a pen. "Here. It's worth giving them a call."

"Thanks so much." Melinda tucked the lead into her purse. It was a start, at least. Uncle Frank and Aunt Miriam had been back from their Hawaiian vacation for a few weeks now, and Melinda's routines at both Prosper Hardware and her farm were slowly returning to normal. But there was always something happening in Prosper to divert her time and attention. And for a town with only two hundred people, that was pretty amazing.

Or maybe not. Because this rural community moved to the rhythm of everyday life, the comings and goings and the ups and downs. Melinda hated to think of it, but when she lived in Minneapolis for all those years, her world had actually been much smaller than it was now. Her circle of awareness hadn't extended beyond her close friends and coworkers and, quite honestly, herself. But here, everyone was connected. And the smallest change or challenge set up a ripple effect that drew so many into its wake.

Along with all that, there was so much happening in just the next few weeks. A crew would arrive Monday to repair Prosper Hardware's roof, and the store's inventory was still transitioning to its summer stock. Frank and Miriam would move in a few weeks, and their Victorian on Cherry Street still had to be prepped for its eventual sale. Melinda hadn't even started to work up her garden plot. The pasture fence needed to be checked for new holes. And then, there was that recuperating donkey in her barn ...

A small hand grabbed hers, and she looked down at the little boy whose inquisitive brown eyes were so much like his father's.

"Did you find some plants?" Aiden eyed the display of greenery with the awe of a five-year-old awash in new experiences. This was his first visit to Prosper, and the first time he'd met Melinda. He lived with his mom, two hours away in Elkton, which meant he only saw his dad every other weekend. But rather than be overwhelmed by everything that was unfamiliar and strange, the little boy seemed to be soaking up the day.

Melinda found herself giving Aiden's hand a little squeeze. "Yes, I did! See the ones there on the ground? Those are all ... ours."

Aiden's eyes widened. "They are? Are we going to plant them?"

"We sure are. Once we get back to the farm, you and your dad are going to help me."

She'd been very reluctant to meet Josh
Vogel's son, as she and Josh had only been
dating for four months. But now, Melinda was
so glad she'd finally agreed. Sure, it had been
nerve-wracking to see Josh's truck come up
her lane just a few hours ago, but Aiden hadn't
been one bit shy to meet his dad's friend. Of
course, Hobo's enthusiastic greeting
smoothed things over considerably. Even
Stormy and Sunny, who often kept an eye out
for arrivals and departures from the
weathered boards of Horace's old picnic table,
had tolerated Aiden's eager pets.

Josh's veterinary clinic was in Swanton,
about ten miles away, but he'd started a call-
sharing program with Prosper's office several
months ago. That meant he was a familiar face
in town, and he'd been momentarily sidelined
by someone seeking free advice. Aiden's
excitement grew when his father reappeared
at his side. "Dad, look what Melinda got!
There's so many!"

"I see. She's going to keep us busy this
afternoon." Josh smiled at Melinda and, for a
second, she thought he might kiss her, right
there in front of everyone. The woman behind
the table eyed them with curious amusement.

"Why, Doctor Vogel, isn't it a beautiful day?" She motioned to her husband, who gave a wave of greeting. "I can't thank you enough for what you did for Tiny. I don't know what she ate, but my goodness, was she sick!"

"Oh, it was no trouble. I'm glad she's on the mend. You'd be surprised what dogs can get into." He gave Melinda a knowing look. "Cats, too."

She smiled as she recalled a frantic trip to Josh's clinic that, in the end, had more than one happy outcome. "I'll go get the totes, if you two care to stand guard until I get back."

"I'll help!" Aiden was quick to volunteer. "I can carry some."

Josh ruffled his son's hair. "Well, you're big and strong. I'm sure Melinda would like that."

I do, she thought as they wound their way through the growing crowd in the park, Aiden still clinging to her hand. *In fact, I like all of this much more than I thought I would.*

But she was relieved when they finally made their way out of the crowd and reached Lizzie, Horace's old truck. The sight of Melinda Foster, forty-one and childless, walking through the park with an unfamiliar child clutching her hand had drawn quite a crop of curious smiles and nosy stares.

"Lizzie's temperamental, but I'm glad I brought her along," she told Aiden after she finally dropped the tailgate. The brown paint did a passable job of disguising the plentiful pockets of rust, but Melinda was reminded of them every time she tried to slide the latches. "We'll have lots of room for all of our plants."

"I like Lizzie," Aiden said. "Can I ride home with you?"

Melinda shook her head. "I don't think your mom and dad would like that. Your car seat's in Dad's truck, remember? It's only six miles to the farm, so it's not far to go." But she knew what might make the little boy smile. "How about, once we get there, I'll park Lizzie in the shade and you can sit behind the wheel for a bit? Hobo can join you; he likes Lizzie, too."

Melinda let Aiden take the smallest empty tote while she carried the rest. They had just started their return trip when a familiar voice called her name. She turned to find August Kleinsbach, the owner of Prosper's co-op, suddenly stationed at her elbow.

"Hey, Auggie. How's it going?"

Sometimes, there were advantages to having nosy friends. Auggie was known for his knack at gathering gossip, but that skill worked both ways. It wouldn't take him long to spread the truth about the little boy following her around. Melinda made introductions, and Aiden reached out to shake Auggie's hand.

"Well." Auggie raised his eyebrows, impressed. "Someone's raising you right." He turned to Melinda. "Here, let me take some of those. That's a lot to carry."

They're empty, Melinda wanted to remind him as he helped himself to three off the top. But it was no use. Auggie would tail them as long as he could, eager for the scoop on this new little face in town.

"I saw Emmett and Patricia this morning, working inside the barbershop." Melinda shifted the totes in her arms as they strolled slowly, mindful of Aiden's much-shorter legs. "Looks like they're painting. How's the inside coming along?"

"What do you mean?" Auggies brown eyes snapped with humor behind his thick-rimmed glasses. "I'm not part of the project, you know."

"Oh, come on." Melinda gave her friend the side-eye. "Main Street's only four blocks long, and there's rarely anything new happening along it. I don't believe for one minute that you haven't somehow scored access to see the renovations."

Melinda knew Auggie well, and he sighed. "Yeah, OK. Here's the deal."

Even though the storefront had been vacant for years, the black-and-white, hexagon-shaped floor tiles were still in great shape. There was a lot of natural light, and plenty of wall space for the counters and sinks. The plumbing and electrical needed upgrades, but wouldn't break the bank.

Auggie missed nothing, but that also meant he saw the potential in everything. "In short, it's the perfect space for a barber shop."

"And since he bought it from the city for a song, it's worth it."

"Exactly. Of course, the place is still dirty."

They'd reached the hostas table, and Josh helped Aiden fill his little tote while Melinda scooped up more of her new plants. "Well, that's easy enough to fix," she told Auggie. "Grandma Shrader always said, 'soap's cheap and water's free.'"

"She was a wise woman." Auggie had worked at Prosper Hardware during high school. "But I don't know about water being free these days. The council's raising the rates, I hear. Highway robbery! We business owners are already paying more than our fair share."

"Hey! It's a beautiful day. Don't start in about that." Jerry Simmons, Prosper's mayor and a retired school principal, had joined their group. Jerry was as disappointed as everyone else when Prosper's middle- and high-school students moved to Swanton several years ago, but he often sported a purple-and-white cap to support the teams.

"You know how it is. The city's costs are always going up, and that includes water and sewer."

"Yeah, I know." Auggie crossed his arms. "You have to pass it along." Then he noticed what Jerry had in his hands, and it wasn't a flat of plants. "What are you doing with those?"

Jerry fanned out a ring of paint chips to display various shades of soft green, pale blue and white. "Taking an informal survey." He peered up at Prosper's water tower. "You know that thing needs work. If I wasn't mayor, I'd say it looks like crap."

Auggie narrowed his eyes. "Don't tell me

that's why you want to raise our water rates! For a facelift?"

"Nope. This is a side project, and we've put it off for too long as it is." Jerry turned to Melinda, seeking the support his longtime friend apparently wouldn't give. "Don't you think it's a good idea to get some feedback from people today? I mean, look at this crowd."

Melinda used to work in marketing, but she wasn't sure what to say. There were a lot of people enjoying the plant swap, but many of them were probably from out of town. Like so many of the community's events these days, it was organized by Vicki Colton, proprietor of Prosper's only gift shop, Meadow Lane. And whenever something was happening in their little community, Vicki made sure the news spread a good thirty miles in any direction. If people came to Prosper for any reason, there was a chance they'd spend some money there, as well as time.

Even so, Jerry needed a little encouragement. And Melinda knew how daunting it was to stare at paint samples and search for just the right color. Her farmhouse was white, and would remain so. But she had dozens of shades to pick from.

"Well, it's always a good idea to give people some say in a project. But you have a lot of choices there. If you give people too many options, they get overwhelmed and can't decide. Maybe have the council members pick their favorites, then do an online survey."

Jerry's frown made it clear he had no idea how to set up such a poll, and Melinda instantly wished she hadn't suggested it. Because if he followed through on the idea, Nancy Delaney would have to do all the work. As city clerk and librarian, she was the town's only full-time employee. And she had enough on her plate.

Except today. Melinda spotted her friend on the other end of the park, wandering through the large booth set up by Swanton's commercial greenhouse. Richard Everton was with her, and Nancy was clearly having a great time. Nancy was divorced, and Richard was widowed; why shouldn't they enjoy each other's company?

Josh and Aiden had taken the first filled totes to the truck, and Melinda motioned for Auggie and Jerry to help her sort the rest of the hostas into bins. If they had their hands busy, they might be less likely to argue. At least, it was worth a try.

"Anyway, Jerry, maybe you'll want to focus on some other color choices today," Melinda suggested. "It's time for the hanging baskets to go up on Main Street. Have you talked to Miriam?"

Melinda's aunt was unofficially in charge of the planters, and she and Jerry had often clashed when it came time to pick out a palette. She was at home today, packing for the move, determined to resist floral temptation until she and Frank were settled.

Jerry raised his chin. "I sure have. Purple and white is the theme this year." He pointed at his team-spirit cap. "Just as it should be. No pink, red, peach, whatever. Just because impatiens come in a rainbow of colors doesn't mean we have to get too crazy. The greenhouse says they'll drop the plants off at the store this afternoon."

"Perfect." One more item could be crossed off Melinda's to-do list. Well, almost. "Esther and I hope to plant on Monday. I think Mom's going to help us."

Josh and Aiden were back, and it was time to go. "And Jerry?" Melinda pointed at the ring of paint chips before she picked up the last tote. "I live outside of town, so I don't officially get a vote. But I really like that light celadon green."

Lizzie roared to life after her usual two-sputter cough. Melinda kept an eye out for pedestrians as she edged away from the curb. The post office's flags snapped in the breeze, and several people enjoyed the spot of shade provided by Prosper Hardware's dark-green awning. Meadow Lane looked to be as busy as her family's store, as its paned front windows showed it was packed with customers.

She saw Emmett Beck washing the front windows of his soon-to-be-relocated barber shop, and gave Lizzie's horn a toot. Crossing the railroad tracks caused her to tap the brakes, mindful of the plants bumping along in the back. Prosper Feed Co.'s towers stood tall and proud on the west edge of town, and its lot was packed with trucks and cars.

There was just enough time to get home, have a bite of lunch, and plant the hostas before Aiden would probably need a nap.

Home.

The thought made Melinda smile as Lizzie chugged out into the countryside, the truck's flatbed half-packed with hostas and her heart overflowing with anticipation and hope. Another summer stretched out ahead, just like this two-lane highway. She cranked down Lizzie's window and turned up the radio.

But what she saw in her rearview mirror made her laugh.

Prosper's western boundary was marked with a large mural. Its painting of Main Street was more colorful than the real thing, but just as charming, and capped off with the town's unofficial slogan: "Prosper: The Great Little Town that Didn't."

"Some towns have a slogan on their water tower." She smirked and stepped on the gas. "But while Jerry's game to give ours a facelift, I don't think that's what he has in mind."

2

Melinda breathed a sigh of relief when she spotted Auggie's truck in front of Prosper Hardware Monday morning. He always prided himself on getting to the store by the time she rolled in at seven; but today, he'd promised to do more than start the coffee pot.

Two of the roofing company's trucks were already parked in the back gravel lot. And Auggie, who prided himself on knowing everything happening in town, was aware of just where the patches needed to go.

"His nosiness isn't always welcome," Melinda reminded herself as she gathered up her lunch tote and a pan of cinnamon rolls. "But when the crew's itching to get started, it's good to have a know-it-all already on the scene."

Auggie waved from his metal folding chair, a steaming cup already in his hand. "The guys are upstairs. I reminded them to give the ceiling another look, make sure they haven't missed anything, before they get on the roof."

He was perched in his favorite spot: close to the vintage sideboard, so the brew and any treats would be within easy reach; yet in front of the right-side window, so he wouldn't miss anything that moved along Main Street. Which wasn't much, especially at this hour. But then, it was better to be prepared.

"What's in the tote bag?" Melinda frowned as she set her things on the oak showcase that served as the store's counter. "I told you on Saturday I planned to bring treats today."

"Oh, I didn't bring snacks." Auggie hid a smirk behind his mug. It looked like he'd swept the floor, and the showcase was already polished to a shine. Which meant that Melinda, as well as the rest of the guys, would be able to give him their undivided attention.

She waited for him to say more, he waited for her to press him, and she quickly gave up. Whatever it was, she'd find out as soon as Auggie had a full house.

An ominous rumble erupted over their heads, then a string of profanities and a crash echoed down the open stairwell.

"They're supposed to fix the roof, not wreck

the floor," Auggie muttered.

"Sorry!" someone shouted above their heads. "Nothing serious."

Melinda ran to the foot of the stairs, where she was met by a young guy with a plastic tackle box in his hand. "Brad's a klutz this morning, he backed into these." He held up his find. "I'm afraid your nice stack is ruined. What are these, anyway?"

"They're small tool kits, something special for Mother's Day. There's a screwdriver set inside and a cute pair of work gloves."

He snapped the kit open. "Hey, these are nice. You know, that's Sunday, and I haven't gotten anything for my mom yet."

Of course he hadn't. And neither had most of the males in and around Prosper. It was the reason the tool kits, which had been steady sellers since Melinda and Esther dreamed them up last month, were flying off the end-cap display by the register.

"It comes with an apron, too." Melinda smiled, as she was about to make another sale. "Green with white lettering, says 'Prosper Hardware' on the front. You can't get them anywhere else."

"I'll take it." He snapped the lid closed.

"Actually, I'll take two. Grandma might like one."

Melinda took this opportunity to tell him about Meadow Lane next door, and Vicki's generous selection of greeting cards. This young man wasn't Vicki's target customer, but the next-closest place to buy a card was ten miles away in Swanton.

"Great! Oh, while you're at it, could you guys please bring down a bunch more of those kits? I need to refill the display. I keep the aprons at the counter."

A few minutes later, three sheepish men came down the steps with full arms. Still apologetic about the commotion they'd made, they even arranged the boxes in columns based on color. Just as they were finishing up, the bell above the front door jingled and veterinarian John "Doc" Ogden raised his eyebrows at Melinda.

"Did you hire more help?" He pulled off his work boots and left them on the mat. Based on how dirty they were, it was clear Doc had been in at least one barn already that morning. "Or just find some young guys to do your bidding?"

"The latter, I guess." Their task completed,

the trio disappeared through the metal door into the back of the building, which housed the wood shop. "They're actually here to patch the roof, but I caught them just in time to give me a hand."

Doc went straight to the sideboard and pulled two rolls from the pan. "Oh, thank you! I'm famished. Took an energy bar when I left home but that was about three hours ago." He rubbed his eyes as he checked the large round clock on the wall. "But these expectant mothers, they like to take their time."

"Don't I know it." Bill Larsen came up from the back, his tool belt already wrapped around his waist. As the store's only other full-time employee, he spent most of his time filling custom lumber orders. "Emily's feet are already killing her." The Larsens were expecting their third child in the fall. "Takes her forever to get out to the car."

Melinda shot him a look.

"I know. I need to shut up. It's just been a long week, that's all."

"It's only Monday." Doc groaned as he dropped into his chair. "We're just getting started."

Bill grabbed a cup of coffee. "I hear ya.

Tommy's had an earache since yesterday morning; I was up with him most of last night." He good-naturedly pointed at Melinda. "See, I'm not trying to be the worst husband of the year. So, Doc, who's the new baby today?"

"A calf." Doc took a hearty bite from his first roll. "Lots of little ones lately. We had a litter of piglets yesterday that needed some help. And then last night, Karen went out north of town to deliver a foal." Doc had caused quite a stir among the local farmers when he hired a female veterinarian, but Karen Porter had quickly earned their respect.

Auggie was strangely quiet, and Melinda wondered how much longer he could keep whatever news he had to himself. George Freitag, the group's elder statesman at eighty-four, had just arrived, and Jerry and Uncle Frank soon completed the circle. Once the usual gossip about the weekend and the weather quieted down, Auggie reached for his tote.

"What do you have there?" Frank was curious. Auggie was always full of news, but rarely brought in any supporting evidence to back up his gossip.

"Oh, something I've been carrying around."

Everyone waited. Finally, George sighed with irritation. "I'm too old for this suspense. Why don't you just tell us what's going on?"

Auggie pulled out a thin stack of paper, then unfolded it to reveal it was one large sheet.

"What's that?" Jerry was already out of his chair, determined to get a closer look. "A drawing? Looks like blueprints."

"Not yet." Auggie carefully smoothed the panels across his lap. "Just a little sketch."

Frank leaned over. "Looks to me like more than a sketch. Hold that up so the other guys can see."

It obviously was the cue Auggie was waiting for. With a huge grin, he quickly complied.

Doc let out a low whistle. "Is that the co-op's lot?"

George motioned for Auggie to pass the drawing around, and Auggie reluctantly agreed. "Yeah. Now, don't wrinkle it. I've been working hard on this thing, and I'm not done yet."

Auggie had whipped the area's residents into a frenzy at the New Year's celebration with his announcement that he planned to add a non-diesel gas pump to Prosper Feed Co.

The community hadn't had a true gas station in thirty years, so the promise of even one pump for their cars and trucks was something people in the area were eager to embrace. Swanton had several convenience stores, since it was a metropolis of ten thousand and also the county seat; but the only other place nearby to get gas was Eagle River, a good ten miles in the opposite direction.

"There's a lot of stuff on here." Jerry was now behind George's chair, taking it all in. "Where do you expect the pump to go, exactly?"

"Current plan is, there on the north side. Might still change it, though. I've decided, we might as well have two. Go big or go home. My guy has to come out and dig, either way, to install the underground tank."

Frank frowned. "I saw the two diesel pumps in the back, like now. I thought the new one would go there, too."

"Oh, I changed my mind. With two, we'll need more room." Auggie's excitement was contagious, and the guys were all ears. "I'll extend the drive around to the north, see. People will come in the front, just like now, drive past the entrance, then hang a right and pull under the canopy."

Jaws dropped around the room, including Melinda's.

Auggie stared at his friends like they were daft. "Who wants to pump gas in the rain and snow? The farmers don't mind, but my new customers will want to fill up in comfort."

"That's nice," Frank finally said. "I see what you're saying. But that's a big change. It's going to be quite a bit of work."

Auggie shrugged as he paused for a bite of cinnamon roll. Doc, who used to serve on the city council, glanced at Jerry and shook his head. The mayor, looking as if he'd aged a few years in the past few minutes, settled back in his chair and turned in Auggie's direction.

"A gas pump is one thing, but this is a whole other ball of wax. You're going to need the council's approval to make this happen." Which meant that Frank, and at least two of the other five members, would have to greenlight Auggie's proposal.

"Seriously? It's just a canopy. It's not like I'm putting up a building."

"Still. You'll need to submit a revised site plan. Who's your engineer?"

That had Auggie stumped. "Hmm. Well, the

Eagle River co-op guy gave me the name of someone to install the canopy. I'll see who he recommends." The drawing was back in Auggie's hands, and he held it out for one more proud examination. "Are you sure all this fuss is necessary? I mean, we're just talking about little Prosper here. This isn't Mason City."

Jerry's smile was a bit strained. "State code; it'll get you every time. Nope, we have to play by the rules around here. Two new pumps, an expanded drive, a canopy ... geez, Auggie, anything else?"

"Actually, yeah. I'm not adding on to the building," he said quickly. "At least, not right now. But I think I'll freshen up inside. I think I'll take out the old coffeepot table, and ..."

"Are you serious?" Melinda couldn't stay quiet. "Your regulars will mutiny. I bet that corner's been that way for years!"

"At least sixty," Auggie admitted. "But this will be better. I'll put a booth by the big window, so they can still see all the action outside. And once the multi-temperature beverage station goes in, they'll forget how it used to be."

Melinda stared at Bill, hoped he'd jump in

with something, anything, that would knock Auggie back a notch or two. But he didn't like confrontation, and just picked at his cinnamon roll.

George finally spoke. "Those guys only care that their coffee is hot and black. Just like you. What are they going to think of this ... beverage-station thing?"

"It's a step up for Prosper Feed Co. More options for more customers." He turned toward Melinda, who leaned against the counter. "Diversification is good, right?"

He wanted her to back him up. She decided to try, but chose her words carefully. "If people come to the co-op for gas, some of them may simply pay at the pump. If they want something to drink, they might come inside. But what if they don't need feed or animal supplies? Can you really make enough money off them to pay for these upgrades?"

"You already sell pop," George reminded Auggie. "Got a case, just like here."

"Melinda's right, I'll need to sell more stuff to more people to make this a going thing." Auggie checked the time, then made sure there were no customers on the sidewalk that might try to slip in early. "I know I can trust all of you to keep this part under your hats for now. I'm thinking about converting a section of the far aisle to carry people stuff, not animal stuff. Bread and cereal, a few toiletries. Not much, but a little taste of those big convenience stores."

Frank turned pale, but said nothing. Melinda suddenly felt sick.

How had Auggie's plan morphed from an extra gas pump to such elaborate renovations? And something that was sure to compete with Prosper Hardware? In a town this tiny, her family's store had long ago cornered the market on day-to-day necessities. Sure, the store sold so much more than that, and a wider variety than what Auggie could pack on a few cleared-off shelves, but ...

"You have some big ideas there." Doc's tone was cheerful but guarded, and Melinda couldn't tell exactly where he stood. He let his diplomacy slip, however, when he offered Frank a quick eye roll.

You know Auggie, the look said. *He always has some crazy idea up his sleeve. Don't worry, he'll get bored with it soon enough.*

Jerry drained his mug. It was time to go; not just because the clock's hands inched toward eight, but because of the chill that had settled between Auggie and Frank. "Well, I need to get across the street. Auggie, you'll want to get those blueprints together in the next few weeks. It could take a while for them to be reviewed."

"By whom?" Auggie's face wore the mad-owl expression that always appeared when things weren't going his way. "There's five council members, and then yourself, by my count. Shouldn't take that long."

"And the city attorney, and the planning and zoning experts. We have 'people,' you know. We call them when we need them."

Melinda's spirits sank further. Auggie's plan wasn't just bad news for Prosper Hardware. Outside consultants had to be expensive, and little Prosper's accounts were far from flush. This was going to cost the city a pretty penny, even if the proposal was never approved.

Auggie folded down his dreams to a more-manageable size and returned them to his tote, then marched to the sideboard and gathered the cups and spoons. He might be stubborn and outspoken, but he always made good on his pledge to wash up.

"All this red tape," he muttered as he

started down the aisle to the utility alcove, the metal tray gripped tight in his hands. "One thing after another! Makes it hard for a guy to get ahead around here."

Everyone looked at each other, their faces grim despite the sunshine outside Prosper Hardware's windows. It was going to be a beautiful spring day, but it was certainly gloomy inside the store.

"Well, now." Doc fought back a yawn. "I wasn't expecting that this morning."

"Nothing ever stays the same, I guess." Jerry crossed his arms and leaned against the sideboard.

George let out a low chuckle. "A town this small, in the middle of nowhere; you might think it would."

"This isn't nowhere." Frank stared at the oak floor, then around at the store that had been in Melinda's family for over a century. "This is home for so many people, including us. Including this business."

"That's not what I meant," George said kindly. "I love this town as much as anyone else. Lived here my whole life." He rubbed his lined hands together. "Guess I have some news of my own. Or rather, a big favor."

"Might as well ask." Jerry sighed. "It can't be worse than what Auggie wants."

Memorial Day was coming up, and George was the head of the town cemetery's committee. The same guy would mow the grounds again this year, but there was more work to be done before the holiday ceremony. The side gate's latch was broken, countless twigs needed to be picked up, and there were weeds all along the fence and around the flagpole.

"Lots and lots of weeds. It's good exercise." George tried to make it sound appealing. "Who's in?"

"I'd rather fight with Auggie about his quest for world domination," Frank muttered. "And my back agrees. Sorry, George."

Melinda had an idea. "Why don't you call over to the elementary school? Maybe the kids could do it during their PE classes. Call it a community service project, or something."

"Free child labor." George's blue eyes twinkled. "I like that." He looked at Frank. "So, that's it, then. You and Auggie are officially fighting?"

"I don't know." Frank ran a hand through his hair. "I guess we'll see what happens."

The men folded their chairs and put them back against the wall. Jerry took care of Auggie's chair, too, and that's when Melinda realized Auggie had his tote over one arm when he went to wash up.

The cups and spoons waited on the counter by the sink, scrubbed and rinsed and wiped dry, but not returned to the sideboard. Sure enough, he'd slipped out the back.

Bill had already made his escape into the woodshop. Frank and Melinda waved off the rest of their friends, then Melinda put the dishes away.

"If he goes through with this, where does it all end?" Frank whispered, even though they were alone in the store. "He's my friend, I want him to grow his business. I just never thought he'd take things this far."

"You know how he is." Melinda grabbed a fresh dust cloth and attacked the counter. It was already clean, but it gave her something to do.

"He gets an idea and can't let it go. It was almost funny, though, how ignorant he is about site plans and permits and such. I want gas here, too, but maybe the red tape's going to be enough to make him change his tune."

There wasn't any more to say. At least, not for now. Except for one thing.

"Are you going to tell Miriam?" Melinda asked.

"Do you think I should?"

She thought for a moment, looked out to where the light posts waited for their hanging baskets. Those had to get planted, along with everything else that needed to be done around here. And Miriam and Frank were getting ready to move.

Another day was about to begin at Prosper Hardware. But Melinda suddenly felt like Doc, as if she'd been up for hours and hours.

"Maybe not." She shook out the dust cloth, and her mind was made up. "You know what? This can wait. It's only the interior renovations we're worried about, and Auggie said that's still a secret. There's always a chance he'll dial things back when he figures out what it's going to cost. A good chance, actually. He dreams big; but in the end, he's a cheapskate."

"You're right about that." Frank flipped the sign in the front door's window. "I'll keep it under my hat, for now. One thing at a time."

3

The whoosh of the watering can brought Sunny and Stormy over to supervise, but neither cat wanted to get too close.

"It sprays up a bit, huh?" Melinda stepped carefully between the two rows of new hostas. "Unlike your buddy Hobo, you two don't like to get your feet or coats dirty." She glanced toward the windbreak that ran along the north and west sides of her acreage. "I bet that's what he's doing right now, whether he's tracking a rabbit or just rolling in the dirt."

She took a moment to survey last weekend's work, and smiled at how two of the hostas were slightly out of alignment.

"Aiden insisted those were their new homes, remember?" She paused to give Sunny's fluffy-orange coat a quick pet. "Josh and I suggested we move them over a few inches, but no. Somehow, I think he's going to be as stubborn as his dad one day."

It was a rare Saturday off from Prosper
Hardware and, even more unusual, the second
in a row. Frank and Miriam had insisted
Melinda shift her schedule away from the
store's busiest day for at least a few weeks,
given the extra hours she'd clocked while they
were in Hawaii. She suspected they'd missed
the store more than they wanted to admit and,
at least temporarily, were willing to spend
extra time there. And, at least on Frank's side,
procrastinate on packing more boxes for their
upcoming move.

Melinda and Josh had hoped to get away
for a weekend, even if it was only a two-hour
drive to one of the Mississippi River towns.
But they'd decided they were too tired, and too
busy, to make it happen. And Melinda was
pleasantly surprised to discover she didn't
mind at all. What mattered was that they
spent at much time together as possible. Being
with Josh turned even a trip to the superstore
in Swanton into a fun outing. If that made
them boring, well, so be it.

But they still managed to get out and about,
once in a while. They'd gone to Mason City
last night with Karen and her boyfriend for
dinner, and Josh had left after breakfast this

morning. Tomorrow was Mother's Day and, since they'd given up plans for their trip, both of them were free to spend the holiday with their families. And it all worked out that Melinda had this afternoon free as well. Because one of the Schermanns called yesterday with astonishing news.

Melinda had been determined to track down the records for the Fulton Friendship Circle, a ladies' club that had thrived in the township decades ago. Anna Schermann had been a longtime officer in the club, and Ada Arndt, the youngest of the eight siblings, suspected the files were in the storage room at Melinda's farmhouse. But the boxes had never been found.

Anna had apparently passed the files to another of her daughters years ago. Because Edith Clayton had discovered them in the basement of her home in Hampton. She had been a widow for several years, and was now downsizing to an apartment. Her granddaughter, Jen, was getting married in July, and Jen and Andrew were going to buy Edith's home.

Edith offered to bring the records out to the farm that afternoon. The occasion was sure to

turn into an unofficial Schermann family
reunion, but Melinda didn't mind one bit.
Their family had owned this place for more
than a century; Horace's grandfather built the
house. Just because she rented it from him
two years ago, and eventually purchased the
property, didn't mean their memories weren't
still firmly planted in this land.

By Melinda's count, five relatives were
visiting today. Hampton was forty miles away,
and Edith, now in her late eighties, didn't
drive out of town. Jen would bring her to the
farm. Ada and her son, Kevin, were coming
down from Mason City to get their first
glimpse of the mysterious files, and had
promised to stop at Scenic Vista in Elm
Springs to pick up Horace.

While Melinda was excited to see the club's
past come to life through its records, the
group's future looked to be spotty at best. The
search for the files had sparked the
imagination of Fulton Township's current
residents, and the ladies had gamely tried to
jump-start the neighborhood tradition. But
while enthusiasm was plentiful, time was
always in short supply. The women had
ultimately decided to honor tradition with a

wink and a nod, and simply meet for coffee, lunch or a volunteer project whenever some of them could fit it into their hectic schedules.

Hobo dashed past on his way to the water bowl, which waited in the shade under the picnic table. His brown coat was passably clean, but his white feet certainly were not.

As she emptied the last of the watering can's contents into the phlox bed next to the back porch, Melinda swept her gaze around the farmyard and admired its springtime beauty. Horace probably wouldn't have much interest in the women's club records, but his still-keen eyes would be quick to notice everything around him.

The trees were fully leafed out now, and the lawn was, at last, a brilliant green. Clusters of coneflowers and other old-time perennials now peeked out around the foundations of the house and garage, their tender shoots promising riots of color when summer rolled around. The lilac trees down by the road were just about to bloom, as were the peonies nodding in the bright sun along the driveway.

Tiny plants lined the lengths of the recently turned garden, and the chickens clucked and strutted as they sashayed from their coop to their run and back again. Fresh laundry snapped on the clothesline, and the air was filled with birdsong. Her eight ewes enjoyed the tender pasture grass, and Pepper the donkey flexed his oversized ears as he peered out the top half of his barn door.

Yes, this was a wonderful time of year for Horace to visit his former home. Hobo popped through his doggie door without a care in the world, but Melinda sighed as she went into the enclosed back porch. "If only the inside of the house was as presentable as the yard. They're all going to be here in an hour. I'll have to make a mad dash."

As usual, the kitchen was the worst. Dirty dishes were stacked on the counter, and muddy paw prints were clearly visible on the faded linoleum. Hazel, one of Melinda's house cats, looked up from her napping spot in the cyclone of half-read newspapers covering the kitchen table.

Melinda patted Hazel's long brown coat, then gently set her on the floor. "I know you get away with that sometimes. OK, a lot. But company's coming, so pretend you don't know how to do that."

Grace, Hazel's sister, soon appeared in the

open doorway into the dining room. She was also only half-awake, but her fluffy calico tail twitched once, then twice, before her piercing green eyes landed on Melinda's face.

"Yeah, I know. It's a mess around here." Melinda took a few seconds to crease the newspapers into a neat pile. Horace might want to read them. "Sorry, Princess Grace, but your maid's been busy outside this morning."

The first load of laundry, clean and folded in the basket, still waited on the floor by the dining room's built-in buffet. More newspapers and magazines littered the coffee table in the living room, and the tops of the bookcases flanking the fireplace were cluttered with too many things that needed to be put away.

Melinda whipped up a coffee cake and popped it in the oven. If she hurried, she might be able to gulp a sandwich for lunch, speed-clean the downstairs, and squeeze in a shower before her guests arrived.

What a difference forty-five minutes could make. The hardwood floors were swept, and the rooms tidy. A pitcher of fresh tea waited in Horace's ancient refrigerator, and the welcoming aroma of cinnamon filled the kitchen. Some of the windows were thrown open to the warm breeze, and Hobo's paws were clean enough to make him presentable to guests. Grace and Hazel were often wary of visitors and, after a thorough inspection of Melinda's hurried sorting and dusting, had decamped to their safe space under Melinda's bed.

Hobo also knew something was afoot, but remained on the couch. He stared out the picture window, his searching brown eyes trained on the gravel road, as he waited for any sign of company.

"Horace is coming, isn't he?" Melinda stuffed her dust cloth under one arm long enough to give Hobo a hug. "You always know when to start watching."

Ada's car soon appeared, a plume of gravel dust trailing behind it. Hobo sprinted through the house, barking all the way, then ran outside and down the back steps.

Horace slowly unfolded his long legs from the passenger seat, then reached back for his cane. Kevin stood by, a steadying hand on Hobo's collar. Ada patted down her short white hair and hurried around the bumper to give Melinda a warm hug.

"Goodness, it's windy! Living in town, I forget how it can blow out here. At least it's out of the south, bringing us all this warm weather."

Behind his glasses, Kevin's blue eyes were so similar to his mom's and uncle's. "There isn't anything to block it, that's for sure. Feels good to come out, though. Everything is so green!"

Horace gave his greetings, first to Hobo and then Melinda, then turned to study the sheep. The whole flock was at the pasture fence, watching and waiting. It was obvious where Horace wanted to go first, and it wasn't the house.

"Mom, why don't you go in and get settled?" Kevin suggested. "Edith and Jen should be here any minute."

The sheep started to "baaa" and pace as soon as Horace approached. He instinctively reached for the gate latch, but Kevin gently blocked him with one arm. Horace was fairly steady with his cane, but eight overeager ewes jostling for attention would be too much. Annie, who had been a bottle baby and was still Horace's favorite, pushed her way to the front and demanded his attention.

"Easy, girl, let me say hello to everyone else, too!" Which Horace did, but his weathered hand kept reaching over to scratch Annie's dark forehead. Stormy suddenly appeared, and rubbed his cheek on the leg of Horace's jeans.

"There's one of my boys." Horace wanted to reach down and pet Stormy's gray-tabby coat, but wisely thought better of it. "Where is your brother?"

"Sunny might be inside." Melinda scooped up Stormy and moved closer to Horace. His face lit up as he scratched the cat's ears. "They love that little door you cut in the wall there," she said. "They come and go as they please."

"As well they should." Horace looked toward the barn with a gleam in his blue eyes. "Now, where is this donkey I've been hearing about? Where's Pepper?"

"Right this way."

As soon as Horace disappeared through the barn's front door, the sheep made a beeline for their entrance. Between their shuffling hooves and a chorus of "baaas" and Pepper's answering "hee-haws," the once-peaceful barn was suddenly filled with noise. Hobo began to bark, and Sunny ran down the aisle and jumped up on the grain barrels, yowling his determination to not be ignored.

"Who said the country was quiet?" Kevin asked Melinda while he jokingly put his hands over his ears.

Pepper's arrival at her farm hadn't exactly been expected. His former owners weren't too keen on keeping him, and Doc decided the donkey deserved a better place to convalesce while his back leg healed. Melinda had room, and Josh convinced her to take Pepper in. It had been a rough go at first, but Pepper's mood, along with his injury, had steadily improved in the past few weeks. He didn't even flinch when Horace leaned over the fence and offered a hand for a sniff of greeting.

"Well, I'll be." Horace's lined face was filled with shock and delight, but he was often a man of few words. "We had lots of critters over the years, but there's never been a donkey here, as far as I know." He turned to Melinda. "So, is he staying for good, or what?"

She shrugged, but couldn't keep the smile off her face.

"That's a yes," Kevin teased. "I bet it is."

"Nothing's been decided, OK? But Pepper is welcome to stay as long as he wants. The next project is to get him to share the pasture with the sheep. I've been locking the flock in, every so often, to let Pepper get a little exercise on his own. But it's not ideal."

"I'm sorry we took that fence down," Horace said suddenly. "The one that split the pasture in two. It was in bad shape, and we were down to only having sheep and, well, Wilbur and I decided it was beyond repair."

"Don't worry about it. If Pepper's going to stay, everyone needs to get along. But it's a work in progress."

Jen and Edith had arrived while they were in the barn. Melinda was eager to see what Edith had discovered, but was determined to give Horace a full tour if he wanted one. She gestured toward the coop, which was in the far corner of the yard. "We could check on the chickens, if you want. Looks like everyone's in the run, enjoying this nice day."

Horace hesitated, then shook his head. For someone his age, it was going to be quite the hike. "Oh, I can see them from here. Is Pansy still a pain in the butt?"

"Yes, and proud of it." They started for the house instead, and Melinda was reminded of how the west side was more faded than the others. Bearing the brunt of the sun, wind, rain and snow had taken its toll over all those years.

But how many, exactly? This was the perfect time to find out. "I plan to have the house painted this summer. Do you remember when that was done last?"

"Oh, not so long ago," Horace said mildly. "Maybe in the eighties."

Kevin did the math in his head and widened his eyes at Melinda. Thirty-plus years sounded right, given the looks of things.

"Do you remember where you got the paint?" Melinda pressed on. "I really like this shade of white." Or what's still visible of it, she thought but didn't say. "Whatever I pick, it needs to go with the new roof. I want gray-green shingles, like before, but maybe a little darker."

"How about those ribbed-steel panels?" Kevin suggested. "They come in all sorts of finishes these days, and they're virtually indestructible."

"Hey, that's a great idea."

They stared at the house, lost in the possibilities. Its second story had steep roof lines with dormers, which gave it a cottage-like feel. Gray trim outlined the windows. Melinda could see it now, how wonderful it would be when this house was brought back to its full glory, and couldn't wait to get started.

Horace finally sighed. "Well, I don't know. The paint's just white. White house, red barn; it's always been that way. We went to the paint store in Swanton and told the guy what we needed. It came in those big buckets, so we got the discount. We had a crew from Eagle River do the top half of the house, then did the rest ourselves to save money."

Melinda and Kevin exchanged amused looks. *Of course they did.*

"Since we had enough left, we painted the garage, too." Horace's eyes lit up with hope. "Is there any still in the basement? Or out in the machine shed? Maybe you could match it."

Kevin reminded his uncle the family had cleared out the farm's nooks and crannies last spring, before the auction, and anything considered hazardous waste had been donated to the county's recycling program.

"I guess I get to start from scratch, then," Melinda said breezily, as Horace looked disappointed. Leftover paint, in his mind, shouldn't be given away. You never knew when you might need it.

Hobo could hardly contain his excitement over the old friends now gathered around the dining-room table, but Horace simply wiped his shoes on the mat, filled a coffee cup, and gave his sisters and great-niece a smile and short greeting on his way to the living room.

His old recliner had followed him to Scenic Vista, so Horace always planted himself in Melinda's oversized reading chair next to the fireplace. It was a spot that still felt like home. He picked up a newspaper, and settled in. Hobo took up his old post at Horace's feet, and gave a sigh of contentment as he stretched out on the rug. The reassuring sound of Melinda's voice motivated Grace and Hazel to cautiously pad back downstairs, their curiosity about these guests now too strong to resist.

The Schermanns treated Melinda like family, so she never had to worry about playing hostess. Kevin and the ladies had found her cups and plates, helped themselves to the beverages, and sliced the coffeecake and passed it around. All Melinda had to do was wash her hands at the kitchen sink, pour herself some iced tea, and join them in the dining room.

"I'm so glad you came in when you did!" Jen made a gentle drumroll on the table, and her engagement ring caught the sunlight. "We tried to hold off on opening the box, but we couldn't stand the suspense."

"No time to waste." Edith's aged hands moved quickly through a stack of yellowed papers. She was a tiny woman, but her slight figure held a big personality. "Let's dive right in."

Under the watchful eyes of the garish bluebirds darting across the dining room's wallpaper, a decorating decision Ada claimed her mother later regretted, the club's minutes were sorted and passed around the table.

Kevin held up a faded sheet of lined notebook paper. "These are fascinating! Look at this roll call from a meeting in August 1938. 'Mrs. John Caulding, Mrs. A. Robertson ...'"

"No first names for the ladies." There was a sharp note in Edith's voice. "Hard to believe, huh? Women had the vote for almost twenty years by then! But obviously, not much had changed in Fulton Township."

"These from the sixties have them." Jen pointed at her pile.

Ada set her coffee mug aside to study one

report. "And the expectations changed, too. This one is from 1975, one of the final years, and there's a report on the club's philanthropic efforts. Donations to a women's shelter in Waterloo, and garden produce shared with the new food pantry in Swanton."

"Sounds pretty ambitious compared to the early 1950s." Melinda carefully shuffled her stack and made sure no cake crumbs landed between the pages. "This month's presentation was on arranging cut flowers. But most of the minutes describe the 'lavish and elegant luncheon served by Mrs. B. Watson, one of the club's officers.'"

Edith's jaw dropped. "That's Mabel's grandmother. Good lord, she must have been in her sixties by then. And still serving fancy teas to the neighbor women."

"Do we know when the club actually began?" Kevin wanted to know.

"Not sure, but Mother once said it was going strong long before World War I," Ada replied. "She was a teenager then, and remembered the ladies rolling bandages for the Red Cross."

"I don't recall much about the actual meetings held here when I was a girl." Edith had her spectacles planted on the edge of her nose. "But you should have seen the fluffing and dusting and sweeping that proceeded them."

"And it wasn't like this house was dirty," Ada said proudly. "But nothing was too good for the club. And the food was a whole other undertaking."

Anna had set aside her usual menus to craft dainty sandwiches, elaborate cakes, and special salads to impress her neighbors. Beyond scrubbing the house until it gleamed, the girls had to inspect and wash their mother's best dishes, polish the silver, and starch a set of cloth napkins. Then they buffed their nicest shoes and donned their best dresses before the club's members arrived.

"It was so much work, but it was always a special afternoon," Ada recalled. "Mother was always praised for her efforts, and we took pride in that."

Melinda sighed. "Well, we tried our best to replicate the club. Or really, Mabel did. The only official meeting we had was fun, but people have become too casual, I guess. What really matters now, as it did then, is that the women have a chance to get together."

"Exactly!" With a fresh piece of paper, Kevin turned his efforts to creating a detailed inventory of the box's contents. "And you can do that just as easily through volunteer projects or going out for lunch. Why go to all the fuss and bother?"

Jen slid her engagement ring back and forth. "It must have been hard when you joined the club, then, for the newlyweds. I'm sure expectations were very high."

"Oh, you bet." Ada groaned. "If your mother was an exceptional hostess, the ladies expected you to be the same. And if she wasn't, well ..."

"It was your chance to stand apart." Edith reached for another pile of minutes. "Reputations were at stake."

Kevin grimaced. "All that pressure! I assumed those meetings were fun. But they sound more like walking the plank."

Melinda and Jen exchanged a knowing glance. "You obviously don't spend a lot of time around groups of women," Jen told her cousin. "We're ruthless when we want to be. You should see some of the moms at the bridal fairs I've been to." She rolled her eyes. "And my own mom's not much better."

Edith seemed about to say something, but instead set her mouth in a firm line. Ada passed Melinda a look that told her all she needed to know: Edith and her daughter-in-law weren't always on the best of terms.

Melinda stared at the records in her hands. "I just wish we knew more about the club. These files are so interesting, but we still don't know exactly when the group started, or why it fizzled out. Of course, by the seventies, more women were working away from the farm, and there were more social opportunities than before. But it's still a shame it had to disband."

A blur of calico fur flew across the floor, and Grace dived into the cardboard box at Jen's feet.

"Oh, Grace!" Ada laughed as a defiant paw rose from behind the flaps. "I know it's almost empty, but you shouldn't be in there. Just because I set it down, it doesn't mean it's yours."

"Everything is hers." Melinda lifted a protesting Grace out of the way. "Hazel's, too, but definitely Grace's. Hobo and I just live here."

"There are a few more stacks in the bottom." Jen pulled them out, then checked again. "Hey, look at this!" She held up a small, light-blue booklet with staples down its spine.

"A cookbook?" Ada gasped. "I didn't know the club ever put one together." Jen handed it to her aunt, who opened the cover as a sense of anticipation filled the room. "From 1949, so just after the war."

"Let me see it," Edith reached across the table. "Doesn't that beat all? I wonder why they did a cookbook?"

"Maybe just for fun, for themselves." Jen got up to look over her grandma's shoulder. "Or maybe it was a fundraiser. Does it say anything in the front?"

Edith carefully turned the pages. "No, unfortunately. But I see several of Mother's recipes. Her blueberry pie, and her homemade rolls. Oh, here's something in the back. No mention of the reasoning behind the cookbook, but there is a bit of club history. Looks like it formed in 1889."

Ada's eyes swept the table and its stacks of paper. "How far back do these minutes go?"

"Sorry." Kevin checked his list. "These last ones are from 1910 and 1911. But nothing older. Unless Edith has another secret stash she's not telling us about."

Edith passed a hand over her lined face. "Lord knows what else is in that house. Alvin and I lived there for forty years, and I always thought we kept up on the clutter. But no. Jen, I'm sorry it's such a wreck."

"Don't worry, we'll get things boxed up and donated." Jen gave Melinda a wry smile. "Actually, after clearing out this place last spring, I'm not intimidated by what's left at your house, Grandma."

"Uncle Horace," Kevin called into the living room, "come see this stuff, you won't believe it! And we found a cookbook, too."

"Hmm." Horace barely looked up from his newspaper. "I was a pretty decent cook, back in the day. Kinda miss it. But they feed us well in the dining hall, so I guess I don't need any recipes."

"What's new at Scenic Vista?" Edith called to her brother. "Haven't talked to you since last week. How's that new therapy for Wilbur? Is it helping?"

Horace let out a barely audible sigh, and Hobo thumped his tail on the rug in sympathy. "Oh, I don't know. He doesn't know what day it is, hasn't for some time. But the nurse is really nice, she's patient with him."

The lift in Horace's voice made it clear patience was a quality he greatly admired.

Beyond farming or the weather, Horace wasn't much of a conversationalist. Edith shook her head at Ada, then tried again. "So, what else is going on?"

"Oh, not much. Maggie called last night. She thinks we should get married."

4

Ada's shriek of surprise made Hazel bolt upright from the couch's cushions, her eyes wide with alarm. Hobo studied Horace's face and waited for some sort of explanation, but his friend merely turned the newspaper's page with a steady hand. Nobody else moved.

"Get married." Edith's tone, low and cold, was the opposite of Ada's. "Have you lost your mind? And here I thought Wilbur was the one."

"Well, now, don't get all upset. I didn't tell her yes. Not yet."

Not yet? Kevin and Melinda stared at each other. Jen crossed and uncrossed her arms, unsure what to do. The club's papers were quickly forgotten, and the group drifted into the living room.

"Start at the beginning," Ada demanded, as Horace was unnervingly silent. "Tell us exactly what happened."

Maggie and Horace were in love as teenagers, but time and circumstance pulled them apart. Last summer, Melinda helped Kevin and Ada track down Maggie, who was now widowed, in Cedar Falls. The two saw each other regularly and talked on the phone several times a week. Maggie had pointed out that if they got married, they could share her assisted-living apartment and split the cost. Wilbur's spot in the complex's dementia unit would be expensive, of course, but the care was excellent.

It was a surprise, to say the least. But despite the shock on her friends' faces, Melinda saw the idea might have some merit.

Maggie and Horace were both in their nineties; who knew how much time they had left? Neither Horace or Wilbur had married, and they'd spent years looking after their father, then their mother. And then, Horace was there for Wilbur as dementia slowly took its toll. Horace had done so much for others; why shouldn't he reach for the happiness that was right before him, no matter what anyone else thought?

Melinda knew Horace held power of attorney for Wilbur. But given the wary look that just passed between Ada and Kevin, she wondered if someone would try to get that changed.

"I can't believe this!" Ada threw up her arms. "How could she even suggest such a thing?"

Horace finally set his newspaper in his lap. "Calm down. I didn't say I was going, did I?"

"What do Wendy and Barb have to say about this?" Edith's mind pivoted to a possible counterattack. Ada was still pale, but the mention of Maggie's daughters put a light of hope in her eyes. Maybe someone had some sense.

"The girls told Maggie it's up to us, they'll support her whatever she wants to do."

"That's their business, Uncle Horace." Kevin crossed his arms. "Let them sort that out. What I want to know is, what do you want?"

"Well, Maggie's always been awfully headstrong, she likes to have things her way." Horace shrugged, but the set of his jaw reminded Melinda that, despite his quiet demeanor, he was the same. "Guess I'll have to think on it."

"Well, who knows?" Kevin forced a smile,

but Melinda knew this conversation was far from over. "Jen, maybe you're not the only one in the family getting married this year."

Ada groaned. Edith shook her head. Jen burst into tears.

"What is it?" Melinda reached Jen before Kevin could.

"There's not going to be any wedding." Tears ran down Jen's cheeks. "Everything's a mess! I don't even know where to start."

Edith was quick to tell Jen the house was hers, married or not. If it wasn't working out with Andrew, well, he could just go find his own place to live.

Jen quickly assured her grandma that her relationship was on solid ground. The wedding itself, however, was the opposite. Jen's venue coordinator called last night to say the company was going out of business. It had been a package deal: event site, dinner and drinks, decorations, cake, flowers. Jen and Andrew would get their money back, but that was all.

Jen was a practical woman. But in this case, it had worked against her. She'd put all her eggs in one basket, and now there weren't many left. Melinda's stomach turned over once, then twice. She'd planned her own wedding several years ago, then got cold feet and never made it down the aisle. But here was Jen, ready to take that important step, and now all her plans were on hold.

"Can you find another spot?" she suggested. "I know it's only two months away, but ..."

"Everything's booked up." More tears. "I don't know what we're going to do. I have my dress, we have the rings, and that's about it."

"When I married your grandpa, that's all we had," Edith gently told her granddaughter, then pointed at the fireplace. "Why, we tied the knot right there. Mother served a nice lunch, and that was it."

Melinda was pleasantly surprised. "I guess I assumed you got married at the church down the road."

"Well, we thought about that. The Schermanns were founding members of First Lutheran. But we only wanted a few friends and close family. Things weren't like now, everyone putting on a big show. It just seemed easier to have the minister stop by." She put a hand on Jen's arm. "Honey, all that matters is you have a special day with the man you love. I wish my backyard wasn't so small."

"What about your parents' place?" Kevin offered.

"I haven't even told Mom yet, I'm dreading it. She's going to freak out. I'd like to have a Plan B in mind, first."

And then, Melinda had an idea. She took a mental step back and considered it carefully, as Kevin, Ada and Edith continued to offer Jen support and suggestions. She looked out at the expanse of grass and the lush trees, and remembered how lovely her acreage was in the full bloom of summer. There was plenty of room for a tent, the guest list wasn't outrageously long; if they had to, people could park in town and carpool to the farm.

Even so, it was a big commitment. Melinda couldn't do it alone, would never have considered it. But she knew people who would love to help. And Horace, who had been sitting there quietly, taking it all in, now gave her a look that said he might be thinking the same thing.

Maybe Jen's big day wasn't going to be a big bust, after all.

"Jen," she finally said, "there might be something I can do. In fact, if this works out, I'd love to do it." Melinda took a deep breath.

"What would you say to having the wedding here? A tent, food, dancing, the whole works."

Jen blinked. "What? Oh, no, we couldn't ask you to do that." But a cautious smile soon appeared on her tear-stained face.

"Do you think you can pull it off?" Kevin tried to keep his excitement in check. "Count me in for whatever you need, if you do."

"The Schermanns always find a way." Ada smiled at Jen. "If this idea doesn't work out, we'll just drum up something else."

Edith considered their options for a moment. "Melinda, you're a gem. Only trouble is, will people want to drive out here? It's forty minutes from Hampton."

"Most of them won't mind," Jen decided. "And if some of them don't want to, well, that'll cut the list down a bit. Maybe we could have a celebration at a bar later on, for our extended circle of friends." She gave Melinda a hug. "And here I thought we would end up at the courthouse! Let me talk to Andrew tonight, but I think we might be interested."

Melinda went to fetch more iced tea, and Kevin followed her into the kitchen. They leaned on the counter and tried to process everything that had just transpired.

"Wow." Kevin shook his head. "Where do I even start? It's a good thing you're already looking at paint and roofing options. If Jen takes you up on your offer, you'll have a deadline to meet. Of course, this place is charming, no matter what."

"Oh, no, you're right!" She glanced at the calendar by the refrigerator. "Their date's the weekend after the Fourth of July. That only gives me two months to get this place showplace-pretty." She lowered her voice to a whisper. "As for Horace, I can't imagine him marrying Maggie. She's sweet, but I don't know what to think."

"Well, there's still time for him to come to his senses." Kevin clearly had his doubts. Then he laughed.

"Be careful, or you might take on more than you bargained for. A double ceremony, right here at the farm! But somehow, I don't think that's Jen's idea of a dream wedding."

"And I'm glad." She motioned for him to grab the cookie jar. There was so much to discuss; additional treats would be a must. "Because it sounds like a nightmare to me. I want Horace to be happy, but ... one wedding at a time."

5

Paintbrush in hand, Melinda stood back to evaluate her work. Horace's old mailbox had seen a rough winter, between the ice and snow and one very unfortunate side-slap from the county plow.

She'd managed to get the wooden post back to almost-straight once the ground thawed, then packed more dirt and, finally, gravel around its base. And now, with the temperatures just warm enough at night, it was time to give the metal box a real facelift.

After spending yesterday afternoon with Mom and Miriam, she coated the post with brown paint, then gave the container a good scrub and smoothed on a primer to cover the gunmetal gray.

Tonight was the first coat of cream paint, and the project was really starting to take shape. Once it was completed, her mailbox would transform from one of the dullest on her rural route to probably the prettiest. Her mind had already run ahead to how a simple stencil could add a contrasting border or accent design to the box. But given the rough life it had here at the end of her lane, with no protection from the elements, she probably shouldn't get too carried away.

There was no doubt, however, that she would plant marigolds around the post again this spring, just as Horace always had.

While the mailbox was going to look wonderful when it was done, she couldn't say the same about herself. It had been so warm lately, she'd chosen shorts instead of jeans before painting the post yesterday. Since her shins and knees were already scratched and scabbed from crawling around in the gravel, she'd pulled on the same frayed pair of shorts tonight and her legs were now smeared with dirt and grass stains.

Her faded tee shirt was dotted with bleach-worn holes as well as swipes of paint. She tried to improve things by pushing her frayed ball cap back far enough to wipe the sweat away, and was only successful in dribbling paint on her face.

Sunny, however, was a regal as ever. His

long orange coat was soft and immaculate despite his expeditions in the wild, which tonight included a sojourn through the gangly weeds in the ditch. "My little lion." She shook her head in awe. "How do you not get that hair full of weed seeds and burrs?"

Melinda stretched her back, then planted her downtrodden sneakers in the gravel dust and flexed her calves. She'd been stooped over for too long, and needed a break before putting the finishing touches on tonight's part of the process. And besides, this spectacular view was worthy of more than a passing glance.

It was the violet hour, that quiet time before sunset when the fields were bathed in golden light. Every stem and leaf seemed sharper in focus, every whisper of the gentle breeze could be heard through the grasses and trees.

A quarter mile up the road, the metal side rails of the creek's bridge took on a soft glow, their dings and dirt smears momentarily invisible. The evening light was just as kind to her faded farmhouse. The gathering shadows softened its faded exterior to show her what it must have looked like long ago, and how it could again.

The field behind the mailbox was thick with new grass, which was being enjoyed by the ten jersey cows that had arrived last week to spend their summer in the rented pasture. Most of them grazed along the fence, keeping an eye on Melinda's handiwork, and the rest loafed in the shade of the open shed in the far corner of the property.

The wild rose bushes just south of the mailbox were setting buds for the season. A patch of Queen Anne's Lace suddenly began to sway, which told Melinda where Sunny had made his latest trek into the weeds.

On her side of the road, as Melinda thought of it with a swell of pride, the lilacs were about to burst into bloom, and the freshly mowed lawn rolled through the gentle ditch and up toward the house.

Chattering birds were everywhere, from the sharp-eyed blue jays gathered at the maple tree's feeders to the robins and cardinals winging their way over the fields. Several sparrows had a party line going on the electrical wires above her head, and the distinct chirps of a red-winged blackbird told Melinda she was being watched from a small scrub tree along the pasture fence.

It was time to get back to work, make the most of the light she had left. At least sunset wasn't until after eight now, and the days would grow even longer in the coming weeks. And Melinda would need every minute she could spare to get ready for Jen's wedding.

She'd already called a few leads on reputable painting crews, including the one offered by the kind woman at the plant swap, and hoped to have estimates by next week. Roofers were next on Melinda's list, but it looked as if management of the celebration itself had landed in Vicki's very-capable hands. She'd jumped at the chance to play wedding coordinator and make sure everything came off without a hitch.

Jen and Vicki were already working their phones, scouring the region for places to rent a tent, tables and chairs even though wedding season was already under way.

Adelaide Beaufort, a neighbor renovating a once-grand farmhouse surrounded by beds of heirloom perennials, offered to handle Jen's floral needs. The owners of the Watering Hole, Prosper's only restaurant, were on board to serve up a simple supper of sandwiches and sides. And Angie Hensley, who lived just around the mile section and already baked sweet treats for Meadow Lane's coffee bar, would create the cake.

As for Horace and Maggie, Kevin's joking prospect of a double wedding seemed highly unlikely. Once he'd shared his news from Melinda's reading chair, Horace had refused to discuss the proposal further, at least for now. Ada called last night to say she'd finally thrown up her hands and decided to stop worrying about it.

"I can't imagine they'll go through with it, really. They're both so stubborn, and they had a terrible falling out before." She and Kevin would keep Melinda posted, but the best plan of action seemed to be none.

"He's a man of few words, even when the conversation's not so personal. The more I press, the more he clams up. I've decided that, until he makes some sort of announcement, I'm going to just let it go."

Melinda stirred the silky cream paint, maybe more vigorously than needed, and picked up her brush again. A smooth, level stroke to the left, then one back to the right, and the mailbox's old dings slowly began to disappear.

As she worked, Melinda decided to take Ada's wise words to heart. Because along with the excitement of hosting a wedding, and the thrill of a challenge, there was a pang of sadness Melinda didn't want to share lest it dampened everyone's enthusiasm for Jen and Andrew's special day.

Melinda had called her wedding off just in time, and for the right reasons. She had no doubts about that, then or now, but the sting came back when she least expected it.

"Craig and I never would have lasted, it wouldn't have worked." She dipped the brush in the paint again. "And I never would have found the life I have now."

Melinda was determined to stay in today, and focus on the future. Which, with Josh in her life and her other numerous blessings, was very bright indeed. As for Jen's wedding, it would all get done, somehow. There were too many helping hands determined to make it happen.

The red-winged blackbird's occasional chirps changed to a warning staccato, and Melinda looked up to see Hobo sauntering down the road, his tail held high. He loved exploring down at the creek, and by the looks of the matted fur on his legs, had recently waded in it. She checked both ways down the gravel, as far as she could see. No one was coming, of course; it was a busy day if even five vehicles passed her driveway. Even so, she cringed and shook her head. Why couldn't he at least run on the shoulder of the road, rather than all over the middle?

"He has no sense, does he?" she asked Sunny, who narrowed his eyes and flipped his fluffy tail when Hobo gave him a nose-bump "hello." While all the cats loved Hobo, it was pretty obvious which species at the farm they felt was the superior one.

"Well, look who's even dirtier than I am!" Melinda set the paint bucket behind her, hoping to avoid yet another mess. "How did you get mud all the way up to your belly? The creek's not even that deep these days." She sighed and looked down at her faded, paint-splattered clothes. "We're quite the messy pair, aren't we?"

Hobo nosed around while Melinda continued her work, the mud on his haunches drying to a thick crust. He soon flushed out several irate birds and one confused striped gopher. Melinda winced as Sunny quickly pounced on his prey. The law of the jungle ruled out here, as much as she sometimes wished it didn't.

Just as she was about to put the finishing touches on this round of paint, she heard the rumble of tires on gravel. Sunny was safety out of the way, gnawing his disgusting snack on the edge of the ditch, but she reached for Hobo's collar as they waited to see who it could be.

"Don't recognize the car." She squinted against the lowering sun as the vehicle crossed the creek's bridge. "Looks new and expensive, though. Well, that rules out any of our neighbors, huh?" Hobo danced at her feet, eager to find out for himself, but she tightened her hold.

While the sedan might have been showroom-clean not long ago, two miles on the gravel had changed that considerably. It slowed as it reached her driveway, and Melinda instinctively waved. "They must be lost, have to be. Who else would be out here, anyway?"

Sure enough, the car rolled to a stop. She was surprised, though, when the young man behind the wheel shifted into park and opened the door. Melinda sensed a salesman, and Hobo's polite growl said he assumed the same.

"Well, hello!" The man extended an immaculate hand. "I sure hope you can help me out."

Melinda wiped her dirty paw on her paint-splattered shorts, and accepted his greeting. "Sure, if I can."

While his teeth were blindingly white, the young man's smile was not overly sincere. The sleeves of his expensive dress shirt were rolled up just-so, and his khakis were perfectly pressed. But the gravel dust had already knocked down the shine on his shoes.

"I'm lost, I'm afraid. I turned off the blacktop and, I don't know, I think I've gone three miles. But you know the roads out here aren't exactly on a grid."

Melinda smiled. They were, actually, square miles all around. Of course, this road made a meander before it reached the creek, then swerved back again. She supposed it could be enough to throw someone off balance. Someone who was out of their comfort zone.

"You're two miles down." She pointed south. "The next corner makes three."

"Oh, good." The poor guy gave such a sigh

of relief that Melinda almost laughed. Was it really so terrible to take a drive down a rambling country road on such a lovely spring evening?

"That means I'm almost there. I'm looking for the Wildwood place. Would I take a right at the corner?"

She blinked. Why would this guy want to visit Bart? He was in his eighties, a sour-faced man with a mean streak. His wife, Marge, had dementia and finally moved to a nursing home two months ago. Melinda couldn't imagine Bart welcoming any visitors, especially one as smooth as this guy.

"Yes, that's right," was all she said. And then, she couldn't resist. "Is he expecting you?"

She got a sheepish grin in return. "Well, not exactly."

Her eyes must have popped open, as the young man hurried to explain. "No, really, it's OK. See, Bart's selling his acreage and his son called me. I went to school with his son. Lenny's son, I mean. Bart's grandson." Melinda's silence obviously made him nervous. "I'm a realtor, in Mason City," he added proudly. "Just got my license in the fall.

I haven't listed a rural property yet, but there's a first time for everything, right?"

"Yes. There always is."

And a first time for getting yelled at by Bart, and possibly finding the bumper of your expensive car peppered with BB pellets.

"So, Bart's decided to sell, huh?" She couldn't imagine Bart willing to do any such thing. In fact, the couple's grown children had been trying for weeks to get him to move to town, to no avail. And Bart wasn't one to change his mind.

"That's what I hear." He shrugged. "Lenny says it's time, wanted me to meet him out here to get things started." His eyes lit up with curiosity. "I'm told the Wildwood residence is likely the oldest in the township. Must be quite the place, huh? I bet it's full of that country charm everyone's looking for when they leave the hustle and bustle of the city behind."

Melinda nodded slowly. "Charm" wasn't a word she'd use to describe Bart's house.

"Decrepit," "neglected" and "depressing" might be better.

But it was obvious this guy had already started on his marketing copy for the listing, and she wasn't going to be the one to set him straight. Bart would handle that on his own.

She gestured around them at the peaceful evening. "Well, it is a beautiful part of the county." The young man was only half listening, his lip curled with disgust as he watched Sunny rip a back leg off what was left of the striped gopher. "I grew up around here, in Swanton, and moved back from the Twin Cities two years ago. I rented this place, at first, but eventually bought it."

It was the young man's turn to look shocked. He took in her ragged clothes, skinned-up shins and the dirt-crusted dog lounging at her feet. Pepper, who was enjoying some solo time in the pasture, offered a "hee-haw" of warning from the other side of her fence. Now that he'd settled in, he was a better guard dog than Hobo.

"Oh, you did?" He stared up the lane, and frowned. "Your place is, uh, full of potential."

She raised her chin. "Yes, I think so."

He reached for his wallet. "Here, might as well take my card. Not saying you're in over your head, or anything." But his withering glance told her otherwise. "If you ever decide to move on, give me a call." The bright smile returned. "Never too soon to build up that client list. Mason City's not that far away."

It was, actually. Forty minutes in good weather. But Melinda only tucked the card in the pocket of her frayed shorts and smiled again. "Thanks. You'll be my first call."

He thought he'd closed the deal, and bigger and better things waited down the road. "Well, I should go. Don't want to keep Bart and Lenny waiting." He turned back toward the car, then stopped.

"Oh, can you tell me, just in case: There isn't a mean dog at the Wildwood farm, I hope? Had a bad run-in the other day."

"Oh, no; no mean dogs there." *Other than Bart himself.* "No dog at all, hasn't been for years."

Melinda again reached for Hobo's collar with one hand, and waved her goodbyes with the other. Once the car disappeared in a plume of gravel dust, she let out a deep sigh. And then, she started to laugh.

"He has no idea what he's getting himself into, huh?" She rubbed some of the dirt off Hobo's head. "Bart's about to get ambushed, and he's sure to come out swinging."

Melinda knew why Lenny invited this

unsuspecting realtor out to the Wildwood farm in the evening. The place was in terrible shape, but the waning light would smooth some of its rough edges.

But not Bart's. Melinda couldn't imagine what, if anything, could do that.

It was time to quit for the night. And suddenly, Melinda's mounting to-do list didn't seem so long, or so difficult. She looked off to the southwest and shook her head. "That guy has no idea what he's in for."

As she gathered up her supplies and gently shooed Stormy's twitching nose away from the can of paint, Melinda weighed whether to call Mabel with this latest bit of neighborhood gossip. It was certainly interesting and, more importantly, verifiably true. If the deal panned out, everyone was going to be pleasantly surprised. Stunned, more like it. But despite the young agent's show of confidence, she doubted Lenny's plan would even get off the ground.

Melinda kept an eye on the road as she moved around her farmhouse, tidying up. She wasn't surprised when, barely thirty minutes later, she saw the same car roll past, headed for the highway, making its escape.

6

The library's meeting room was already bustling by the time Melinda arrived with her pan of chocolate-walnut brownies. It was the book club's May meeting, the last one before fall, and the members had decided to pull out all the stops with their snacks.

The console along the wall was already full of dishes, and more food was quickly taking over the main table.

"I'm starving." Nancy filched a tortilla rollup from a tray. "I swear, I had at least seven of these before I left the house. I never should have made them."

"And I would have been very disappointed if you hadn't." Sam Holden, who ran the insurance office next door, helped himself to the appetizers. "They go perfectly with the barbecue beef I brought." He pointed at the slow cooker and the package of buns. "Help yourselves."

Amy Westberg, a teacher at the elementary school, added a pasta salad to the spread. "Everything goes with those rollups. In fact, everything here goes with everything else. And I have to say, it was fun to meet at the community center last month, but it's great to be back at the library."

Nancy had asked the club to make a trial run of the new space, which was just a block away in a former bank. Making good use of the members' keen eyes and sound judgement, she'd been able to get a list of last-minute fixes that, once they were addressed, meant the community center was truly ready for its first guests.

Karen arrived, her long blonde hair in its usual ponytail. She was still wearing her "Prosper Veterinary Services" polo shirt. "I agree. This is our spot. Sorry I didn't have time to change."

"As long as you're remotely clean, we'll look the other way," Sam said with a twinkle in his eye. "Besides, you brought garlic bread. All is forgiven."

"Well, to tell the truth, my shirt isn't in such bad shape. That's because the one I left the house in this morning experienced an unfortunate incident on a farm call. I only put this on maybe two hours ago."

Shelby Dunlap, the music teacher at the elementary school, had just come in the door. Bev Stewart, a retiree who now worked as a part-time carrier for the Eagle River post office, was right behind her.

Nancy looked around. "I think we're only missing Vicki. I'm sure she'll be here soon."

"She's out front." Bev set a veggie tray on the table. "In fact, I'll hustle out and help her. She had her arms full. Two tote bags and a tray to boot."

"How much food did she bring?" Shelby asked. "We all promised to bring one dish."

"You know Vicki." Sam's lined face broke into a smile. "She's an overachiever. But we'll all benefit, I'm sure."

"Here we are," Vicki sang out as she came into the room. Bev trailed behind with little Francesca in her arms. The sight of Bev, a stocky, no-nonsense woman, cradling a Pomeranian with a pink bow in her hair was almost too much. Melinda took a big bite of her sandwich and refused to return Karen's amused look. She wasn't going to laugh if she could help it.

But Francesca was more than a doggie fashionista; she was so cute and friendly, she'd quickly become a hit with Meadow Lane's customers. So much so, that Vicki now included her little dog in the store's social-media posts.

Vicki set out a selection of single-serve cakes and brownies in clear plastic containers. "I've been in such a rush lately, I didn't even try to make something from scratch." Melinda instantly recognized two of the confections, and knew they all came from Angie's at-home bakery.

Eyebrows went up around the table. Vicki was never one to take the easy route. She must really be crunched for time.

"So I grabbed some things from the shop's coffee bar. Now, if you don't find something you like, I can always run across the street and get more."

"Goodness, no, you don't need to do that," Amy said kindly. "I'm going to take that slice of carrot cake off your hands, right now, before anyone else claims it."

Vicki settled Francesca on the chair next to her, then lifted the last tote bag into her lap. "I know we're here to talk about the book, and stuff our faces, but Melinda, I just had to show you a few ideas I found." She beamed at her friends. "In case you haven't heard, I'm taking on a new role: wedding planner!"

Before the gasps ever got rolling, Melinda held up a hand. "No, no, I'm not getting married!"

She filled everyone in on Jen's situation while Vicki unpacked a tall stack of inch-thick bridal magazines. There was a stuffed-full binder, too. No wonder Vick needed Bev's help; she was certainly carrying a heavy load.

"The magazine tabs are color-coded," Vicki explained. "Blue for centerpieces, yellow for flowers, green for guest favors." Her brown eyes sparkled as she opened one thick tome to a marked spread and handed it to Melinda.

"Look at this! It's an archway threaded with roses and lilies. I know these aren't Jen's colors, but I know we could replicate this, easy-peasy! It would be perfection. Your garden will be in the background, and then we can line up the chairs east-west. Or, no; maybe set them on the diagonal. What do you think?"

A quick count showed at least six or seven dozen roses on the metal-framed trellis. Adelaide had promised to do the flowers, but it would depend on what was blooming in early July. Jen, a no-nonsense bride grateful to be getting married at all, didn't care about sticking to a specific theme.

"Well, it's very colorful," Melinda managed to say. Bev took the magazine from her hands.

"Goodness, this thing is heavy! Vicki, you'll need a wrist brace if you're going to carry these things around. I agree, this is a nice idea, but it seems a little fussy to me. The real question is, what does Jen say about it? I don't think it matters what Melinda thinks. No offense."

Melinda shrugged.

"Oh, I haven't shown it to her yet." Vicki picked up the next magazine. "I want to narrow some options first. You know, not overwhelm my client with choices."

"If the wedding's less than two months away, I'm afraid you won't have to worry about that," Shelby said. "Most take a year to plan. I did mine in six months, and it was crazy. I can't imagine what Jen's going through."

"All we really need is a tent, and tables and chairs." Melinda tried to keep Vicki on track. "The rest is, well, the icing on the cake."

"And a portable dance floor," Vicki reminded Melinda as she pulled out her phone and checked her messages.

"A small one, of course, just enough room for a few couples at a time would do. I'm tracking down a lead on that yet tonight. Jen thinks she may have found a tent for rent, but she's staying on the waitlist at several places. Trouble is, this is prime wedding season, and everything's booked and taken."

Nancy took a sip of lemonade. "I can't believe this, but the community center has something going on every weekend through the end of August, already."

"Including Ryan's graduation party," Amy reminded her. "I'm so glad you were able to jump the list. It will be so much better than trying to host it in your garage."

Nancy hadn't wanted to take advantage, but Jerry had wisely encouraged her to do just that. She'd spent over six months shepherding this challenging project for the community; why not, just this once, make things easy for herself? No one had complained; at least, not that Melinda had heard.

"And we even have a few weddings at the end of the summer," Nancy added. "I wish I could offer Jen a date, but there's nothing to be had."

"I figured as much. And besides, she's really thrilled to have it at the farm. Edith, her grandmother, was married there, too."

Vicki had been listening to the conversation, but not really. A sudden smile lit up her face, and she pulled a pen and notepad from her purse and jotted something down. She might take things too far sometimes, but Vicki had the creativity and determination to make sure Jen's big day didn't turn into a big bust.

The conversation moved on to the book, at last, and the group enjoyed a spirited discussion about how the novel's various plot points worked, or didn't. A few members were eager to read more by the same author over the summer, but others were certainly "one and done." They all threw in suggestions for September's book, and Bev's was the winner.

"It's four hundred pages," she admitted after Nancy pulled her slip of paper from the bowl. "Just beware."

"That doesn't bother me," Amy said. "September's four months from now. That will give us all plenty of time to get the book read.

I also have a stack of 'beach reads' I've been waiting to dive into."

"Chick lit, you mean." Sam rolled his eyes.

"No, not really. Some of them are mysteries." Amy tapped her phone. "Here, let me send some of them to you. They aren't westerns, your usual faves, but who knows?"

"I don't know where the school year has gone." Shelby sighed. "After Founders Day next weekend, all that'll be left are the end-of-year concerts and ceremonies."

Some of the elementary students had been tapped to perform a small play Vicki wrote about Prosper's early days. While she had been disappointed with a few of the pioneers' morals, she'd managed to set her judgement aside and craft a simple, warm-hearted story of determination and community spirit. The production was set for Saturday in the school's auditorium, with all the proceeds benefitting the elementary's music program.

"Two more run-throughs, then the dress rehearsal is Friday morning." Vicki fed Francesca a doggie treat out of her purse. "Once we get the play out of the way, I'll really be able to focus on giving Jen the wedding of her dreams."

Karen and Melinda exchanged looks. If Vicki ramped up her efforts even more, what might happen?

"Nancy, is anything wrong?" Bev looked concerned. "You seem awfully quiet, all the sudden."

"Have you had a fight with your boyfriend?" Sam asked in a singsong voice. Richard and Nancy's secret hadn't stayed that way for long.

Bev rolled her eyes. "Seriously. Are you sixty-three, or just three?"

"Oh, Richard and I are fine." A smile crossed Nancy's face, but quickly disappeared. "It's just that, well, something's come up with the council." Prosper's panel only met twice a month, and the meetings rarely lasted an hour. Unless something was brewing. And from how worried Nancy looked, there had to be.

"What is it?" Vicki put down her phone. "This can't be good."

Nancy gave something several moments of consideration. Then she pushed back her chair. "Everyone, please stay put until I get back." She began to mutter to herself as she crossed the room. "It'll be all over the internet, it's all public information, it's not like ..."

Their dessert options were momentarily forgotten. "Well, I don't know about the rest of you." Bev crossed her arms. "But this oughta be good. Or bad. Right now, you couldn't blast me out of here."

"She went next door." Amy hovered by the room's entrance, and refilled her plate while keeping an eye on Nancy's whereabouts. The library and city hall were connected by a cased opening, and Nancy soon reappeared with a large roll of paper in her hand. She shut the meeting room's door behind her, even though the library was closed.

"Now, please, I want all of you to promise to say nothing about this until tomorrow, once it's online."

The book club members stared at each other. "Sure. When will that be?" Karen wondered.

"Sometime before noon." Nancy cleared a space at the end of the table. "And don't worry, you'll know when it happens. Because the buzz will be swift, and probably deafening."

Melinda's heart almost skipped a beat when Nancy unrolled the drawing. She stayed silent, and tried to look as surprised and curious as the rest of the book club's members. Which wasn't that hard to do, really.

She'd seen this before, if a less-detailed version. But every piece of Auggie's grand scheme was clearly in place. He hadn't backed down, not one bit. And for all his grumbling about bureaucracy and costs, he'd still found the motivation and money in the past week to get a professional to refine his ideas so he could submit them to the council.

"Well, look at this." Sam leaned over the table. "Auggie's moving forward with his expansion plans. He's been quiet about it lately. I was starting to think it was just a bunch of bluster."

"Auggie?" Bev rolled her eyes sarcastically. "Never."

"A bit of disclosure." Nancy weighted one corner with Amy's copy of that month's book. "Nothing will happen on this for several weeks. All the council will do Monday is vote to file the plans for consideration. There won't be discussion or time for public comments until a later date. You all know the agenda is posted on Friday, but Auggie asked Jerry to get this out there as soon as possible so people can start talking about it."

Vicki pointed to one of the store's front corners, and raised an eyebrow. "Look at that. He wants to renovate inside, too? Seems like an awful lot to take on."

"What's so bad about this?" Shelby wondered. "Isn't this what everyone's been wanting? When he said at the New Year's party that he was going to offer gas for everyone, it felt like Christmas all over again."

"But it's going to feel like Halloween for Prosper Hardware if he succeeds." Sam frowned. "The interior upgrades will let him expand the co-op's merchandise. That means competition for others in town."

He gave Melinda a look of sympathy as gasps echoed around the room. Auggie had made the coffee group promise to stay quiet on that part of the plan, had insisted no one else knew about it. But if Sam did, he probably wasn't the only one.

Melinda's frustration flared. Not only was Auggie going forward with his full plan, despite its drawbacks, but he hadn't been straight with some of his closest friends.

"All of us business owners support each other." Vicki rubbed her temples. "Or at least, we try to. But in a town this small,

competition isn't a good thing. It's important
we all stay in our lane."

Bev crossed her arms. "The pie's only so
big. You can only cut the slices so small before
someone's left out in the cold."

"Well, there's more." Nancy slid a stack of
papers out from behind the drawing. "It's bad
enough he's trying to encroach on another
business' territory, but that's not the only
thing that'll cause people's blood pressure to
skyrocket. He wants incentives to make it
happen."

"Incentives?" Sam narrowed his eyes,
instantly suspicious. "What kind of
incentives?"

"Tax breaks." Nancy clipped off the ends of
the words. "Reduced taxes on the additional
value of his property for, oh, as many years as
he can get. There are state laws that cap it, but
this town needs every dime that comes in."

"Everyone needs to pay their fair share."
Vicki's eyes were suddenly cold. "You know
Arthur and I poured some serious money into
our building, and we didn't ask for anything in
return."

"And you've done wonders with the place,"
Bev said. "What an asset to the community

Meadow Lane has been. Auggie needs to take a page from your playbook."

"Wait. What is this?" Melinda reached for another document. "Wetland restoration credits?" Her jaw dropped as she scanned the proposal. "Oh, come on! This is insane!"

In his quest to gather as many kickbacks as he could, Auggie had requested the low-lying corner of his property be designated a wildlife area. Despite the fact it held just a few trees, and only collected water during a short period in the spring.

"Lucy and Desi aren't even a protected species!" Bev was incredulous. "Sure, they're cute, but they're just ducks. If people didn't feed them corn all the time, they wouldn't hang out at the co-op in the first place."

"I suppose the trees draw some owls," Sam said drily. "And you know the mice are thick out there, in and around the grain towers." Then he laughed. "Hey, Nancy, I need to repaint my office's front steps. Can I send the city an itemized bill and get reimbursed? Two gallons should do it."

Nancy closed her eyes for a moment. Then she quickly rolled up the drawing, as if doing so could somehow make the drama disappear.

"All I know is, this isn't going to sit well with folks."

Jerry was very upset, she reported, torn between the need to grow the town's economic base yet protect other businesses' bottom lines. Being friends with everyone involved just made the mayor's role that much more difficult. And then, there was the city's marginal financial situation to consider. And how Auggie's requests for incentives smacked of charity.

"He and Auggie have had it out, several times already. Jerry's been clear about what the public reaction's going to be to that part of the plan. But Auggie's so full of big ideas, I don't think he really cares."

"But he should." Sam's tone was ominous. "Sure, Prosper Feed Co.'s been around forever. But there's a co-op in Eagle River, and another in Swanton. If he burns bridges, he'll be sorry. People might get their gas there, but the farmers will rethink their loyalties. And, no matter what else he adds, grain processing and storage is still the vast majority of his business."

Melinda snapped the lid on her leftover brownies. Suddenly, she was more than full;

she was sick to her stomach. "Do the council members know about this yet?"

Nancy glanced at the clock. "Yes, by now they do. Jerry was going to call everyone tonight, after supper. Let them get in a good meal before he had to break the bad news."

Vicki returned to her place at the table and gathered up her bridal magazines. Each glossy-covered volume made a thud as she stacked them in a pile.

"Doesn't he know how this could backfire on him? I thought he had more sense than that." Suddenly, she reached for her notebook.

"Another idea for the wedding?" Sam asked.

"I wish." Vicki frowned as she scribbled some notes. "I need to figure out how I'm going to address this with customers tomorrow. Everyone's going to be talking about it, and I need to be careful what I say."

7

Once Jerry confirmed Auggie's proposal would come up at next week's council meeting, Frank was forced to tell Miriam everything he knew.

She was momentarily furious that he'd kept it from her, but finally understood. Like Melinda, Frank had hoped Auggie would at least drop the idea to expand the co-op's inventory.

Not long after she got home from book club, Melinda got a call from Aunt Miriam. While she was upset about the possibility of Auggie stealing business from Prosper Hardware, Miriam was more hurt by what she saw as an act of betrayal.

"That man got his start at our store. My parents taught him everything they knew! Oh, scratch that. The part where he's stabbing us in the back? That's all Auggie. One hundred percent."

Understanding that a united front would be critical in the coming weeks, Melinda's family hashed out their own plan. It was decided the best course of action would be to talk about Auggie's ideas as little as possible. Whenever it was brought up by a customer or anyone else in the community, they would simply say Auggie had a right to expand his business, and the fate of his proposal would rest with the city council. That still put Uncle Frank in a difficult position, but it was the best they could do.

The next morning, Frank and Jerry took care to keep the coffee group's conversation as far away from that topic as possible. And true to his new, secretive nature, Auggie was also silent on the matter. Melinda claimed to be behind on inventory counts and spent her handful of free moments before the store opened cataloging the grocery aisle. Or, if truth be told, hiding from her friends.

She breathed easier when the group broke up just before eight, but caught herself watching the clock. After all, Nancy promised the news would be posted on the city's website and social media page by noon. Melinda worked the register and restocked shelves, while Esther gave the display window a seasonal overhaul. It was now mid-May, and time for the gardening gear and rain boots to make way for coolers, fishing rods, and the store's small selection of patriotic-themed housewares.

Memorial Day was just around the corner, and the Fourth of July would arrive before Melinda was ready. Of course, Jen's wedding was the weekend after that, and ...

"Glenn incoming!" Esther shouted just after eleven. "And he's mad as can be, by the looks of things."

Her announcement caught not only Melinda's attention, but that of every customer in the store. And so it was that Glenn Hanson, Prosper's longtime postmaster, had a captive audience by the time he stormed through the entrance. Melinda was glad Frank kept the hinges on the oak front door well-oiled, because Glenn shut it with an unusual amount of force.

His face was red, even though the day was pleasantly cool and the post office was just next door. But Melinda knew why he was so riled up: the sheet of paper clenched in his beefy hand.

"I can't believe this!" Glenn marched up to the counter and slapped down the notice he'd printed off the city's website. "He's got some nerve, I tell you! Even the feds don't play this dirty, and that's saying something."

Prosper's post office was moving to limited hours in the fall. It wasn't closing, thankfully, but it had taken weeks of protest from the town's residents, and some sly maneuvering by Glenn and his union representative, to keep the door open.

"He's crazy, don't you think?" Glenn shouted to the woman placing her purchases on the end of the counter. "Connie, I know you have plenty of sense. Can you believe it?"

Connie, who obviously had yet to hear the news, only blinked and clutched her package of toilet paper to her chest.

"Uh, Glenn." Melinda leaned over the counter. "She's trying to ..."

"What? Oh, sorry." He hurried to help Connie unload her handbasket. "I'm just in a state of, oh, I don't know. Complete outrage, I guess."

"What's going on?" A man carrying a pair of work boots came up the main aisle. "Who's playing dirty now?"

"None other than Mr. August Kleinsbach, current proprietor of Prosper Feed Co." Glenn handed over the notice. "And I do mean 'current.' If he keeps up these shenanigans, he might find himself running short of customers, gas pumps or no gas pumps."

The printout soon went hand-to-hand around the store, and returned to the counter so battered that Glenn would have to press it under a stack of heavy books before he could tack it on the post office's bulletin board.

Just as Nancy predicted, Auggie's demands for special treatment were met with howls of laughter and outbursts of anger and frustration.

"I know this comes as a surprise to us all." Melinda measured her words carefully. "But it'll be up to the city to decide what does, and doesn't, happen. And remember, nothing will be decided Monday night. It's just the start of the process. Everyone will have a chance, later on, to speak to the council on this issue."

"That's right. Everyone needs to keep calm, and carry on," Esther called from the display window. "Oh, by the way, new items have been added to the seasonal clearance racks by the stairwell."

The chance to save money was always appealing, and several shoppers were quick to shift their focus. While Auggie's proposal was still being discussed in the aisles, the store's emotional temperature dropped by a few degrees.

When his audience scattered to work through their shopping lists, Glenn began to calm down. "Well, I still can't believe it." He checked the clock, then sighed and started for the door. "Pete's watching the counter, and I'm starving. I better get back."

"I understand why Glenn's so upset," Esther told Melinda as she passed by on her way to the stairs. "Glad to see, though, that he's not letting such shocking news get in the way of his lunch."

* * *

"He's outdone himself this time." Mabel swatted away a fly as she and Melinda waited for more of their neighbors to arrive. "Auggie's built that co-op into a far-more-profitable business than the guy that used to own it. But this new vision sounds more like a nightmare."

"And not just for Prosper Hardware, but for

himself. The court of public opinion is now in session, and Auggie's not faring so well. Oh, good, there's Adelaide and Lauren. Angie should be here soon, and then we can get this over with."

Melinda had enlisted some of her friends to help shepherd Pepper's official introduction to the sheep. The critters had studied each other across the barn aisle, but had never been in the pasture together. This evening, that was going to change.

Stormy appeared around the corner of the barn, apparently back from one of his pasture expeditions, and demanded Melinda pick him up. He soon vibrated with contentment, and his comforting presence made her feel better. That, and Mabel's assessment of the situation.

"Oh, I wouldn't worry too much about Pepper." She smiled as she pulled on her chore gloves. "Like Auggie, he's just one more in a very long line of stubborn males. Pepper seems pretty mellow for a donkey. I can't imagine he'd kick up enough mischief to cause any real trouble. Besides, the ewes have him outnumbered eight to one."

Melinda was glad to see Lauren again, and to hear she enjoyed her new job as a traveling rural nurse. One of Jessie's cousins, she'd needed a place to stay after ending a volatile relationship, and Adelaide and Mason had offered to take her in. The Beauforts hoped to eventually turn their elegant farmhouse into a bed and breakfast, and Lauren was the perfect first, unofficial guest. Angie soon arrived, and the rebooted Fulton Friendship Circle was unofficially in session.

"We don't have a quorum, but I still say this counts." With her auburn curls now up in an elastic, Angie was ready to take on this challenge. Along with her burgeoning in-home bakery, she and her husband farmed and raised cows. "Pulling weeds in a cemetery, wrangling livestock, it suits me just fine. Just as fun as fancy tea parties."

"I think Donna wants to schedule lunch in Swanton sometime next month." Melinda gave into Stormy's latest demand, and put him down. "That's probably as formal as we're going to get."

"So." Adelaide flipped her gray braid over her shoulder. "What's the plan?"

The ewes were grazing in the front of the pasture, down by the road. Melinda decided to leave them there for now, and let Pepper out

on his side of the barn. While some of the
ladies kept an eye on Pepper, the others would
bring the sheep around with a promise of corn
snacks. What would happen next? Well, they'd
find out soon enough.

Melinda thought it best not to halter
Pepper, as it would make him combative from
the start. She would just stay close to him, and
be prepared to step between him and the ewes
if there were signs his curiosity could cross
into aggression. And she had another tactic in
her back pocket, literally: a little bag of
carrots, a treat Pepper never turned down.

The top half of Pepper's pasture door was
already open. The moment Melinda reached
for the bottom latch, he launched into a string
of brays she now recognized as his song of
excitement.

"Easy, now. You get to roam around
tonight, but you won't be alone for long.
Promise me you'll behave."

The unfamiliar women around him only
drew a few curious glances from Pepper.
There was so much to explore; who cared if
these people wanted to stand around, telling
him what a good boy he was?

Hobo, for once, wasn't the center of

attention, and glumly watched the show from the other side of the fence. Sunny and Stormy lounged in the freshly mowed grass several feet behind him, not sure if they wanted to be too close to the action, but unwilling to miss out.

After a few mouthfuls of thick grass, Pepper kicked up his heels, just a bit, and started to trot around in the refreshing evening air.

"You're doing the right thing." Adelaide nodded her approval. "Look at how happy he is already. We've never had a donkey, of course, but you know there are goats, a pig and a few sheep sharing our pasture. It always takes time, but eventually, everyone gets along."

Annie and one of the other ewes had already ambled up to the south side of the pasture and now waited there, a bit cautious but mostly curious, as Pepper continued to explore. But when the donkey barely gave them a look, they soon went back to grazing themselves.

"Well, if Annie's on board, maybe this will be a piece of cake." Adelaide shielded her eyes to study the rest of the flock. "Let's get the corn, and bring everyone together."

Annie recognized Mabel, and was now getting her forehead scratched. "Angie and I can stay here with these girls. Pepper's around back, pleased as can be. I don't think he's going to charge. But we'll keep watch, just in case."

When the ladies returned with the other ewes in tow, nothing had changed. Angie and Mabel continued to visit as Annie and her friend grazed. None of the sheep showed interest in running around the barn to face off with Pepper.

"So far, so good." Melinda ratted her corn bucket to bring all the ewes her way. "Well, let's take everyone around back. This will be the real moment of ..."

She rounded the barn, and stopped. "Wait. Where's Pepper?"

Mabel shielded her eyes to study the west edge of the property. "Hmm. The pasture's not huge, he can't be far. He must be in that little stand of trees, way out in the corner. But I think we would have seen him take off in that direction."

There was no sign of Pepper. Or Hobo, for that matter. But then, Melinda spotted a sign of something else.

The back pasture's walk-through gate now stood open.

Annie saw it, too.

Before Melinda could corner her, or even get out a shout, Annie barreled her way toward freedom. Her "baaas" of excitement alerted the rest of the flock and, with Annie as their self-appointed leader, the whole crew followed in her wake.

"Head them off, if you can!" Adelaide shouted to Angie and Lauren, who were closest to the fence. But Annie was too quick, as were two of her friends. Waving her arms and shouting, Lauren jumped between the rest of the sheep and the gate, and Angie snapped the latch just in time.

"I didn't know they could move that fast." Melinda told Mabel as they hurried across the pasture. "I mean, look how fat they are."

"Curiosity is a dangerous motivator." Mabel wiped the sweat from her brow when they reached the fence. "Are you sure the gate was closed?" Then she groaned. "Oh, no! Do you think Pepper figured out how to lift the latch? Donkeys are incredibly smart. I don't know of any other way he'd be able to get out."

Melinda shook her head. "His previous

owners told Doc he was an impulse purchase from the Eagle River auction barn, and that he'd become a nuisance. Now I'm thinking they conveniently left out the part about Pepper being an escape artist."

The walk-through gate had a simple latch, just a curved piece of metal that dropped down around the adjacent fence post. An easy lift with his strong teeth, then a small nudge of the gate, and Pepper had set himself free.

The three misbehaving ewes only made it as far as the thick grass along the machine shed, and were content to stay where they were. But Pepper was nowhere to be found. Adelaide caught up with Melinda and Mabel as the other ladies used the corn buckets to draw the other five sheep away from the fence. "The question is, where did he go?"

Melinda tried to peer into the windbreak, which was now filled with evening shadows thanks to its canopy of new leaves. "I don't know if he's in there, or not. What if he went on through, and trotted out into the field?"

"Oh, no!" Mabel pointed to the other side of the yard. "There he is in the garden, stomping around with those big feet of his. Didn't you just plant everything?"

They met up with Hobo next to the chicken house. The hens paced in their run, flustered by the recent sight of a strange animal galloping past their coop, but Hobo seemed content to lounge in a spot of shade. "Some guard dog you are," Melinda scolded him.

Pepper stopped snacking long enough to notice the women's approach. Those big ears soon pointed toward the sky.

"Hee-haw! Hee-haw!" He stomped a front foot, and Melinda cringed as a fragile tomato seedling disappeared into the dirt. After a few of the cucumber plants were tasted and discarded, Pepper turned to the flowering bushes on the north side of the garden.

Melinda put a hand over her eyes. "Oh, not the bridal wreath! The blooms will be gone before Jen's wedding, but the hedge stays beautiful all summer long. It won't, though, if we don't get him out of there."

Angie had stopped in the barn for Pepper's halter, and met up with the ladies by the chicken house. "Well, what do you think?"

"I think we spread out slowly." Adelaide put her hands on her hips. "And then move in, very slowly. If he spooks, he'll get down to the road before we'll be able to head him off."

Mabel reached for Hobo's collar and guided him to the other side of the garage so he couldn't be a distraction. Stormy and Sunny now watched from a nearby flower bed, and Melinda was sure both of them were smirking. They expected a rodeo.

She reached for Pepper's halter, but Angie shook her head and gave a sideways smile. "He thinks it's going to be you, not me. He may be bigger than the sheep, but he's still smaller than our cows. I think I've got this."

Lauren stationed herself in the front yard, prepared to head Pepper off before he reached the lilac bushes. Adelaide covered the space between the house and the garage, and Melinda stayed near the coop. It took Angie a few tries, but she finally cornered Pepper and took him into custody.

Getting him back to the barn turned out to be the most difficult part of the process. The carrots worked, but only for a while. And the more Melinda tugged on his halter, the more determined he was to plant his hooves and shake his head.

"This donkey's as stubborn as a mule," Adelaide muttered, then gently slapped his rump. "Get along there, Pepper! Melinda has

raspberry iced tea and lemon cookies waiting
for us."

Once Pepper was finally back in the barn,
Annie and her two friends were guided into
the pasture with less fuss.

Melinda double-checked the latch on the
bottom half of Pepper's barn door, and
decided it was too heavy and too difficult for
him to manipulate. Even so, the front side of
the pasture had a walk-through gate identical
to the one in the back. Both would need
Pepper-proof reinforcements before he could
safely roam again.

Melinda wondered how long it had taken
Pepper to figure out the gate latch. He'd been
solo in the pasture only, what, maybe five
times? Just enough opportunity, she decided,
for him to locate the gate closest to his barn
door, and chew around on it and see what he
could accomplish.

The women washed up and settled on the
screened-in front porch, where Melinda
offered her gratitude along with the treats.
"No one has earned this more than you ladies.
I suspect the former Fulton Friendship
Circle's monthly programs never focused on
donkey wrangling."

"You got that right." Mabel had been a member in the final years before the original club disbanded. "The funny thing is, though, that for all their dresses and curls and heels, they went home and changed back into their farm clothes to tackle just that kind of task. Or worse."

"I think I've earned at least two cookies." Adelaide took the plate when it came around. "Oh, animals! They make farm life so interesting. I would guess we've had the most excitement of anyone in the township today."

Mabel accepted a paper towel from the stack shared in lieu of napkins. "True. But you know, there's always something happening."

"I hate to gossip," Angie said, "but I thought one of you might know. What is going on with Bart? Is he moving to town, or isn't he?"

Melinda didn't have to decide whether to share her encounter with the real estate agent, as two of her neighbors had already heard what happened. As she'd suspected, Bart hadn't taken kindly to the agent's arrival, or his son's behind-the-back attempt to make him move. But apparently, Bart and Marge's children weren't ready to give up.

"He's finally agreed to a senior apartment

in Swanton. Clarence thinks they'll end up having an auction." Mabel took a bite of her cookie and let that news sink in while she chewed. Clarence Murphy lived just west of Bart, and he talked to Ed frequently. "Bart's admitted he shouldn't be out here anymore, but he's dead-set against all the fuss of listing the place."

"I don't know how marketable it is." Adelaide shook her head. "Our place needed work when we bought it, and we're still at it. But it had good bones, was in decent shape. Bart's, however ..."

"Isn't much more than an eyesore." Angie refilled her glass from the pitcher on the side table. "I love old houses, and I'm sure it had some charm back in the day. But maybe it's just too far gone."

Melinda had to admit Angie was right. "But it's a nice piece of land, or would be once it was cleaned up. There's so many hardwood trees, and a tributary of the creek runs through the back corner."

"Either way, we're likely to find ourselves with new neighbors," Adelaide reminded her friends. "Now, that would certainly get people talking."

"You won't be the newbie, then," Angie told Melinda.

"I'll be happy to pass the crown along when that time comes." She got to her feet. "Oh, before you go, I have something to share."

Melinda soon returned with the club's cookbook, and Adelaide gasped when it was placed in her hands. "Oh, wow! Was this with the meeting minutes?"

"It sure was. I've flipped through it a few times. It was printed in 1949, but I suspect many of the recipes go way back." She turned to Mabel. "There's one in particular I want to ask you about. It's on twenty-eight."

Mabel wiped her hands on her paper towel and carefully turned the pages. A smile soon spread across her face.

"Well, now, you would be correct! My coconut cake is well-loved, but I guess I can't take all the credit."

The decadent dessert was always requested when the Bauers were invited to a potluck, and it made frequent appearances at family birthday dinners and holiday celebrations. Melinda had not only found the recipe in the Fulton Friendship Circle's cookbook, but a very-familiar name attached to it as well.

"Did you get the recipe from Anna Schermann? When I saw the contributor, I was so excited."

"Truth be told, I got it from my mother." Mabel studied the ingredients carefully. "But, yes, this is it!"

"So it's a Schermann family recipe, as well as your family's." Angie leaned in for a look. "Melinda, are you thinking what I'm thinking?"

Angie had been tapped to make Jen's wedding cake, which through discussion had evolved into a set of layers for ceremonial purposes, then cupcakes for the guests.

"Well, Jen just wants a simple white cake," Melinda said. "Why not?"

"Does she like coconut?" Mabel wanted to know.

"I'm not sure, but we can find out."

"We could always make some chocolate cupcakes in case a few guests don't care for this flavor," Angie decided.

"But I can't think of a better way to honor tradition than serving Anna's special recipe at her great-granddaughter's reception. Mabel, if Jen's in agreement, I'd be honored if you'd help me out."

"You couldn't keep me away," Mabel promised. "And it's really not that difficult to make. Oh, won't this be fun!"

Melinda promised to copy the small book and share digital files with her neighbors, but saw another opportunity within its pages. One of the current club's loosely defined goals was to purchase signs to mark the location of the former hamlet of Hawk Hollow, and maintain its pioneer cemetery.

A second edition of this cookbook, rounded out with additional recipes from current and former township residents, would be a way to generate money for those projects. And with the club's records now in her hands, she could add to the historical information in the back of the book.

As always, Melinda had little time to spare. But she had the skills to update the cookbook, and had already researched economical ways to get it printed. Her neighbors loved the idea, and a plan quickly took shape to gather more recipes. In addition to reaching out to current residents, many former families still had ties to the Lutheran church. Angie was an officer in its women's club, and promised to spread the word.

And there was another chance to cast a wide net for submissions.

Prosper's inaugural Founders Day was that coming Saturday, and Nancy and Melinda had organized a historical photo display at the new community center.

"So many people are going to come through the exhibit," Adelaide said.

"If Nancy would let us set up a table, we could take advance orders for the cookbook and provide forms for people to send us more recipes. There's just enough time to get this in Friday's newspaper, and out on social media."

Melinda was thrilled her neighbors were willing to get on board. If some of them helped with publicity, she would have more time to compile the expanded cookbook.

"I'm sure we could sell a few copies at Prosper Hardware. And Nancy might be willing to offer them at the library and city hall."

Adelaide saw another possibility, as well. "The county historical society is sure to get on board. The proceeds from their holiday party gave us a great start toward our goals for the cemetery project. Hawk Hollow has certainly captured the imagination of everyone around here; I'm sure people would be interested in this, too."

Angie was completely engrossed in the cookbook. "See something you like?" Lauren asked.

"I sure do." Angie reached for her phone and snapped a picture of one page. "Now I know what we're having for supper tomorrow night."

8

Two familiar faces were at the store by the time Melinda arrived Saturday morning, but they didn't belong to Frank and Miriam.

Friday had been moving day, and her aunt and uncle were still trying to get settled in their new home. Melinda's parents, Diane and Roger, had helped with yesterday's efforts, and now would work the store on its busiest day of the week. And since it was Founders Day and the start of the farmers market season, it promised to be even more hectic than usual.

Roger had planted himself in the coffee circle, and Melinda hoped his easygoing ways might diffuse the tension caused by Auggie's project. Based on the forced smiles, however, that was going to be a tall order.

"How's your back?" Melinda asked her dad. "Mom said it was a tough go yesterday."

"I'm better. Good thing they hired that crew

for the heavy stuff. But Frank thought he had to get in there and help, and I couldn't let him do it alone." Roger shrugged, or tried to, then winced and rubbed his left shoulder. "Oh, yeah; that's stiff, too."

"Ice first, then heat," Doc suggested. "That's the way to go."

Diane came down from upstairs with a box of additional merchandise. "I grabbed a little of everything. Sunscreen, bug spray, and more Prosper Hardware caps. It's really feeling like summer out there. If people are going to mill around in the park, who knows what they'll need?"

Melinda reached for the dust cloth and began to buff the counter. "This is only the celebration's first year, but I think it's going to draw a decent crowd. It's impressive how many activities Vicki was able to pull together in such a short amount of time."

In addition to the children's play at the school, a woodcutting artist had been tapped to demonstrate techniques in the park. Members of the county historical society were eager to support the new festival, and one of the women volunteered to set up a soap-making station. Two of Shelby's musician friends would play fiddle-and-banjo tunes that afternoon. A few food vendors would also be on hand, in addition to the regular farmers market booths.

Melinda hoped to find time for some of the park's activities, but she was most excited about the historical photo exhibit. Thanks to the robust collection in the historical society's archives, Nancy had dug up photos from nearly every decade of the town's past. Scanned and enlarged, the prints had been matted in simple frames and now lined the walls of the community center's main room.

Along with the photos, the center itself would also be on display. While a handful of private events had already been hosted there, today was the first time the renovated space's doors were officially open to the general public. Between the photo exhibit, and the opportunity to satisfy their curiosity, Melinda expected the center to be packed.

From his chair by the sideboard, George saw something outside that piqued his interest. "What did Vicki do to her hair? And her dress. She looks ... different."

The rest of the guys craned their necks to stare out the front windows, and Melinda almost burst out laughing. The men debated every topic imaginable, but beauty and fashion were never on that list.

Melinda found herself watching, too, as Vicki came in the door. Her long brown hair had been piled high and rolled into a sleek bun in an obvious nod to the day's festivities. A short-sleeved, V-neck tee let her prairie-style skirt take center stage. It would take several yards of fabric to create those luxurious tiers, and Melinda guessed the fashionable confection had cost Vicki more than what most Hartland County settlers had in their pockets when they arrived.

"I love your look," she told Vicki. "But, where's your corset?"

"And shouldn't you be wearing long sleeves?" Diane teased.

Vicki laughed. "I had to draw the line somewhere, and comfort was the line. Besides, I ran out of time to order an authentic costume. But I think this gives a nod to the period while still looking stylish." Her leather tote, however, was definitely modern as well as expensive. She set it on the counter and pulled a binder from its depths. Then another. And a third.

"Wow." Diane studied the stack. "You have a lot going on there."

"As always." Vicki shuffled the pile and set one binder aside. "That's the early plans for the Fourth of July festival. Now, this is today's agenda." She opened the next cover, scanned the first page, and gave a nod of approval. "Good. On track."

The last binder was so large, it made a thump on the counter. "Here we are, Jen's wedding. Melinda, I have a few things I want to run past you, if we have time. But first, where are you with upgrades at the farm?"

"I am happy to report a painting crew has been decided upon and hired." Although the men had pretended to ignore what was going on at the counter, Melinda's announcement brought a round of applause from across the room.

"Two days, three bids, and one winner." She acknowledged her friends' cheers with a quick nod. "In the end, it wasn't much of a contest."

"They're that good, huh?" Vicki smiled. "That's exciting! You know it'll get done right, and on time."

"Yes, thankfully. But really, the other two didn't have a chance."

The first contractor had glanced at her farmhouse's narrow clapboard siding and, despite his profession as a painter, tried to talk her into covering it with vinyl siding. His brother was in that line of work, and maintenance-free was really the way to go. The windows looked terrible, and needed to be replaced immediately. No worries, though, because he knew a guy ...

The next contender wasn't much of one, either. It was clear he doubted Melinda's assessment of the situation, and the number of gallons he insisted it would take was more than double what the owner of Swanton's paint store had estimated. Sensing a con, she leveled with him: She needed someone reliable who wouldn't waste paint, and the job had to be done by the end of June. With a wedding at the farm just a week later, there couldn't be any delays.

"So, you're getting married?" He'd nodded and crossed his arms. "Makes sense, though. It's not right, a woman living out here in the country all alone. Well, I guess if you want a written bid, give me your man's email and I'll send it over."

She sent him packing, instead.

Thank goodness for the woman who sold her the hostas. Hank was polite, friendly and knowledgeable. He had experience with older homes, and was delighted that many of the farmhouse's period details were still intact. But he recommended a complete scrape-down of the exterior, not just the areas with the most peels and flakes, and Melinda had to admit he was right. More time and labor meant more expense, but she didn't want to cut corners. The good news was, Hank's crew could start in a few weeks and meet the deadline with a little room to spare.

"What about the roof?" Vicki asked. "Do you think that'll be done in time? End of June would be a good target there, as well, in case of last-minute delays."

Melinda didn't bat an eye at Vicki's directive. They'd talked about this several times, and Melinda was the one who'd insisted both projects be completed before Jen's wedding. It would be so rewarding to have the farmhouse shined up before the big event. And besides, she'd been planning these upgrades for a long time; she didn't want to wait until after the ceremony to get started.

"That's a tall order." Auggie inserted

himself into the conversation. "All new paint, and a new roof, too. Melinda, if you have to pay extra to get it all done before the wedding, Jen should reimburse you for those fees. That's only fair."

Suddenly, things were moving in an awkward direction.

"The roof's not going to be a problem at all." Melinda gave everyone a big, no-worries smile. "The company that fixed the store's roof will replace mine. It'll only take a few days, and I'm already on their calendar."

"Well, I don't know about everyone else." Roger's tone was especially cheerful as he took his empty mug to the sideboard. "But I can't wait to get up to the park and see that wood-carving demonstration. I hear the guy's really talented."

"Looks like a great day, huh?" Doc folded up his chair, and the other guys took the hint. "I have farm calls to make, so I better get started."

* * *

Just like Diane said, summer felt like it was just around the corner. Or had arrived a little early. Before Melinda left for the photo exhibit, she pulled two quarters from her purse and plunked them into the vintage, round-topped pop machine in Prosper Hardware's back lot. She couldn't think of a better way to honor her family on Founders Day than to sip an orange soda on her short stroll to the community center.

When Prosper's last grocery store closed several decades ago, Grandpa Shrader rolled the dispenser out of the store's back room and across the gravel, then chained it to this oak tree on the edge of the alley. It was his way to ensure residents could still get a refreshing drink, day or night. The store still sold pop inside, of course, but residents enjoyed the nostalgia of the machine even more than what it offered for sale.

Her path took her out to Third Street, then she wandered up to Main. Kitty-corner from the post office, the community center's tall windows sparkled in the sunlight.

Melinda felt a sudden surge of pride at how far the former bank had come in barely six months. While too many of Prosper's commercial properties were deteriorating, this two-story brick structure now welcomed visitors with freshly painted front steps flanked by pots of geraniums.

The photo exhibit had just opened and, given the number of people streaming in and out of the grand building's vestibule, it was sure to be well-attended. Conversations echoed through the high-ceilinged front room, where the dark oak floors and ornate woodwork gleamed in the glow of the reproduction fixtures overhead. A roller cart offering punch and cookies waited inside the entrance and, in one far corner, Melinda found Adelaide and Lauren staffing the cookbook table.

"Look at this crowd!" Adelaide nearly shouted to be heard over the din. "The photos turned out amazing. And these off-white walls are the perfect backdrop. I could almost believe I'm at a gallery opening in Madison." The Beauforts had lived in the Wisconsin capital for years before returning to Mason's home area.

Melinda laughed. "I was thinking the same thing, but about Minneapolis. I guess Prosper's more cosmopolitan than we think, at least for today."

"Doesn't this place look sharp?" Nancy was barely able to contain her excitement. "I'll run it by Jerry, but I think we should leave the prints up after the open house. They are so striking, and the perfect artwork for this historical building. We'll take them down, of course, for any renters that request it."

Melinda leaned in. "What about Delores? Do we need to get her approval?" Delores Eklund's generous donation had made Prosper's community center possible. The retired teacher had also appointed herself the project's interior decorator, and no surface in the building had escaped her scrutiny.

"Oh, I think she'll come around." Nancy shrugged. "She loves this town, and is proud of its history. I think that'll be more than enough for her to overlook all the nail holes we put in the plaster."

Now that they were enlarged and framed, the photos' significance and emotional impact was fully on display. Melinda wandered over to the generous bank of front windows, and started with the oldest prints in the collection. One was an 1880s shot of the train depot, which was now only a storage shed on Auggie's lot. The other showed the first-known photo of Main Street, taken shortly after the town incorporated in 1890.

It was fascinating to see how the small business district had evolved over the years. While Prosper Hardware always looked the same, so many of the other buildings had changed hands, and purposes, several times.

There was the once-bustling drug store, which was now a vacant shell of its former self. And another bank, one Melinda wasn't familiar with. Was that the last resident of the dusty-windowed brick building in the next block? It had been empty for years, and she couldn't imagine it polished and tidy, buzzing with commerce. She studied a vintage photo of the former gas station, which showed a smart-capped attendant washing a car's windows, and remembered how the business closed after the 1980s farm crisis.

While many of the prints were a sobering reminder of how precarious small-town businesses could be, others gave her hope. There was Meadow Lane, way back when it was a butcher's storefront. A dry-goods store Melinda pegged as the soon-to-be-home of Emmett's relocated barber shop. On the end of the first row, she found the shot of the town's first mercantile, a grand limestone structure that had fallen into disrepair before the city purchased it for a dollar and renovated it into the current city hall.

The last third of the exhibit happened to be Melinda's favorite. Instead of landscapes of Main Street or the exteriors of individual businesses, it was filled with slice-of-life photos from Prosper's past. Along with school activities and holiday celebrations, there were people enjoying watermelon on a hot summer's day, a group shot of the town's long-ago baseball team, even pictures of damage from when a tornado grazed the edge of town in the 1950s.

Karen met up with Melinda as she turned the last corner. "I love these casual shots! I was so excited when you found them in the archives. They really bring the past to life."

"I wish we'd had room for more. This isn't even a third of them." Melinda pointed to a photo showing the inside of Prosper Hardware in the 1940s. "There's my great-grandpa, lounging against our oak showcase, with one of the clerks. Look how high everything goes on the back wall! Grandpa pulled some of those shelves down when he renovated in the sixties. Said it looked less cluttered, but Mom claims he was just tired of going up and down that rolling ladder to fetch things."

"I think this is the vet clinic." Karen pointed at a sepia-toned print from the east end of Main Street, which showed a modest, single-story structure with a small barn on its back lot. "Doc says it's been remodeled several times over the years. He thinks its original purpose was as a livery and harness shop, and I bet he's right. Look at all those horses lined up for the photo."

"That fits. And you still have the barn! Speaking of animals, we have about forty cats on the list for next week's spay clinic. I'm so glad we can hold them here now. It's easy to set up, and clean up at the end of the day. A better location than the council chambers."

Along with club meetings, anniversary and graduation celebrations, and family reunions, the community center was now the official home of the area's nonprofit cat-care program. The initiative focused on curbing overpopulation among ferals and barn cats, and made sure those felines also received at-cost vaccinations and basic medical care.

"Can you believe it's only been a year since we had our first clinic?" Karen shook her head in awe. "We had no idea what we were getting ourselves into, just that we wanted to help."

"It's amazing how it's taken off. Just goes to show there was a real need in the community. I'll double check, but I'm pretty sure we'll see our five-hundredth patient sometime next month. Can you believe it?"

Karen did the math. "Yes, that sounds about right. What a milestone! What are we going to do to celebrate?"

Melinda had to put that question on the back burner for now, as she'd promised to watch the cookbook table while Adelaide and Lauren took a break. Before she could head in their direction, someone tapped her on the arm.

"There you are!" It was one of the women from the historical society. "Adelaide asked me to come find you, right away. Oh, this is so exciting! I couldn't believe it at first, but the proof's right there. You have to see it!"

Adelaide was about to burst with some sort of good news. "You'd better sit down." She motioned to a chair, then handed Melinda a sheet of paper that was blank except for a photocopy of a small, black-and-white picture.

When Melinda studied the scene, her jaw dropped.

"How ... where did you get this?"

They had searched everywhere, through old county history books and the society's archives, the Prosper library's meager photo collection and even the dusty files upstairs at city hall. Hawk Hollow merited a short mention in the history books and appeared on a few antique maps, but that was all. If there had ever been a photo of Hawk Hollow in its heyday, the print had vanished ... just like the little community itself.

But here it was. And there was no doubt, as the sign across the front of Hawk Hollow Creamery was clearly visible. Off to the left was part of another single-story building, which had to be the general store.

"Look at the truck, there in the front!" Adelaide nearly jumped up and down with glee. "I'd say it's one from the twenties. The photo could be from the Great Depression era, maybe, but not much later."

Lauren pointed out an elderly woman chatting with another member of the society's board. "She walked in with this, not even ten minutes ago. I just couldn't believe what I was seeing."

The woman's grandparents had lived in

Fulton Township many years ago, about a mile south of the church, and the farm was eventually handed down to others in the extended family. When the farmhouse was cleaned out last fall, there were several boxes of old photos that one cousin hadn't had the heart to throw away. Because the family was originally from Illinois, no one knew for sure where some of the snapshots were taken.

But when the announcement about the Hawk Hollow cookbook appeared in yesterday's edition of the Swanton newspaper, everything clicked into place. The woman had the original at home, but was willing to let someone borrow it long enough to scan it properly.

"We have to put this in the cookbook." Melinda still couldn't believe their good luck. "I was going to include the history of Hawk Hollow, what little we have, since the money raised will benefit the cemetery. But this is priceless."

"Isn't it funny how things work out?" Adelaide leaned over to give the photo another look. "We're celebrating Prosper's history today, but the big excitement comes from little Hawk Hollow."

9

It was a beautiful evening, warm but not too
hot. The farmyard was filled with birdsong,
and the lowering sun was warm on Melinda's
face as she moved down the clothesline, pulled
off the fresh-scented towels and sheets, and
added them to the basket at her feet.

Josh had grilled steaks for dinner, and
there was shortcake and some of her patch's
early strawberries waiting for them when their
chores were through. But really, spending
time with Josh was never a chore, no matter
what tasks were on their list. They could mend
fences, or muck out the barn, and she
wouldn't care. Those weren't exactly her ideas
of perfect date nights, but it was the person
you were with that mattered.

And in her life, the animals, too.

Hobo dashed past, barely missing the
laundry basket, and Charlie was right behind.
Josh's rescue dog was having the time of his

life at the farm, exploring its far-flung corners with his new friend. He was a handsome fellow, with a shaggy black coat highlighted by patches of brown and white, but wasn't afraid to follow Hobo's lead and roll in the garden's dirt.

At least they had enough sense to stay between the rows. Melinda had replanted the seedlings Pepper ruined last week, and crossed her fingers there would be no more jail breaks. Given the sturdy, complicated latches she and Josh installed on both pasture gates, her mischievous donkey was likely to keep to his own turf from now on.

And yes, he was her donkey now. Doc had asked around, tried to find Pepper a new home, but there'd been only a few leads and none of them seemed serious. The donkey had bounced around enough, and he needed a stable environment with some animal friends to keep him happy.

Which, given Josh's grin as he came up from the barn, was meant to be Melinda's farm.

"So far, so good. Pepper's pretending to graze, but he's really watching the sheep out of the corner of his eye. The sheep are staring at him, but nobody's run off yet." He turned back for another look. "Yes! Annie's gone back to noshing, and some of the others seem inclined to take their cues from her."

Melinda reached for Josh's hand and gave it a squeeze. "Excellent work, Doctor Vogel. If everyone can just get along, that's all I ask." She sighed. "Too bad things in town aren't as easy as they are here at the farm."

Monday night's council meeting had been tense but short. Or so Melinda had heard, as she'd deliberately stayed away. There was plenty to do at the farm when the weather was this nice. That, coupled with vague references to planning Jen's wedding, had been enough of an excuse for anyone who'd asked if she planned to attend.

The council voted unanimously to file Auggie's requests, just as Nancy said they would, and set a public hearing for their first meeting in June. Auggie was in the crowd, prepared to address the council if they had any questions, but the members agreed ahead of time not to draw him into their very-brief conversation.

Any grandstanding by Auggie would have stirred up the crowd, and made residents demand a chance to speak their minds, too.

Of the five council members, only three made any comment at all. One of the men raised concerns about Auggie's requested tax breaks, and another simply stated he was in favor of having regular gas available in Prosper again.

But it was Jake Newcastle's remarks that piqued Melinda's curiosity. Jake had read a prepared statement that, while brief, touched on several parts of the proposal. He raised concerns about protecting Prosper's finances, but also insisted he was a strong supporter of local businesses' efforts to expand.

Such premeditated waffling was often the hallmark of a political campaign, and Melinda wondered if Jake was already plotting to once again challenge Jerry for the mayoral post. The next election was over three years away. But if Jake set his mind to something, he was sure to follow through on it.

Frank hadn't said a word. And, other than outlining the upcoming steps for the audience, neither had Jerry.

Given his ties to Melinda, Josh was just as determined to stay silent on the issue.

"I had three people today try to draw me

into conversations about the co-op." He reached for a pillowcase and folded it into fourths. "And I'm proud to report I was able to dodge my way out, every time."

"Aren't you the sly one." She leaned over and gave him a kiss. "Jake's not the only smooth-talker around here, then. Maybe you should run for a seat on Swanton's council. I wish this wasn't an issue for you, but since it is, I'm glad you were able to sidestep all of that. People might think you're biased."

"You know I am." He kissed her back.

Melinda reached for a towel and held it up to her nose. "Mmm, you can't get that fragrance from any bottle. While I was away, I'd forgotten how wonderful it is to hang laundry on a clothesline. When I came out here that first day and saw this, it brought me back to my childhood."

"Swanton's a small enough town that most people still have a line in the backyard. I think my house is one of the few on my block that doesn't."

"Well, you can bring your laundry out and use mine, anytime." She held up a hand. "Already washed, though. Horace's old machine acts like it's about to shake apart during the spin cycle, no matter what I do. That might be next on my repair-and-replace list."

"I'm good with any excuse to come out here, so I might take you up on your offer." He reached for her hand and pulled her behind the screen of sheets that flapped in the gentle evening breeze. "You know, I think I like laundry day; it gives us a little privacy out here."

They kissed for several minutes, and Melinda was too pleasantly distracted to point out the obvious. But when they finally broke apart, she had to laugh. "Honey, it's not like anyone can see us. There's no one within a half mile, at least."

"I know." He kissed her neck again. "We have this whole place to ourselves."

"Well, not really." Melinda pointed to the laundry basket, which Stormy had taken over during the past few minutes. The soft, sweet-scented towels made a perfect cat bed, but Melinda wasn't about to let him stay.

"I don't know where you have been lately, and maybe it's just as well." She lifted him out of the basket, but he didn't protest. "I'm going to take my chances and not wash those again."

She added the clothespin bag to the bin, and they started toward the house.

"I have whipped topping and vanilla ice cream; which do you want with your shortcake? Or really, we could get crazy and have both."

"Ice cream sounds good, thanks."

Melinda set the laundry basket on the back porch's bench. "Oh, since you're here, I need your help with something else. I think one of the chickens chipped her beak on something. Could you give her a quick look, first?"

Hobo and Charlie trailed them to the coop, and lounged in the grass while Melinda and Josh went inside. The hen was one of the oldest of the flock, one of Horace's girls, and didn't mind a quick examination.

"Doesn't look too serious." Josh gently set the hen back in her brooder box. "It'll grow out, eventually. As long as you see her eating and drinking like normal, I wouldn't worry."

Pansy strutted over and pecked at one of the feed pans, then glared at Melinda.

"Oh, please." Melinda rolled her eyes. "There's plenty of snacks in there, and more out in your run. You're just mad you're not the center of attention."

But something else had caught Josh's. He grimaced and pointed to the underside of the chicken house's roof, where a beam of evening light slipped through a crack. Melinda looked harder, and saw another one not far away.

"That roof." Josh shook his head. "It's in rough shape. If it gets to leaking bad, you're going to have a mess. And there's nothing madder than a wet hen."

With the chicken house's door latched tight to make sure Charlie and Hobo didn't get any ideas, Josh and Melinda went around to the back of the coop. The steep slope on this side of the roof faced north, and caught the worst of winter's winds.

The thicket of wild black raspberries was tall and lush, and made it hard to get too close. But even to Melinda's untrained eye, now that she studied them closely, the gray shingles were worn in several places. And the joints where they met the now-unused chimney didn't look much better.

"I'm so glad you saw that crack," she told Josh. "I've been in such a rush lately, at chore time. I wonder how long it's been there?"

"It's small, so it may have just opened up this spring. And the other one, too. It's been dry lately, the lack of humidity makes everything shrink back."

Melinda sighed. "I need to fix this before the wedding. Not because the guests are going to care, but because it can't wait."

"Some replacement shingles should do it." Josh took her hand as they started toward the house. "That's my farmer-boy assessment. But I'm afraid I don't have the skills to help you fix it. At least, not fix it right."

"Neither do I. And it's important to know what you can tackle, and what you can't."

The coop's roof needed repairs, and there wasn't money to spare. The roofers weren't coming for several weeks yet, and she knew they'd charge a hefty base fee for what looked to be a simple patch job. What she really needed was someone who'd work for a few bucks and maybe some pizza.

A handyman. Two would be even better.

Suddenly, the situation was looking up. "I think I know just who to ask."

* * *

Kevin and Melinda ducked under the awning of Scenic Vista's front entrance to stay out of the hot sun.

"I didn't call Dave yet, but I know he'll want to do it." Kevin kept his eyes on the driveway, as some of their guests had yet to arrive. It was Memorial Day, and the nursing home was hosting a program to honor its residents' military service. Wilbur, at ninety-six, was the oldest World War II veteran at the facility.

"I know Jen wanted to pay you something for hosting the wedding, and you wouldn't let her. Having her brother fix your coop's roof would be a good trade. Dave either has leftover shingles he can use, or he'll get them for you." Kevin raised his chin. "And I'd love the chance to come out and lend a hand."

At her surprised look, he laughed.

"Yeah, even a college professor can do it, when the time calls for it. It's not my best skill, but I threw a few shingles here and there when I helped Horace and Wilbur on the weekends. When the machine shed's roof needed work, I put those spares on, up along the ridgeline."

Melinda was impressed. "I hadn't noticed."

"That's the point." He grinned. And then, his expression turned wistful. "Really, let me help. This may be my last chance to leave my mark out at the farm."

Melinda understood. Her farm had been more than the Schermann family's home base; it was a place Kevin had poured hours of sweat equity and lots of love into over the years. "Please do. We'll make a party out of it. Well, I'm happy to report I've chosen the paint color for the house."

"Let me guess: white?"

"Of course! My plywood samples tell me it's a shade warmer than what's on there now, but it's as close as I could get. Oh, good, here's Josh."

Veterinary emergencies never took a holiday, and there had been two last-minute patients to attend to that morning. Which meant Josh had missed the Memorial Day ceremony at Prosper's cemetery, and lunch at Frank and Miriam's new house.

George had made good on his promise to have the town's plot ship-shape for the holiday, thanks to the nimble hands of the fifth-graders from Prosper's elementary school. The ceremony was followed by donuts in the fire department's shed behind city hall, but Melinda had somehow also found room for the massive spread Miriam fixed for the family's noon meal.

And she wasn't done eating yet. Scenic Vista's celebration would be capped off with cake and ice cream, and then she and Josh were grilling out at Roger and Diane's that evening. If she kept eating like this, Melinda wasn't sure she'd fit into the sundress she bought for Jen's wedding.

But all those snacks weren't the reason she felt a bit queasy. Horace had invited Maggie to today's program, and her daughters were driving her up from Cedar Falls. It would be nice to see Maggie again, as well as Wendy and Barb, but it was anyone's guess how this gathering would go.

Maggie claimed her daughters supported her idea, but Melinda wondered if that was really true. Kevin and Ada still weren't fully on board. And to make matters worse (or better, depending on how you looked at things) Horace wasn't, either. And while Horace and Maggie talked on the phone several times a week, they hadn't seen each other since Maggie tossed out her marriage proposal.

"There they are!" Kevin's voice was cheerful, but Melinda sensed the tension in his shoulders. Josh simply raised an eyebrow at Melinda, and shrugged. He was serene and detached from the situation, and she resolved to do the same. As much as she felt like a member of the Schermann family, this wasn't her battle. Horace was her friend; she would simply support whatever he decided to do.

"Hello, everyone!" Wendy's smile was genuine when she got out of the car. If she was in such a good mood, the situation must be somewhat under control. Kevin, however, had to know.

"Any word?" he whispered.

Wendy lowered her voice and rolled her eyes. "Well, my impression is, they can't seem to make up their minds what to do. And at their age, maybe that's not such a great idea. Too much stress, if you ask me."

"Horace has clammed up on us," Kevin explained. "We've just quit asking. Mom's already inside; she hopes that today, with everyone here, he might give some indication which way he's leaning."

A small crowd had started to gather on the nursing home's east lawn. Folding chairs were lined up in front of a temporary platform decorated with patriotic bunting, and easels parked on each side showcased vintage photos of residents in their military uniforms. The ceremony didn't start for more than a half hour, but the guests were taking the opportunity to enjoy the nice day and each other's company.

"That's all I want for today." Wendy gestured at the smiling faces around the stage. "Just the chance to catch up with all of you, without any fuss. He called her cell when we were about halfway here, and she got so excited. I swear, I don't think my girls were this dramatic when they were teenagers."

"Young love." Josh smiled. "I guess it never gets old."

"Well, they chatted all the rest of the way here. On and on, this and that. And they'd just talked the night before last." Wendy looked over her shoulder and frowned. "Barb was going to help Mom with her walker. I wonder what's taking them so long?"

She motioned for Melinda, Kevin and Josh to follow her. As they approached, Melinda could see Maggie in the backseat. She wore a tasteful red dress, and her white curls were immaculate despite the heat. Her outfit was bright, but her expression was the opposite.

"No!" she told Barb. "No, I'm not going!"

Barb threw up her hands in frustration,

then came around the bumper. "You know how they were all lovey-dovey on the phone, we couldn't get them to hang up? At the last minute, she told Horace that since she was coming today, they should take this opportunity to make their plans while everyone is together."

Kevin and Melinda exchanged worried looks. Horace hated ultimatums. It had taken a complex web of pleading and plain luck to get him to agree to a temporary stay with Wilbur. Then more emotional maneuvers to make Horace think it was all his decision to remain at Scenic Vista.

"And what did he say?" Josh asked. Melinda was afraid she knew the answer.

"Well, I didn't hear his end of it, but I can about guess." Barb crossed her arms. "She got angry, started crying. And now, she won't even get out of the car."

Kevin closed his eyes for a moment. "I'll bring him out here. Thank goodness the ceremony doesn't start for a while yet. Josh, how about you come with me? Maybe Melinda can find a way to talk some sense into her."

"Me?" Melinda took a step back.

"Yes, you." Wendy patted her arm

encouragingly. "She thinks the world of you, and not just because it was your detective work that brought them together after seventy years. You're smart, and independent, and ..."

"Very single." Melinda cringed. Was that what Wendy wanted? For her to talk Maggie out of this idea?

Wendy gently pushed Melinda toward the car. "Please try, at least. We keep telling her: 'You and Horace are happy just the way you are; why mess with a good thing?' But she won't listen to us."

"Hey, Maggie." Melinda slipped into the backseat with a smile. Even with the doors open, the car was already stifling inside. "It's good to see you. So glad you came today. I'm sure it means a lot to Horace. And Wilbur, too."

"Humph!" Maggie looked away. "Poor Wilbur, I doubt he even understands what's going on. As for Horace, well, I doubt he cares. Not about me, at least. Not one bit!"

Wendy and Barb shook their heads at each other. Their weariness was one important piece in a puzzle Melinda was now trying to solve; and apparently, on a deadline. She'd assumed Horace's silence about Maggie's proposal was simply stubbornness on his part, a way to protect his privacy while he considered what was in his heart, and how best to balance that with Wilbur's needs. But it was becoming clear the lovebirds had been fighting on and off since this all started. Were things really that strained between them?

Maybe no one needed to worry about a wedding, anymore. Because given how upset Maggie was, there was a real chance these two might be on the verge of breaking up, instead.

"He says he's not ready!" Maggie's eyes filled with tears, which began to roll down her weathered cheeks. Even with the heat, she'd put on face powder for this special day. Wendy found a tissue in her purse, and handed it to her mother.

Melinda glanced toward the entrance. Oh, if only Horace would get out here! He was rather spry with his cane, but it would be a few more minutes. "Well, maybe he needs a little more time." She struggled with what to say next, but Maggie didn't.

"More time?" Her voice cracked with anguish. "He's had seventy years to know if he really loves me or not! This is exactly why we broke up the other time! 'I don't know what to do,' and 'this is a big decision,' and 'my family needs me.' I've heard it all before; I can't go through this again."

Melinda was about to suggest Maggie back off on this whole marriage thing, and just enjoy spending time with Horace. Did a ring really matter that much? Wasn't it more important to give Horace some space? If she had to browbeat him into a commitment, was it even worth it?

But then, Melinda realized that was her idea of a healthy relationship. Not only were Maggie's ideas rooted in the past, but her life had been full of ups and downs. Maybe she saw this as her last chance at happiness.

When Maggie and Horace broke up seventy years ago, her life went into a tailspin. She'd become pregnant by someone else, then offered her baby boy up for adoption. Maggie had barely spoken about this to her daughters, but they'd extracted enough information to make attempts to find their half-brother. Their search was still unsuccessful, and they feared it was likely to stay that way. And while Maggie eventually married, Wendy and Barb hinted their parents' relationship had seemed to be built mostly on friendship.

There wouldn't ever be anyone else for Maggie. Horace was her great love, and they'd lost decades to time and circumstance. And now, there wasn't much time left; no wonder she wanted to spend every moment with him. But if he wouldn't commit, her wounded heart might not be content with what Horace still had to give.

Maggie gave an irritated sigh. "My mother was right. Oh, I hate to admit it now, but she was! 'Horace isn't good enough for you,' she kept saying. 'Move on, find someone else. Someone more educated, who can give you a better life.' Well, I tried, and look how that turned out."

"Mother!" Wendy gasped.

Barb was on the verge of tears herself. "Maybe you didn't love him back, but Daddy loved you. Always!"

There was no remorse on Maggie's lined face. Instead, Melinda saw relief; relief that, finally, she had spoken her truth. But this family was about to unravel, right here in Scenic Vista's parking lot. And there was Horace, slowly making his way in their direction with Kevin and Josh trailing behind. Melinda had to do something, and quick.

"Let's go, huh?" Her tone was cheerful, but carried the hint of an order. "It's terribly hot in here."

Maggie merely wiped her cheeks again, and turned away. Melinda couldn't take one more minute, and gave Maggie's arm a little pinch. "Get out of the car."

Maggie stared at her in shock. Before she could offer a challenge, Melinda raised her voice. "I've had enough. It's suffocating in here, and I'm not going to miss Wilbur's big moment because of your temper tantrum. Get out. Now!"

Wendy swooped in, relieved Maggie of her purse and set the walker next to the car. "Stop it, Mother! You are embarrassing us." The parking lot was filling up with cars and, just as Wendy hinted, this melodrama was attracting quite a bit of attention.

"I don't give one whit for what people think," Maggie hissed. But when Melinda glared at her again, she edged toward the door. "Fine. Let's get this over with."

"What is going on?" The lines on Horace's forehead deepened when he saw Maggie's tears. "Honey, why are you still out here? The ceremony is about to start."

"How can you ask me that? You know how upset I am!"

There wasn't much privacy in a parking lot, but they tried to give Horace and Maggie some space. Wendy herded everyone into the shade of some nearby trees, and they watched as the lovebirds pecked at each other by the side of the car. Hand gestures were few, as he kept a grip on his cane and she maintained her hold on her walker, but it was obvious they were both frustrated. And yet, still in love with each other.

Finally, Horace motioned for Kevin to help Maggie navigate the curb. And he had a small smile for Melinda when he passed her on the way to the ceremony. "Well, hello! Nice of you to come. Kevin says you have the paint picked out for the house."

"Why, yes." She blinked at the unexpected direction of their conversation. "It's ... white."

"Just as it should be." He pointed to the stage. "Good, Ada has Wilbur all settled. Edith is late; but then, they probably hit road construction on the way." Before Melinda could press him for details, Horace moved on.

Josh touched her arm. "Wow, he's so calm. He could have had a lucrative career as a professional poker player. You'd never know they just had a fight. Do you think it's over?"

"Hardly. He's just hit the pause button. There are other things to focus on right now. Let's go find a seat."

Melinda easily found Wilbur's portrait in the photo display, and marveled at how young and handsome he looked. Wilbur's girlfriend jilted him while he was overseas, Horace had said, and he gave up on the idea of marriage altogether.

And while Horace's young love had found him again, their future seemed as uncertain as it was before.

Horace and Maggie finally agreed to sit next to each other, at least. Ada stayed on the platform with Wilbur, who smiled every time the audience erupted into applause. But from the vacant look in his eyes, it was clear Wilbur didn't understand what the ceremony was about, or that he was one of the honored guests.

When it was Wilbur's turn to be recognized, Melinda saw Maggie reach across the gap between their chairs and grasp Horace's hand. A smile passed between them, and Melinda wondered what they were thinking.

Maybe, just like that, the fight was over. They'd already lost seventy years. Why waste another moment?

Josh saw it, too. "Life's full of surprises, huh?" he whispered. He put his arm around Melinda, and she let her head fall against his shoulder.

10

Jerry stood at Prosper Hardware's front windows, just taking in the view. But then, something caught his eye. Or rather, someone. "What's Emmett up to?"

"Working on the barber shop, even at this early hour." Doc settled into his usual chair, coffee cup in hand. "Tomorrow's the first of June, he's really counting down the weeks to the grand opening. I saw him inside, when I drove past."

Jerry turned back to his friends. "Not anymore, he's not. He's coming this way."

A guest at coffee hour? Melinda smothered a laugh at the surprise on the men's faces. Roger was there that morning, but her dad showed up often enough to almost be a regular. Just as he had during Frank and Miriam's vacation, he was working part-time the next few days. The Langes were settled into their new home, but there was plenty to do at their Victorian before it went on the market. Miriam had taken time off to do just that; and Frank, given the ongoing tension with Auggie, had never seemed so eager to clean in all his life.

"So, what's the news today?" George gestured to the extra folding chairs by the sideboard when Emmett walked in. "Help yourself, the coffee's on."

Emmett waved and poured himself a cup, while Jerry and Doc scooted their seats to widen the circle. When Emmett rummaged in the drawer for an extra spoon, Auggie squirmed at the sight of someone rifling through his stash. And he nearly came out of his chair when Emmett took the second-to-the-last blueberry muffin.

"Funny you mention it, George, as I do have news."

"You've set a date to open?"

"Not yet. It'll be sometime next month, after the Fourth. But, no, my news is bigger than that. I'm going to hire a female stylist!"

Eyebrows shot up around the circle. Melinda let out a cheer, but the guys were too stunned to notice.

Auggie frowned. "Are you serious?"

"I certainly am! She works at a place in Swanton right now; you know, the one on the square? Well, she's talented, smart, and looking for career advancement. I'll retire someday, someone's going to need to take over the shop. She'll start here in late summer, so not right away."

"A lady barber." Jerry was coming around to the idea. "Who would have thought we'd see the day, right here in little Prosper!"

"Wait a minute." Melinda put down her dust cloth and came around the counter. "Who says she's only going to cut men's hair? I'd love to just walk down the street and get a trim."

"Bingo." Emmett winked. "That's exactly the plan. Sure, she'll have male clients, too. But this is the perfect way to expand the business. I've been only serving half the people around here, all these years."

Doc nodded his approval. "You've said most of the guys at your Swanton shop are willing to come over here for a cut. But you're right, this is a great way to broaden that customer base."

"Mary will be pleased." George got up for a refill. "She drives to Charles City to get her hair done, has for years. If this woman is as good as you say, it'll make things so much easier for her. Who knows? I might give her a try myself, once she's settled."

"You would?" Auggie was surprised.

"Well, yeah. Why not?"

"Oh, I don't know." Auggie's brow furrowed as he sipped his coffee. "I don't know if I'd be willing to chance that. Nothing against you ladies," he quickly told Melinda, "but I don't trust my locks to anyone but Emmett."

"What locks would those be?" Doc snickered. "You have less left than I do. But seriously, I doubt she'll have much trouble fitting in."

Jerry polished off the last of his muffin. "I think it's exciting. Doc, I remember when you hired Karen. First female veterinarian around here in, well, forever. Sure, some of the guys were surprised, but they came around quick, once they saw how good she is. No reason this woman can't do the same."

Emmett had a long day of work ahead of him; another cup of coffee was exactly what he needed. "I just thought I'd stop in," he said as he went back to the sideboard. "I wanted all of you to be the first to know."

"Glad you think so highly of our group." Auggie was pleased. "We always have the pulse of everything going on around here."

"Oh, I know." Emmett chuckled as he returned to his seat. "I figured it was the best way to get the word out. I mean, if a business plans to expand, this is the place to make an announcement."

Auggie chuckled, too flattered to notice the hint of sarcasm. Emmett was being tactful now, but he'd told Melinda last week he was furious about Auggie's request for tax breaks to renovate the co-op. Just as Vicki and Arthur had next door, Emmett and Patricia were rehabbing a vacant storefront with no handouts from the city.

Jerry, who'd either had the same conversation with Emmett or simply suspected his stance on this issue, seemed to shrink back into his chair. Melinda gave her dad a look, and Roger swung into action.

"Well, now, did everyone see this?" He smiled brightly as he held up that morning's edition of the Des Moines newspaper. "Looks like the crops are hanging in there statewide, even though it's been dry. Auggie, how are things holding up around here?"

Jerry's shoulders dropped in a visible show of relief. Auggie mostly loved to talk about himself, but the crops and the weather were next on his list. Doc, who spent a great deal of time driving the area's back roads, could also be counted upon to have insight into the situation. And George, with decades of farming under his belt, would provide the historical commentary.

The store was packed with customers all morning. Bill was trapped in the back, busy with custom lumber orders, so Melinda was glad Roger was skilled at ringing up purchases and stocking shelves. When Esther arrived at eleven, Melinda finally had a chance to water the baskets of impatiens swaying on the light poles out front. They needed a daily drink, even with the recent rains, but Melinda didn't mind. It was a chance to step away from the counter for a few minutes and gather her thoughts.

Getting a haircut in Prosper was more than she could have hoped for. When she moved home from Minneapolis, she'd had to adjust to driving several miles to access many day-to-day necessities. When Emmett expanded his new barbershop, and if Auggie put in his gas pumps, everyone would think they had it made. Now, if a pizza place would just open up in Prosper, and offer delivery ...

But, no. Even if one did, they wouldn't deliver all the way out to her farm. And besides, such a place would be competition for Jessie and Doug and the Watering Hole. More options might be handy for residents, but Vicki was right: in a town this small, everyone needed to stay in their lane if all the businesses were to have a chance.

Melinda moved the ladder to the next lamp post, then reached for the watering can and started her climb. Her family was obviously worried about how Auggie's merchandise expansion would hurt Prosper Hardware, but only a few people had mentioned that specific concern in the past few weeks.

It was the tax breaks they were against. And his crazy request for a wetland designation, which was nothing more than a blatant cash grab. People could see that from a mile away. She couldn't believe anyone on the council, including Jake, would ever support that idea.

Melinda decided this all came down to the simple principle of everyone paying their own way. Auggie had a right to grow his business, but it seemed like he was trying to cheat the system. And that, to people around here, was the worst offense of all.

She sighed as she moved on to the last basket. Because right below her was an unmistakable reminder of how tight Prosper's city budget had always been. Main Street's margins were pockmarked and rough, and there were plenty of cracks in its asphalt.

The thoroughfare really needed to be repaved, but that wasn't going to happen anytime soon. Even though Main was part of a county highway, and the county would cover some of the cost, Jerry said Prosper didn't have the cash to pay its share.

No matter what happened, it was a lovely day. Before she came down the ladder, Melinda took a moment to admire the view. Prosper had its financial problems, but it was still a charming little town. In the next block, she could see Emmett and Patricia hard at work on Prosper's newest business. Vicki kept talking about organizing a chamber of commerce.

That seemed like a big step for a town this small, but if more people saw its potential and put down roots here ...

The roar of a speeding truck disrupted her thoughts. A blue pickup barreled down Main and barely slowed to bank the corner at Second Street. Prosper didn't have a police force, and instead relied on drive-throughs from a county sheriff's deputy, but most people obeyed the speed limit. Then she spotted an SUV roaring into town from the opposite direction, and it also turned off Main.

Something must be wrong. The volunteer emergency department's shed was behind the other two city buildings. If these people were reporting for duty, no wonder they were heavy on the gas. Bill was on the crew, he would know what was going on. But before Melinda could fold up her ladder, she saw Bill's truck run the stop sign by the post office and head in the same direction as the others.

Roger met her at the door, his face pale. "It's Doc. He got charged by a bull, not ten minutes ago. From what Bill said, he's hurt pretty bad."

* * *

Everyone hovered at the counter and listened to the wail of the ambulance's siren as it rushed east out of town. Their shopping lists forgotten, customers got on their phones and tried to piece together what happened. When everyone knows everyone, someone always knows something.

"My husband's on the crew, but he's not on call today." One woman wiped her eyes and scanned a text. "Word is Doc's leg is broken. They called ahead to Mason City, so they'll be ready for them."

"They're taking him that far?" one man asked. "That doesn't sound good."

"A broken leg could be handled in Swanton, I'd think." Esther worriedly rubbed her hands together. "Unless there's more injuries than what we're hearing."

Glenn had hurried over to get the latest. If anyone needed stamps or a package mailed, they'd have to wait. "He could've been kicked in the head, too. Or hit his head when he fell."

"Now, don't say that!" Esther was in tears. "That could be ..."

The next word out of her mouth was sure to be "fatal." Given the collective anxiety rising inside the store, Melinda decided it was time to step in. "We don't know for sure how bad he's hurt. All we can do is pray for him and the first responders, and wait."

"Best crew around." Glenn picked up on her hint and tried to find a smile. "And Doc's a member himself, as you all know. Nobody better than them to help Doc, or any of the rest of us, in our time of need. And Mason City's top-notch. They'll take good care of him. Why, he'll be back in the saddle in no time, I'm sure."

The shoppers slowly went back to their browsing, and Glenn finally returned to the post office. Melinda jumped when her phone buzzed in her back pocket. It was Auggie. The accident happened only thirty minutes ago, but discussion at the co-op had already netted him the exact location of the farm, the bull's name as well as that of the property owner's, and the fact that this animal had a history of aggressive behavior.

"Where are you getting all this?" Even for Auggie, this was fast work. "Sharon should hire you to work for the newspaper."

"Word travels fast, and I have my sources."

Auggie reported Doc did indeed break his leg. It was a compound fracture, but at least it was the smaller bone below the knee. He had several scrapes and bruises, and hit his head when he fell. Doc was going into surgery as soon as he got to Mason City's hospital, and he had a long recovery ahead of him. The bull's owner, as well as his son, had sustained minor injuries, but had been successful at keeping Doc from taking a direct hit.

Precautions were taken, Auggie heard, but things still went wrong. The bull had been shooed into a pen, and Doc and the farmers were outside the stall. The animal was even wearing a halter anchored to a sturdy post.

No one was sure how the bull slipped loose, but between his rage at being tied and the stranger in his midst, he busted through the wooden stall gate and escaped outside.

Neighbors were called to corral the bull, but he was too agitated to approach safely. He ran to the far corner of the pasture, and it was decided to let him work off some steam before anyone tried to approach him again.

But Auggie was already looking for a way to channel his frustration in: Even with health insurance, Doc's medical bills would be steep. He didn't have it all figured out yet, but the co-op was going to find a way to raise money for Doc and his family. "Don't tell anyone what I told you," he cautioned Melinda. "It's all off the record, at least for now."

"I promise. Thanks for letting me know, though. I'm sure Bill will have more details when he gets back."

Bill later confirmed all of Auggie's gossip, and then some. Doc had also sprained the opposite elbow, which took the rest of the impact when he fell. And there was a nasty bump on his head, but he never lost consciousness. Melinda almost did, however, when Bill described how badly Doc's leg was broken.

"He's lucky that concrete floor had a layer of straw on it. As banged up as he is, it could have been so much worse." Bill sighed as he reached for his safety goggles. He was done playing the hero; time to get back to work. "If that had been Karen out there, and she'd taken that kind of hit? She's tough, but she's small. I don't know what would have happened."

Esther dabbed at her eyes. "Poor Doc. He's always there when people need him, day or night. We're lucky to have someone like him in our community. Karen, too." She smiled at Melinda. "And Josh."

Melinda tried to focus on stocking shelves and ringing up purchases, but it was difficult.

Especially when Doc's accident was all anyone wanted to talk about. And once she knew Doc was in good hands, all she could think about was Josh. What if it had been him, instead? And that made her feel guilty.

At his own clinic, the biggest threats were a nip from an anxious dog, or some scratches from an impatient cat. But Josh had been working with Doc and Karen for several months now, and sometimes took large-animal cases when the other two veterinarians were booked. Until today, Melinda hadn't had cause to think about how dangerous those farm calls could be.

She'd seen him last night, and they'd texted that morning. But now, it wasn't enough. As soon as four o'clock rolled around, she was in her car and driving out of town. At the junction with the state highway, she took a left and headed for Swanton.

Josh's truck was at his clinic, just where it was supposed to be, but she still breathed a sigh of relief. He was finishing up for the day, and she'd wait if she had to. But oh, she hoped she didn't.

"Melinda!" Norma was surprised to see her. "Are you OK? Has something else happened?"

"No, thank goodness." She realized how worried she probably looked, and gave Josh's vet assistant a reassuring smile. They'd all had enough bad news for one day. "I'll be fine. I just ... I'm waiting for Josh, is all."

Norma bit her lip and nodded. She understood. "He's almost done with the last patient. I'll let you know as soon as you can go back. How's Doc? What's the latest?"

"Anne said the surgery went well." She couldn't imagine how Doc's wife was holding up through all of this. And how would Karen manage until Doc returned to work? Despite her business partner being in the hospital, Karen had carried on with the rest of the day's appointments. Those animals, and their owners, still needed help.

A man and two women were at the counter. "I don't care how much that bull is worth." The man set his mouth in a firm line. "They ought to put him down! If he charged Doc like that, who knows what else he might do?"

An uneasy silence settled over the waiting room. The cat in the carrier next to Norma's desk began to howl.

"Here's Sparky's rabies certificate." Norma tried to keep her voice cheerful as she handed the paperwork to one of the women. "I gave him his vaccinations, and Doctor Vogel checked that lump on his leg. No cancer, just benign."

"Well, that's one bit of good news for today."

Finally, Norma handed Melinda a patient's file. "Here, why don't you take this back to him? He should be wrapped up by now. I bet he'll be glad to see you. It's been a long day."

Josh's smile lit up his face when she walked in, but it quickly dimmed.

"I'm fine, nothing is wrong." She took a deep breath. "Or, nothing else is, I should say. I just had to see you, that's all." She set the file on the counter and wrapped her arms around him. His scrubs smelled of disinfectant and cat urine, but she didn't care.

Josh brushed her hair with one hand. "Whoa, what's all this?"

"I'm just so grateful you're OK, that you're not having surgery because some mad bull tried to trample you."

He laughed softly. "Well, it gets a little crazy sometimes; but yeah, that's not likely to happen here. Livestock's a whole other ballgame, though. I've been out of the loop for a few years. It's good I've been helping Doc and Karen, it'll keep my defensive skills sharp."

Melinda swallowed the lump in her throat, as well as the next thing she wanted to say.

I want you safe, and in one piece. I wish you'd just focus on your own practice and keep yourself out of harm's way.

But she couldn't lay that on him. This was his profession, his calling, and he'd help any animal that was in distress. And now, with Doc out of commission for weeks, it was likely Josh would be taking more of those farm calls.

Beyond her worries about Josh's safety, there were other things to consider. The three veterinarians were busy as it was. How would Josh and Karen manage on their own? And what about the cat clinics? It was a blessing that a veterinarian from Charles City also volunteered for the program, but they already had a full slate of patients for the summer ...

"What are you thinking about?" Josh whispered, then kissed her quick. "Something's going on in there, I can tell. I'm just not sure what."

"Logistics." She kissed him back, then hugged him tight before she made herself pull away. "I need to run home and do chores. I'll be over to your place as soon as I can, maybe by six? Let's go out to dinner somewhere, my treat."

"Sure thing. Am I going to hear about this, whatever it is, over dinner?"

Melinda gave a rueful laugh. "Depends on how much I can get worked out between now and then. I'll ask Annie and Hobo for their feedback. How does that sound?"

11

It would take a game of musical chairs to keep both veterinary practices afloat while Doc was on the mend. Much to Melinda's relief, her mom agreed to occupy one of the seats.

Diane was a retired teacher, and had decades of experience in communicating effectively, dealing with a variety of personalities, and doling out compassion. She and Roger lived only a few blocks from Josh's clinic, and Diane was soon installed at the front counter. That freed up Norma to pinch-hit at Prosper Veterinary Services. As the larger practice of the two, it was in dire need of someone who could handle vaccinations and dental cleanings, as well as fill prescriptions.

Melinda did whatever she could to fill in the gaps. She worked the Prosper clinic's front desk during her lunch hours, and filled Karen and Josh's freezers with casseroles. When

Josh's schedule was especially hectic, she drove into Swanton to take Charlie for walks and play fetch in the backyard.

The plan wasn't perfect, but it worked well enough. Other things seemed to be moving in the right direction, too. Frank and Miriam were settled in their new home, and the painters would arrive at Melinda's farm next week to start on her house. Vicki and Jen were making great progress on the wedding plans. A talented friend of Vicki's college-age son was now on board to serve as photographer, which was one of the last items on the must-have list for the big day.

Of course, Auggie was still full-steam ahead with his expansion plans. But miracles still could happen: Bart had not only found an apartment in Swanton, but had agreed to hold a farm auction in a few weeks.

Melinda wasn't quite ready to take a victory lap, but her confidence was growing that things would work themselves out, one way or another. It would have been nice to spend Sunday afternoon napping or reading, but she had another problem that needed her attention: fixing the chicken house's roof, with Dave and Kevin's help. Or really, the other way around. She would mostly fetch supplies and tools, but Dave promised to get her up on the roof to replace a rotten shingle or two.

Dave shielded his eyes with one hand as he looked it over. "Hmm. Doesn't look too bad, I guess. I've seen worse."

Kevin snorted. "Are you sure? I tried to ask Horace how old these shingles were, and all he said was, 'well, they're older than the ones on the house.'"

"Which are?" Melinda wanted to know.

"A good thirty years." Kevin shook his head. "Three decades is a long time! And just think, that's only a third of Horace's life. And this land's been in our family for much longer than that."

Before Melinda could gently correct him, he laughed. "Sorry, old habits die hard." He squeezed her shoulder. "And then you came along."

"And that's just about as good," Dave chimed in.

"OK, enough with the fawning. Your payment is the same no matter what you say. There's beer and pizza for dinner when we're done, and I've pulled rhubarb for both of you to take home."

"Let's get after it." Dave put on his tool belt. "It's hot out here, but this is going to be kind of fun."

Melinda watched the cousins, joking around in their old jeans and tee shirts, and a lump formed in her throat. Kevin was right about old habits. And while the Schermann clan was always welcome at her place, this was probably the last time any of them would fix something around the farm. The cracks in the plywood sheeting were an easy fix: nail up scraps from inside the coop. And Melinda could handle that on her own another day.

Of course, she and Kevin were good friends. And Dave could tackle just about any odd job. Melinda had learned many skills since she took over this farm, but a second set of hands was always welcome. Or a third. Maybe she could find them something to do, once in a while, to give them another excuse to spend time together out here.

Dave picked up one of the aluminum ladders leaned against the coop, and started at the northeast corner. Kevin took the south side of the roof, just above the hens' fenced-in run. As she adjusted her straw hat and lifted fresh shingles from the pile by her boots,

Melinda was nearly giddy with anticipation. Where was the woman whose favorite Sunday-afternoon pastime was browsing the best boutiques in downtown Minneapolis? Dave was right, this could really be fun. And she'd have so much satisfaction when the rain and snow arrived, knowing she'd taken steps to keep her small flock dry and warm.

Hobo didn't care too much about the chicken house's repairs, but he was overjoyed to see Kevin and Dave. He'd since settled in the nearby shade of the windbreak, out from underfoot. Sunny wasn't anywhere to be found, but Melinda spotted Stormy lounging on a low-hanging branch just above Hobo, the perfect perch to have a bird's-eye view of the project.

Dave reached for his pry bar and tackled the first worn shingle. "Speaking of Uncle Horace, what's really going on with the girlfriend? Grandma said there was some dustup before the Memorial Day program, but she got there too late to see it go down. Did they really make up as fast as they started to fight?"

Kevin tossed a curled shingle on the ground. "Yep. A one-eighty. I told Jack later, I hope we fight like that when we're ninety: get mad, get over it quick and move on. But it was kind of sad, in a way. Every moment counts, at their ages, and I hate to see them argue."

Melinda hadn't wanted to wade too far into the family drama. Even so, here was her chance to get some answers. "I know it's not really my business, but doesn't Horace have power of attorney for Wilbur? If he decides to move to Cedar Falls with Maggie, and take Wilbur along, is anyone going to be able to stop him?"

"Jeez." Dave looked up in alarm. "I hadn't even thought about that."

"Oh, Mom's talked to him." Kevin hit a nail on the head, maybe more forcefully than needed. "It was difficult, but she made it clear that she and Edith must be consulted if he even considers it. He agreed, said he only wants what's best for Wilbur."

Melinda pointed out another worn shingle to Dave. "Good, I've been worried about that. Horace is thoughtful and grounded, at least."

"Which is more than I can say for Maggie." Kevin laughed. "She's a spitfire, even at her age. And those two are like oil and water. I see now why they broke it off, way back when."

"Seventy years apart." Dave shook his head in awe. "Why not try to spend their last ones together? But then, if they squabble like old chickens, maybe it's best to leave things as they are."

"Well, he says he hasn't decided." Kevin took the stack of shingles Melinda handed his way. "But I don't think that will happen anytime soon."

"I'd be happy to attend their wedding, if there ever is one." Melinda looked over her shoulder at the house. "Just as long as I don't have to help plan it. I have my hands full getting this place ship-shape before Jen and Andrew's big day. Five weeks and counting."

"All I have to do is help set up, and then show up." Dave's breezy tone said he was thrilled with that arrangement. "Oh, Kevin, by the way: Jen's decided the groomsmen and ushers aren't wearing jackets. We might even lose the ties. It's going to be hot, and she wants everyone to be comfortable."

"Jen's a sensible woman." Melinda picked a stray nail out of the grass. "But what does your mom say about that?"

"Oh, she's fit to be tied. But she'll get over it. Jen tried to tell her we're all going to wear shorts, but she didn't think that was funny."

Once most of the worn shingles had been replaced, Kevin came down his ladder. "I think it's your turn," he told Melinda. "We need a few fixes on this end, and we'll be almost done."

"I'll stay up here." Dave appeared over the ridge of the roof. "I'll walk you through it."

The chicken house wasn't very tall, but Melinda had to take a moment to enjoy the view from its sloped roof.

She'd swap out a few shingles, just enough to say she learned a new skill, then run inside and preheat the oven. A take-and-bake pizza from Swanton waited in Horace's old refrigerator, and it could look after itself while she helped the guys finish up.

Dave gave pointers from across the way, and Kevin handed up supplies from below. Really, it wasn't that hard. Melinda was grinning by the time she had her second shingle replaced.

When she crawled closer to the edge of the roof, determined to fix a few more spots before turning things back over to the guys, she glimpsed a small nest tucked under the nearby eaves. She rarely came around to the back corners of the coop, as the door was on the east side. As she began to pry up another shingle, Melinda wondered what type of bird would raise a family there.

Something tiny flew past her temple, and she shooed it away. All the sudden, she felt a searing point of pain just above her ear. Then another white-hot zap on her neck.

The pry bar fell out of her hand. It bumped down the chicken house's roof, and Dave gave her a strange look. "Hey, what's going on? Oh, my God! Hurry, get down!"

She cried out in pain as she was stung a third time, on her right arm.

"Yellow jackets!" Kevin shouted from below. "There's the nest!"

Another angry buzz, another pinprick of pain. Then more, but she lost count. Her bare forearms scraping over the rough shingles, Melinda managed to slide down until her feet touched the top rung of the ladder. By now, her limbs trembled and she was lightheaded. When did it get so hot up here on the roof? She closed her eyes and tried to focus.

The ladder started to shake, and a hand grabbed the back of her tee shirt. Another hot sting hit her left arm.

"I got her!" Kevin yelled to Dave. "Quick, hold the ladder. Melinda, can you step down? I won't drop you, and it's not far."

With Kevin's help, she started to move. Suddenly she was lifted into the air, then strong hands reached under her armpits. She was back on the ground, but so dizzy she had to lean against Kevin to stay on her feet. Her mouth was dry and her pulse pounded in her neck. And searing pain radiated all over her body.

"We have to get her inside," someone said.

"How many times did they get her?"

She tried to move her mouth, but no answer came out.

"Not sure. She's conscious, at least."

"I want to lie down." She finally found the words. "It hurts so bad."

Dave swore. "I should have checked around first. We disturbed their nest."

They started for the house, Dave and Kevin steadying her from both sides. Hobo ran ahead, but kept turning back to stare into her eyes. He seemed scared, but Melinda no longer was sure why. Her thoughts bounced around as her mind attempted to block the searing pain.

I forgot to turn on the oven for the pizza. Everything hurts. Did I put the beer in the fridge this morning? My arm feels numb.

The guys were saying something about allergies and "how many does she have?" Someone was going to call Josh but he was too far away, what about the emergency room, Ed and Mabel might be home ...

It was wonderfully cool in the kitchen, and the linoleum looked so smooth and inviting, but Dave and Kevin made her march. "Nope." Kevin tightened his grip on her arm. "If Mabel sees you lying on the floor, she'll have my head. To the couch."

Her eyes closed the minute her head hit the throw pillow. It was so peaceful in here, except for the frantic chatter going on around her and the white-hot pain points on her face and arms.

"Melinda!" Someone took her hand. "Do you understand what's happening?"

"I got stung by wasps." Her words were slow but she was able to get them out. "I want to lie down."

"Close enough," the other one said. "She's breathing normally, at least. I count eight. Oh, no, here's number nine."

Some time passed, she wasn't sure how much. And then another familiar voice joined in. "Honey, just lie still." Mabel was there. "The boys checked for stingers. But you need to stay awake for us. Can you do that?"

She tried to nod, but it was too much effort. How was it that she was inside now, in the air conditioning, and those spots were getting hotter by the minute?

Cold compresses landed on her arms and face, and Kevin returned with a glass of water and some pills she was told to swallow. A blob of fluff landed on her stomach and settled on one shoulder.

"Oh, Grace, no; I don't think you should climb up here just now." Mabel was about to lift Grace away, but Melinda insisted she stay. Her presence was comforting, as long as she didn't put any pressure on the welts.

"Where's Hobo?" she mumbled. "I don't want him to get stung."

"He's right over there." Kevin pointed toward the dining room, where Hobo was sprawled out on the hardwood floor. Hazel crouched next to him, her face anxious.

"Just let her sleep," Melinda heard Mabel say before she drifted off. "It's been long enough that if she was going to have a serious reaction, it would have happened by now."

* * *

She couldn't lift her right eyelid all the way, but it seemed like the light in the room had changed. Muffled conversation drifted in from the kitchen, then she heard footsteps.

"Hey, my love." Josh kissed her forehead and wrapped a hand around her wrist. "How do you feel? Your pulse is normal, at least."

"I don't know." She caught sight of her left arm, and stared at it for a moment. The angry welt just above her elbow was more than an inch across, and the one on her forearm was just as big.

"Yep, you're swelling up all over. But that antihistamine kicked in nicely. It's a good thing you were wearing pants. This could have been so much worse."

"Are Kevin and Dave OK? Did we finish the roof? All the animals need to be fed."

"Easy there, Horace." Josh gave her a teasing wink. "Everything is in good hands. Kevin got one sting, but Dave was in the clear. Your mom's making dinner, your dad's doing chores. Ed's going to take care of that nest, maybe tomorrow, but he wants the wasps to calm down first. And I will be your medic for this evening." He squeezed her hand. "Just so you know, I have horse tranquilizers in the truck if you get any crazy ideas about overdoing it."

She tried to roll her eyes at him, but it was difficult. "How bad is my face?"

"Oh, I think it's just fine." He stroked her hair. "Now, if you're talking about the welts, there are two. The one above your right eyelid, then one on your left cheek. And two on your neck. Everything else is on your arms."

Josh said it would take a few days for the swelling to start going down. The itching would come later, and that was actually going to be the worst of it. But as long as none of the welts became infected, she'd feel like herself again soon.

She made it to the kitchen table to join Josh and her parents for supper, then simply held Hazel in her lap as they put away the leftovers and did the dishes.

"It's hard to let people take care of you sometimes," she whispered to Hazel while Josh walked Diane and Roger out to their car. "But you know what? It's really not so bad."

12

"Well, things sure are topsy-turvy down at the vet office." Bev set her eggs and cereal on the counter. "Norma's keeping the ship afloat, though. I can't imagine how tough it is for everyone. How long is she going to be over here?"

"Several weeks, at least; maybe for the whole time Doc is out." The eggs were from Melinda's hens, and she smiled as she rang up Bev's dozen. Her girls' offerings were always in demand at Prosper Hardware; the cartons that arrived via the wholesale truck were clearly second-best in customers' minds. "I'm so grateful Mom's willing to come out of retirement and watch over Josh's front desk. The big shuffle would never work without her help."

"It's good to see everyone pitching in." Bev reached for her wallet. "Doc and Anne go to our church, as you know. There's a rotation for taking food to the house. The important thing is, he's on the mend."

Before she could stop herself, Melinda scratched the still-pink spot on her cheek. All of her welts had improved considerably in just a few days. The swelling was down, and she could move her right eyelid normally again. But Josh was right about the itching. It was so intense that she wore cotton gloves to bed to keep from raking her fingernails over the sores in her sleep.

"I just hope Anne's prepared for what's to come." A woman added her two cents' worth as she studied the rack of garden seeds, which were now half off. "When my husband broke his arm, I had it easiest when he first got home. Once he started to feel better?" She shook her head. "It was nearly impossible to keep him out of trouble. With a break like Doc's, it'll be so important that he doesn't overdo it."

Doc was already counting the days until he could rejoin the store's morning circle, and to when he might be able to handle minor tasks at the clinic. It was good he was trying to stay positive, but all those noble intentions might bring trouble if he wasn't careful. Melinda could see him promising to only answer the phone and process paperwork, but it would be too tempting to get up to greet patients and fetch medicines. He certainly had a long road ahead of him. And so did everyone else, if they wanted him to heal properly.

If there had been any good to come from Doc's accident, it was that the coffee guys found a reason to set aside their varying opinions on Auggie's expansion plans, at least for now. They'd kept Doc company when he was still in the hospital, and arranged for the Ogdens' lawn to be mowed. Frank and Jerry also took turns cheering on Doc's son at his baseball games.

Auggie's fundraiser was generating a lot of buzz (and cash) down at the co-op. Being sensitive to Doc's pride, Auggie refrained from publicizing it on social media and in the local paper. Instead, he quietly spread the word through his extensive web of customers, which held Doc in high regard. And while Melinda was still frustrated by Auggie's grandstanding, his efforts to help Doc were a reminder that, on his good days, he wasn't such a bad guy, after all.

It was nearly time for Melinda to head up to

the clinic so Norma could take her lunch break. The morning's oppressive humidity had just given way to a pop-up thundershower, but given how dry it had been lately, the rain running down Prosper Hardware's front windows was a welcome sight. She was grateful to need her umbrella to get out to the car, and again to make it up the vet clinic's front walk. But the tranquility of the refreshing rain vanished the moment she walked in the door.

The place was an absolute zoo. The phone was ringing, and Melinda grabbed it before she even set down her purse. Norma was waiting on a few pet parents at the counter. Howls from the distressed critters in the back provided off-key harmonies to the low-volume tunes from Doc's favorite country radio station.

"Oh, am I glad to see you." Norma handed Melinda a sheet of paper. "He's picking up lab results for his dog. I haven't had time to enter them in the system yet. She's dropping off Simba for some vaccinations this afternoon. There's three scripts I need to prep; people will be in yet today to pick them up."

Since Melinda wasn't a technician, she

wasn't allowed to fulfill prescriptions from the pharmacy shelves in Doc's office. But typing and waiting on people? That she could handle. "Where's Karen?"

"Two farm calls south of town, back to back. Like always, if there's anything you don't know the answer to, write it on that notepad. I'll get the ones I can, and we'll have to turn the others over to Karen."

Melinda glanced at the growing list, and her heart sank. Even with Norma's help, how would Karen manage until Doc was literally back on his feet?

"Just make sure to eat," she gently admonished Norma as she settled in. "As soon as the scripts are ready, go take your break."

Melinda bounced around for several minutes until everyone was waited on, and then returned several calls requesting appointments for the coming days. At last, the front office was quiet. She took a few deep breaths and pulled out her sandwich and chips.

Everyone was under a lot of stress, but their plan to cover both clinics seemed to be holding up. And her mom's willingness to help at Josh's clinic created the perfect opportunity for the two of them to get to know each other better. Her dad had even volunteered to unload pet food and supplies and, much to Diane's pleasant surprise, tidy up Josh's waiting area and clean his clinic's kitchen.

Melinda was grateful her parents thought highly of Josh. Because while she didn't see him as often as she liked, it seemed they could be heading toward something more serious. But then, it hadn't even been six months since she'd rushed to Josh's clinic on Christmas Eve morning to announce the spay-neuter program had received its first grant. And to let him know she wanted to see more of him.

Through the rain-splattered front window, she spied an elderly man making his way up the sidewalk. His steps were surprisingly quick for his age, but he must have forgotten his umbrella. He didn't look familiar, which raised her curiosity.

Melinda had to laugh at herself. Just because she worked at Prosper Hardware, she didn't necessarily know everyone within a twenty-mile radius of its front door.

When the man came into the vestibule, she noticed the tote in his hand wasn't anything like a canvas bag. It was more like ... a satchel?

He studied the waiting room with keen blue eyes, his curious gaze taking in the comfortably worn chairs and the framed pet-health prints on the walls.

"How can I help you?" Melinda leaned forward, her elbows on the counter. "Are you here to pick up something, a prescription perhaps? Norma's working on them now."

The man chuckled. "No, actually. I'm here to give something."

She shuffled the stacks of paper on the counter and tried to get her bearings. "Oh, did you bring in a stool sample? I know we had a cat yesterday that was having trouble."

The man didn't answer her at first. His buzz-cut white hair was damp from the rain, but the splotches on his blue-plaid shirt didn't faze him in the least. "Hmm. I don't recognize you, so I suspect you don't know who I am, either."

Melinda stared at him. He was turning out to be the odd customer of the day, for sure. "No, sorry, I don't think we've met." She smiled and held out her hand. "Melinda Foster. I work at Prosper Hardware, actually; I'm just helping out here over lunch."

A light of recognition flashed in the elderly

man's eyes as he accepted her greeting with a firm shake. "Frank and Miriam's niece, then." It wasn't a question. "The one who's back from the Twin Cities."

He raised his chin and squared his shoulders. "I'm Thomas McFadden." He waited a second, to see if that name meant anything to her. When it didn't, he began to chuckle.

"Well, Melinda, it's nice to meet you. I have a long history with this practice, and an even longer one in Prosper. I hired John away from his first employer, many years ago, and transferred the business to him when I retired."

"Really? You're serious." She thought of the photos in the Founders Day exhibit, the scenes of Main Street's businesses through the decades. And here was a piece of Prosper's past, standing right in front of her.

"Well, yes, young lady, I certainly am. It's terrible what happened to John last week. He's a great man and an excellent veterinarian, one of the finest." Thomas chuckled again. "You seem surprised. Did you really think 'Doc' has been the one and only 'Doc' in this town?"

"I guess I hadn't thought about it. Wait. Why did you say you were here?"

"I hadn't yet." He set his bag on the counter. "But I'm here to pinch-hit for John."

Melinda couldn't believe what she was hearing. Thomas had to be in his eighties; how could he still handle such a physically demanding job? And veterinarians had to keep their credentials current if they wanted to legally practice their craft. It was obvious he had ties to Prosper, but she'd never seem him before; she was sure of it. Where did he live these days?

It was like he'd just dropped out of the sky. So many questions, she didn't know where to start. Thomas was studying her again, and now had one of his own.

"What happened to your face?"

Melinda instinctively reached for her welts, but pulled her hand away just in time. "Yellow jackets. We were shingling the roof of my chicken house, and all the sudden something flew past, and ..."

"Happened to me, too." Thomas was eager to share his story and, quite possibly, trump the one Melinda was about to tell. "Several times, in fact. The worst was, oh, back in 1968,

I believe. I was out east of town, inoculating some calves at the Bergstroms' farm. There was an old cottage on the edge of the cow yard, had never been torn down. Well, we were just getting started when ..."

"Doc McFadden!" Norma burst through the swinging door that opened into the back of the clinic, three small white sacks in one hand. "Why, whatever are you doing here?"

"He heard about ... Doc." Melinda couldn't bring herself to refer to him as John; it was a habit too hard to break. She gave Norma a wide smile and blinked. "He's here to offer his services."

"Oh, is that so?"

Norma's years of experience had long ago turned her into a cat that always landed on its feet. She set the scripts on the counter and leaned casually against it, as if she hadn't just received the shock of her life. "Well then, we're very glad to have you. So, Tom, tell us how this all came about."

Her sudden informality wasn't lost on Melinda. Or on Thomas, for that matter. Norma was friendly and gracious, but it was clear where Thomas McFadden, DVM, fit into the pecking order these days.

As Thomas apparently loved to talk about himself, it didn't take long to sort out the situation. He'd chatted with Doc a few times in the past week and, well, he knew how tough it was to be down a man at a practice this small. He was retired, of course, but volunteered with several animal rescue groups in and around Mason City, where he and his wife moved several years ago. That meant he'd kept his license current.

As for the forty-minute drive to Prosper ... retirement was rather dull, and he had plenty of time. One of his sons lived in Eagle River; he could stay overnight with him if needed.

Melinda found out later that Thomas had offered his services to Doc only that morning. Doc was grateful for the help, but assumed his former boss would wait for clear marching orders before grabbing his gear and driving down to Prosper. There hadn't even been time to alert Karen to the arrival of this temporary third partner, much less let Norma and Melinda know who was about to walk in Prosper Veterinary Services' front door.

"I'm not sure I should commit to five days a week yet," Thomas said. "I'm not as spry as I used to be. But I think I can fit in three days."

Thomas seemed to be in excellent health for his advanced age, but Melinda still couldn't imagine him crawling around in barns and facing off with agitated livestock. Of course, the cats and dogs that required in-office exams would be more his speed.

"Well, as they say, you're never safe from surprise until you're dead," Norma told him. "I'm sure Karen's going to appreciate your offer to fill in while Doc's out."

"I haven't had a chance to meet her." Thomas waved one hand dismissively, a telling gesture that made Melinda's welts pound with irritation. He had decades of experience to offer, but an outdated attitude about his profession seemed to be part of the deal. "John's still lead partner, right?"

Norma barely nodded.

"Well, then, it's all settled. I was stunned when I heard he'd hired a woman assistant." Thomas shrugged, as if to say, *what can you do about that?*

He noticed Melinda staring at his satchel. She'd never seen anything quite like it, outside of a movie or television show. "I know, it's ancient. I don't really put much in it these days. That's what tackle boxes are for. But I've carried it for sixty years, so why mess with a good thing? It's tradition."

Thomas didn't wait for her reply before he turned back to Norma. "Why don't you show me around, help me get my bearings? I doubt much has changed in twenty years, but you never know."

Norma suddenly smiled, and Melinda knew the gears were turning. "Sure thing. Once Melinda leaves, I'll be busy at the desk until Karen gets back. We have several kennels that need to be scrubbed and sanitized. I think it would be perfect for you to start there."

Thomas opened his mouth to object, but Norma steered him toward the back of the clinic. "Now, tell me how your wife is doing. I haven't seen her for, oh, at least five years. Is she ..."

As the door shut behind them, Melinda felt a headache coming on. Yes, Karen needed help. But this could be more than she'd bargained for.

* * *

"Well, McFadden's certainly livened things up around here." Josh passed Melinda a freshly washed plate. "As long as he plays nice,

I think we'll be able to manage until Doc is back. Karen's made it clear she doesn't answer to him, and Norma keeps him on his toes. For all his bluster, he's still a fine veterinarian. Steady hands, even at his age."

Melinda dried the plate and put it back in the cabinet. She was as much at home at Josh's as she was her own place, and knew just where he liked things to be. And while his bungalow was a few decades newer than her farmhouse, their kitchens had something in common: no dishwasher.

"Karen came in the other day to find him in Doc's office." She accepted a handful of sparkling silverware. "He was certainly making himself at home."

Josh frowned. "It's nice of him to help out and all, but it's not his practice anymore. From the way he struts around, I think he's forgotten that."

"Karen said he'd taken over Doc's office chair. He was just sitting there, basking in the glow of his memories. She's sure the risk of a hip fracture was the only reason he didn't kick his feet up on the desk."

"He doesn't want to make big decisions or deal with the tough stuff, but that's to our advantage." Josh let the water out of the sink, and the drain's gurgle made Charlie look up from his rug in front of the refrigerator. "We need the extra set of hands, and he's getting what he wants: the chance to 'play veterinarian' one more time."

Melinda laughed, but stopped when Josh didn't join in. There was something in his voice that made her turn and study him closely. That, and it was taking him an awfully long time to wipe out the sink.

"What is it?" She laid a gentle hand on his shoulder. "Something's up. Do you want to talk about it? Did something happen today?"

Josh sighed and looked away. "Well, yeah. I hadn't wanted to bring it up yet, but ..."

"Oh, no. Did you lose a patient?"

He shook his head, but put his free hand over his face. She waited, gave him the time he needed to gather his thoughts.

"I got a call today." There were tears in his eyes. "Keith Littleton, my mentor, passed away last night."

Melinda gasped. "Honey, I'm so sorry. What happened?"

"His wife called. I hadn't seen Keith in a few years. His practice is ... or, well, it was ..." Josh blinked back tears. "It's in Brookdale, about ten miles from Elkton. He had cancer, but he never told me. Didn't tell anyone, really. Kathy said he wanted it that way."

He gripped the sponge tighter. "I should have called more often, gone to see him. Maybe he would have opened up to me if I had."

Melinda put her arms around him, and he leaned into her embrace. "Sometimes, people are worried others will feel sorry for them. And sometimes, it takes all they have just to take care of themselves, you know?" Josh nodded, too emotional to speak. "It's so hard, but I guess that's the way he wanted things to be. Is this the clinic you worked at, right out of veterinary school?"

"Yeah." Josh took a deep breath. "Keith taught me everything I know. I'd never had made it this far in this profession if it hadn't been for him. I just can't believe he's gone."

"I know you're so swamped these days you can barely catch your breath. But we'll figure out how you can get away to attend the service. You need to go; you need that chance to grieve."

She didn't know what else to say, other than

the obvious thing she never tired of telling him. "I love you. I love you so much. Tell me what I can do to help. How can I help you get through this?"

"I don't know what I would do without you." Josh pulled back and touched her face. His brown eyes were puffy now, but the warmth in them held Melinda's gaze. "I love you. You are my rock, Melinda. You know you are."

"Hey. I'm not going anywhere." Melinda's breath caught in her throat. Josh was grieving, obviously, but the tension in his arms told her there was more going on. "Something else is wrong. Please tell me."

"Kathy said they talked it over, when Keith knew he didn't have much time left." Josh wiped his face with the back of his hand, the kitchen towel forgotten on the counter. "He wanted me to have first dibs on his practice."

Melinda felt as if the air had been knocked out of her. Brookdale was two hours away. Surely Josh wouldn't go; he'd built a life here in the past year, between his growing practice, the partnership with Doc and Karen, his friends, this house, and his love for her. But Brookdale was only minutes from Elkton ...

and Aiden. His son held a special place in Josh's heart that Melinda could never fill. And that was just how it should be.

Josh didn't try to explain all this to Melinda. He didn't have to; he could see her working through it in her mind.

"It would be crazy to walk away from my practice here. I love it, and I love you." He squeezed her arm. "But it's a fair price; more than fair, actually, given how successful the business is." He started to cry again. "I don't know how I could ..."

A question hung between them in the quiet kitchen. One Melinda was too afraid to ask, and Josh maybe wasn't ready to answer.

He hadn't said yes. But he hadn't said no, either.

She swallowed the sob about to escape from her throat and looked out into the backyard, where the soft evening shadows gathered on the lawn and the fireflies glowed in the warm, humid air.

"When ... how long do you have to decide?"

"She said there's no hurry." Josh closed his eyes for a moment, relieved to have shared his burden. "A month, at least; maybe two. There's an assistant vet, and two techs, they can keep things running for a while on their own. The estate has to get settled. And I told her about Doc. I can't leave him and Karen in the lurch. He'd have to be back on his feet, literally, before I could even consider such a move."

Josh took her face in his hands. "Melinda, you mean the world to me. But no matter what happens, I could never, ever, ask you to give up what you have here for me."

Melinda's eyes widened with shock. She was still trying to process this. But it was clear Josh had studied all the angles.

How could she even think about such a thing? She couldn't. Her life was here. She'd worked too hard to become part of this community again, and had invested so much time and love into her little farm. She was proud of how she'd reestablished her roots; but now, they could cause her to lose Josh. She liked to think they'd make it work somehow, but it wouldn't, not in the long run. Two hours was too far. Josh knew it, too.

"You cannot leave here. Even for me." He kissed her. "Just tell me you need me to stay, and that's the end of it. I'll call Kathy tomorrow, tell her I'm not interested."

For a second, she was flooded with relief. Josh wanted to stay, she didn't have to lose him. Everything would be settled, and they'd go on as if this had never come up.

And then, she realized what Josh was asking her to do.

"How could I do that?" She backed away and threw up her hands. "You just said you'd never ask me to leave here. But now, you want me to turn around and do that very thing? Tell you what to do? It's not fair! What about Aiden?"

"What about him? I still get to see him, none of that changes. I don't mind the drive."

She shook her head. "But if you took this practice, you'd see so much more of him. He's already five, he'll grow up so fast." She put her hands over her face. "I can't ask you to choose me over Aiden! Don't you dare put me in that position."

He looked away. "I'm sorry. I hadn't thought of it like that."

"As much as you love me, as much as you love it here, you're considering this offer. As you should. He's your son! And because of him, part of you wants to say yes. Am I right?"

Josh nodded. "But I don't have to go."

The hopeful, searching look in his eyes was too much, and she had to turn away. This was a great opportunity for Josh, as well as a difficult choice. Part of her wanted to tell him what to do, but he needed to figure this out on his own.

"I can't make this decision for you." Her lips trembled as she spoke. "I just can't. Josh, this is huge; it affects every part of your life." She closed her eyes and took a deep breath. "I love you, and I promise I'll make peace with whatever you choose to do."

That was true; or she wouldn't have said it. But supporting him, and what she selfishly wanted him to decide, were two different things.

13

Melinda stayed over, just as they'd planned, but couldn't rest. She kept rolling over to stare at Josh, whose brow was furrowed with grief and worry even though he was asleep.

He shouldn't leave. She couldn't let him. But what could she do? Aiden meant everything to Josh, and she couldn't stand in the way of that. No matter how much it would break her heart.

Melinda found it nearly impossible to complete anything beyond basic tasks the next few days. She managed to eat, shower, and care for her animals. And go through the motions at Prosper Hardware, nodding and smiling and chatting with everyone like she hadn't a care in the world. When really, it felt like her world was falling apart.

Kathy had given Josh plenty of time to think over her offer, and Josh was going to do just that. He continued to lean toward turning the offer down, which gave Melinda hope but also brought a pinch of guilt. If it wasn't for her, if she wasn't in his life, would he have already said yes?

Maybe not. Melinda knew better than to think she was the only reason Josh said he wanted to stay. But this was a rare opportunity to move closer to his son. She wondered if the rest of it would ever be enough to keep him here.

One thing she did know, however, was that she had to keep this to herself.

Josh didn't want word to get out. He didn't need the court of public opinion to cloud his decision and, more importantly, Doc and Karen were stressed enough as it was without having to worry their business partner might be moving on.

Miriam had asked Melinda and Diane to help her sort through the last of the stuff at the Victorian, and Melinda agreed with a heavy heart. She had so many fond memories wrapped around that house.

The property wouldn't go on the market for several weeks, at least, as Frank and Miriam wanted to make some upgrades that would be needed to attract a serious buyer. Even with those improvements, it would surely take months to find someone willing to buy such a large property in a town as tiny as Prosper.

Melinda wouldn't have to say her final goodbyes quite yet, but she'd been dreading Sunday afternoon. But now, she saw a silver lining. With so much work to do, and her promise to keep Josh's dilemma a secret, she'd be forced to think about something else for a few hours.

But as she reached for a stack of Christmas decorations destined for a consignment store, waves of bittersweet nostalgia swept over her. She swallowed the lump in her throat and reached for the packing tape.

The boxes were stacking up under the dining room's picture window, whose stained-glass header tossed radiant sunbeams across the now-bare oak floors. Her life had been turned upside down, but at least something was getting accomplished here on Cherry Street.

When it came to their emotions, Miriam and Diane weren't faring much better. Miriam set a plastic tote on the stairwell's landing, and looked around with damp eyes.

"Well, this might be the last of it. One more

trip to Charles City, and we'll have all the donations out of here."

"It's been a long couple of months." Diane sighed and put an arm around her sister's shoulders. "I mean, for you and Frank, most of all. Over thirty years here. Just think of all the fun we've had in this house."

"I'm trying not to think about that." Melinda reached for the next box. "It's the end of an era. I like the new place. But it's just not the same."

"Maybe this will help it feel like home." Miriam approached the antique clock that still hung in the front hall. She'd claimed it was best to leave it at the Victorian until the last minute, since it could get damaged in the chaos of moving, but Melinda knew better. When the clock came down, that meant it was really, truly, time to go.

"Oh, come here, you." Miriam carefully lifted it off its bracket. "We'll make sure you get to your destination safely."

Diane had a fluffy bath towel spread out on the end of the dining-room table, ready to wrap the timepiece for its short car ride to its new home. At least the clock had made the cut; several pieces of antique furniture, including the table now used for sorting and packing, had been deemed oversized and out-of-step with the Langes' modest ranch. A Mason City antiques dealer was coming tomorrow to haul them away.

"Oh, the stories this table could tell." Diane reached for a roll of twine. "How many Christmas dinners did we enjoy here?"

"Too many to count." Miriam shook her head sadly. But then, she laughed. "Remember when Mom made that dessert with the flaming cherries, and Uncle Edgar bumped her elbow just as she set it down? I swear, she was more worried she might scar the table than the chance something might hit the rug and start a real fire."

Melinda frowned. "I didn't realize this table was a family piece. If I'd known, maybe I would have volunteered to take it."

"Don't worry, it's not." With the clock now wrapped in its swaddling clothes, Miriam began to fold a stash of unneeded curtains. A house stocked with mini-blinds had no use for the tall drapes this Victorian lady demanded. "I got it at a tag sale, right after we moved in. Besides, the one you found secondhand is perfect for your house. Simple, clean lines;

you wouldn't really want this fussy thing." But it was clear Miriam loved the table, just the same.

"When did you start hosting at the holidays?" Melinda reached for a box of bed linens waiting at her feet. "Seems like Grandma and Grandpa did it when I was little."

"With all this room, it didn't take long for this to become the gathering place." Miriam tipped her head across the wide entrance hall toward the living room, whose paneled pocket doors opened into a generous space that, a century ago, had been a back parlor. "Mom and Dad downsized soon after we moved in here, as you know. I don't recall volunteering to become party central, but ..."

"You loved it." Diane pointed at her sister. "Admit it."

"Well, I suppose. This is a big place, and it was fun to fill it with the people we loved. So many of them are gone now." Miriam glanced at the stairwell, where the vine-covered wallpaper was now missing its collection of family photos.

"The memories will go with us, though." Diane was about to start a cardboard box for the drapes, but reached for a clean trash bag instead. "Here. One less box to tape. They'll get tossed in the wash when we donate them, anyway."

Melinda added her last carton to the pile by the picture window. "Do we think we're done?"

"I believe so." Miriam looked up at the plaster ceiling and sighed. "I'm pretty sure I got everything else out of the upstairs yesterday. Oh, I'm glad this is almost over. I'm so tired."

"I'll go check." Melinda was already halfway to the stairs. Her emotions were getting the better of her again, and she needed a few minutes to herself. "Just in case anything was left behind."

"She's been such a help to us," Melinda heard Miriam say to Diane as she turned the corner of the landing, the tears already threatening to overflow. "Not just with the move; but the store, everything ..."

Melinda tiptoed down the hallway, overcome by the immense silence that filled the second floor. It was dim and a little too warm. Frank and Miriam had the air conditioner in power-save mode, and the hall's only sunlight came from one window on its opposite end. All the doors were closed, and the iron handle of the one for the bedroom above the kitchen was already sticky with humidity.

Inside, the roller shades were pulled low against the summer heat. The space was barren now, every corner swept and the walls pockmarked where the picture nails used to be. As children, Melinda and Liz always shared this space when they spent the night; Mark had his own room next door. If Melinda tried hard enough, she could picture the twin beds along the west wall, cloaked with the ruffled pink coverlets Frank had insisted were real princess bedspreads, come all the way from England.

Melinda leaned against the wall and closed her eyes. She could see herself here with Liz, laughing and sharing secrets. Playing with their dolls, plotting what they would do in the morning once Miriam fed them a hearty breakfast.

Frank and Miriam never had children, and their home and their hearts were always open for their nieces and nephew. Melinda didn't know who would occupy this home next, but she hoped they'd be as happy here as her family had been.

The tears came faster now, but it wasn't only the memories of the good times that had her sobbing. This house was already so empty, so lonely; it showed her how her own farmhouse would look and feel if she ever left it behind.

No matter how hard she tried to push the mental picture away, she could see her home with the rugs rolled up, the comfortable furniture gone, the blank walls staring out over the fields through undressed windows.

She wiped her face with the back of her hand. "I'm not going anywhere, so that's not going to happen."

But the truth was, as she tossed and turned at night, Melinda had considered that very idea. Not because she was unhappy with her life; far from it. But because she was so happy with Josh. She knew she loved him. Had known it for some time now, although she couldn't look back and name the exact moment when it all became so clear.

He'd already told her, more than once, that he'd never ask her to come with him if he left. And she'd assured him that she couldn't leave.

Even so, she couldn't stop wrestling with the idea.

What was she willing to give up, what was she willing to do, to keep him in her life?

Melinda had been surprised at how easily the scenario had come together in her mind. All the animals would go along, of course. She'd never leave anyone, not even cantankerous Miss Pansy, to be cared for by the farm's next owner or, even worse, given away. She and Josh would have to find their own acreage near Brookdale, but she knew he would love that. After all, he'd grown up in the country.

Everyone would adjust, she was sure of it. Hobo and Charlie were already friends. Hobo loved Aiden, and even the cats had all warmed up to the little boy. She and Josh would have a charming farmhouse, just not the one she had now. They'd have their own land, a new life that they started, together.

It could work. Right?

Yes. She was sure it would, if they wanted it to. But was that really what she wanted?

She opened her eyes and looked around the empty room, tried to get past her rose-colored memories to see what was really in front of her. The plaster was cracking a bit, there along the south wall. And while the windows were tall and generous, they were also old and drafty. Despite her aunt and uncle's tireless work over the years, this house would always demand more time and energy than most people had to spare.

It was the same with Josh; she needed to focus on reality. What if the ideal picture in her mind didn't come to pass? And they'd only been dating six months. Would they get engaged? Would she even be willing to move without some promise about the future? And spending the night together, at her place or his, wasn't the same as living with each other. What if they didn't get along well enough to make it work?

And then, there were the other parts of her life to consider. Which, as much as she loved Josh, Melinda still had. In spades.

How could she leave Prosper Hardware behind? Would Bill really want to run it alone, someday, if she left? Despite his eagerness to have a bigger hand in the business, Melinda wasn't sure. She'd let her family down, let herself down, if she walked away. And she'd need a job. No matter how successful Josh's practice might be, Melinda could never see herself without a career.

Helping out at the clinic might not be enough to feel fulfilled; and, she suspected, it might be too much time spent with Josh. Brookdale was a small town; there wouldn't be much professional opportunity there. And her family, her friends ... she'd miss everyone here. Even Auggie.

No, running away wasn't the answer. She had to stay; she wanted to stay. If Josh left, she would give him her blessing. But she would have to let him go.

If it would just get resolved one way or another. But she had to give Josh the time and space to make this decision on his own. And, to give herself enough breathing room so she wouldn't completely fall apart if he left.

Mom and Aunt Miriam were waiting for her, and the afternoon was slipping away. She gave the room one last look, tugged the door closed behind her, then made a quick tour of the rest of the upstairs. Miriam was right; everything was gone.

Melinda started down the steps. At least she had a good reason for her red eyes and flushed cheeks.

"There you are!" Miriam's smile was a little too bright, and Melinda knew they both had been crying, too. "What's the word? Are we done?"

"Yes." Melinda closed her eyes again and took a deep breath. "Yes, we are. At last."

Diane checked her phone. "It's almost five. I don't know about you two, but I'm exhausted. The thought of making dinner is more than I want to deal with." She raised an eyebrow. "A burger sounds good right about now; scrumptious, actually, if I don't have to make it. How about we head over to the Watering Hole? I think Roger can fend for himself. It's so hot, he'll be happy with a sandwich. What about Frank?"

"Oh, I think he can manage. Melinda, can chores wait for an hour or so?" Miriam thought for a second. "Of course, if you're meeting up with Josh ..."

"This is the first day he's had to himself in ages, he's catching up on stuff at home. I'm on my own tonight."

And I might be in the future, too. She pushed that thought away and reached for her purse. "I need to talk to Jessie, anyway. Jen and some of the ladies are coming to the farm next weekend to look everything over for the wedding, and Jessie's going to bring food samples."

"Oh, yes, the wedding!" Miriam laughed, some of her usual good humor returning. "I'd almost forgotten all about it. How are things going?"

"Slow and steady. I'm letting Vicki play traffic cop. I'm trying to finish up the Fulton Friendship Circle cookbook, hope to have the files ready later this week. The painters start Tuesday, and the roofers are coming after that."

"Oh, is that all?" Diane shook her head. "Honey, I don't know how you're going to get it all done. But you will. You always seem to have an answer. And if you don't, well, you go out and find it."

Her mom made it all sound so easy. Melinda desperately wanted to share Josh's dilemma, but couldn't. So she only said, "it's a lot to do, but we'll get there."

Miriam had disappeared into the living room, but soon came back with a large plastic tote.

"Dear me, this is heavy." She carefully deposited it on the table. "Melinda, before we go, I have something for you. Well, a bunch of somethings."

Melinda's curiosity temporarily pushed her worries aside. "What is it?"

"Open it." Miriam was smiling now. "Look and see."

A faint musty smell rolled out when she unsnapped the lid. When she saw what was inside, her jaw dropped.

"No! Are you sure? Don't you want to keep them?"

"Well, I seem to have run out of room at the new place. And Frank digitized the old store records a few years back, as you know. I wasn't about to throw them away."

Melinda lifted out the first leather-bound ledger. "Aunt Miriam, this is a huge piece of our family's history. I'd be honored to look after them."

"Good." Miriam nodded. "Because I have two more totes over there in the corner. I know you have that whole storage room out at the farm. Which will be one-hundred-percent leakproof once that new roof gets installed."

"And there's something else." Diane went into the kitchen and came back with a cardboard box.

"Goodness, it's like Christmas around here." Melinda was touched, but that wasn't the only emotion that made the tears well up again. Miriam entrusting her with Prosper Hardware's historical records was another reminder of her role in the family's business. And of how deep her roots ran in this community. No, she could never leave again. Not even for Josh.

Diane was grinning like a fool. "Come on, open it!"

"The tea set?" Melinda gasped. It was all there, even the cream and sugar holders. Her great-great-grandmother brought the rosebud-patterned dishes from Wisconsin when the family moved to Iowa a hundred-and-fifty years ago. For the last few decades, they'd held a place of honor in Miriam's china cabinet.

"Well, you have the perfect spot to display them." Diane shrugged. "After the Schermanns cleared out most of the breakfront in your dining room. They'll look lovely there."

"And away from Hobo and the kittens' prying paws." Hazel and Grace were about eighteen months old, by Doc's guess, but

Miriam still thought of them as the babies they'd been when Melinda brought them home. "I know you've always admired the set."

"Yes, but ..." Melinda looked at her mom. "Does Liz know about this?"

"Oh, don't worry. She's getting a few vases and that cut-glass bowl she's always had her eye on. We'll send them with her when they come to visit." Liz and her family, who lived in the Milwaukee area, would be back for the Foster family reunion later in the summer. Mark would come out from Chicago, too.

"Frank picked out some of our dad's tools for Mark," Miriam added. "I doubt he'd have much interest in the stuff here in the house." She looked around, her eyes suddenly sad again. "Or rather, what used to be here."

"You're doing the right thing," Diane reminded her sister.

"Well, we'd better be." Miriam tried for a laugh. "It's too late now. Which brings me to a larger gift I have for you, Melinda. Or really, something I hope you're willing to take on."

Melinda glanced into the empty rooms around them. What could possibly be left? "Um, OK. Maybe I'm happy with my old books and my tea set."

"Frank and I want to have company at our new place. But it's a tight fit. I'd like to declare your farm the official Shrader family gathering spot from here on out. Christmas, Easter, birthdays. Well, whenever you feel up to it, at least."

"She's still going to cook," Diane was quick to add. "As will I. You won't be stuck doing everything yourself."

"Oh, I'd be honored." She'd always enjoyed entertaining, even in Minneapolis. Of course, if this torch would pass to her, she'd have to be here to accept it.

Miriam rubbed her hands together. "Then it's settled. Let's go get something to eat."

14

Melinda sighed with irritation as she turned off the blacktop, knowing her hatchback would soon be coated with one more layer of gravel dust.

"We'd better get a nice rain just before the wedding," she muttered. "No one's going to want their vehicle to get this dirty, then risk brushing up against it in their nice clothes."

The plume of dust trailing behind her blocked the sight of the lush, green fields from her rearview mirror, and her mood was just as murky. It had been a long day (a long week, actually) and she was tired, sweaty and fed up with just about everything, and everyone.

The possibility of hosting a Dust Bowl wedding for sixty-some guests wasn't the half of it. Melinda had spent the night at Josh's, which was the next-best thing to having him stay at the farm, but the tension was almost more than she could bear.

She'd done chores after work, admonished Hobo and the housecats to behave themselves, told Pepper and the ewes to head inside if it rained (everyone, including Auggie, promised it would) then packed her overnight bag.

The hoped-for thunderstorm never materialized, but the mood had certainly been gloomy at Josh's house. Even Charlie seemed to sense it. Josh and Melinda talked about everything, and nothing, but the offer from his mentor's family had been too awkward for either of them to broach.

Was this how it would be until Josh made a decision? Every conversation about anything they might do, or might plan, more than a month out was filled with forced cheerfulness and awkward silences. Josh had taken some farm calls off Karen's schedule tonight and, as Melinda admitted to herself with a sinking heart, was probably as relieved as she was to have a good excuse to stay apart.

And the store had been a madhouse today. Cranky customers, packed aisles, and a cash register that refused to ring up several popular sale items correctly. Esther was on a much-deserved vacation, but even with Bill's help, Melinda could barely keep up. If it hadn't been for Miriam putting in extra hours, they never would have made it through.

Vicki was in the midst of a planning frenzy, and it seemed like she called Melinda every hour with some question or update. Along with working out the finer details of Jen's wedding, she was helping Nancy and Jerry put the finishing touches on Prosper's Fourth of July celebration. Melinda hated to do it, but she'd stopped picking up her phone when Vicki's name appeared on its screen.

She just had to get home, and she was almost there. A splash of cold water on her face, a change into cooler clothes and a slice of watermelon, and she'd feel so much better. After chores and supper, she could flop on the couch and try not to think about anything other than what show she wanted to watch, or what book she wanted to read.

Speaking of books, she really should work on the Fulton Friendship Circle cookbook instead. The project's baked-in nostalgia, as well as the thrill of seeing a family member's name in print, had people ignoring the deadline Melinda set for submissions.

But the buzz around the cookbook meant its proceeds might pay for Hawk Hollow projects for years to come, so Melinda gritted her teeth and let the recipes keep rolling in. Mabel had offered to finish typing the items, but Melinda still had to design the extra pages. Adding to the stress was Jen's hope of handing cookbooks out as wedding favors to close family members.

Melinda took a deep breath when she spied the end of her lane. Even here at home, everything seemed to be a mess. Which wasn't really true. But the house? Yeah, it was a disaster zone.

In a matter of days, her farmhouse's appearance had deteriorated from shabby-chic charming into, well, abandoned and haunted. The old finish hadn't been the best, but all the clapboards were now a dull shade of scraped-down gray. And the laid-bare walls made the worn shingles look that much worse.

If not for the crowd of trucks in the driveway and the scaffolding packed with Hank's painting crew, someone could believe no one lived there. Who said Bart had the worst-looking house in the township? Right now, Melinda was giving him a run for his money.

She couldn't believe Horace and Wilbur had

let the house go for so long. Hank had warned her a full scrape-down would give the best results, and she'd agreed to the extra time and expense that would require.

But every day there was a new wrinkle. Or, more exactly, several old boards that were too far gone to be saved. But she was determined to do this right, in hopes it wouldn't need to be done again for a very long time.

Of course, no one really knew what was under all those layers of shingles on the roof. She'd decided to go with the ribbed steel panels for their durability and ease of installation, but found herself tossing and turning some nights, wondering if that was the right choice.

At least the mailbox looked sharp. Melinda pulled to the edge of the gravel, walked across the road, and gathered up the bills and circulars. "It has to get worse before it can get better," she reminded herself for the thousandth time as she got back in the car. The air conditioning was refreshingly cool, but it made the sweat and the dust stick to her skin.

"I guess I should be grateful this project's running on time."

Hank's guys showed up promptly at seven; she met many of them on the gravel as she started into town in the mornings. They chipped away at the house until close to five, and Hank was always ready with the day's updates when Melinda pulled into the yard after work. How they managed ten-hour days in this heat, she didn't know.

She had just reached the garage's welcoming shade when her phone rang. Diane rarely called at this time of the day, and Melinda cringed as she picked up the call.

"Honey, I can't believe this! Are you sitting down?"

Melinda's heart nearly stopped. What now? "Oh, no, what is it? Is everyone OK?"

"Oh, yes, sorry to scare you."

Melinda rolled her eyes. She didn't need any more drama. "What's going on?"

"Well, the paper just came. Oh, I hope Frank hasn't seen this yet." Diane was really worked up about something. "Maybe I should have called Miriam first. It's Auggie. Or rather, it's what he did!"

The Swanton newspaper came out twice a week in the late afternoon, and was delivered on foot in most of the county's communities.

But rural residents got theirs in the mail the following day. That put Melinda at a disadvantage when Prosper Hardware customers wanted to voice their opinions about something in the latest edition.

According to Diane, that day's paper would be the talk of the county within hours. Right there, on the front page, was an overblown feature on Auggie's grand plans to expand the co-op. The can't-miss photo showed the great man himself, arms crossed and with a smug smile, posing in front of the office with the towers pointing skyward in the background.

The article was full of self-serving quotes from Auggie about how his project "is the spark we need to revitalize Prosper's business district" and promises to "set the stage for further growth in our charming community."

Sharon, the paper's editor, at least had listed all the kickbacks Auggie wanted from the city, and cornered Jerry to get his reaction to the project. "Cornered" was the right word, Diane said, given Jerry's evasive comment about how the council was simply considering Auggie's proposal.

Auggie, for his part, went so far as to predict "a record crowd" would attend the upcoming public hearing to voice support for his plans.

"I can't believe this!" Diane was shouting now, and Melinda pulled the phone away from her ear. "He really thinks the whole town is going to storm city hall and insist he gets everything he wants? And Jerry! Why didn't he say more, tell the paper that not everyone's behind this idea?"

"He's the mayor, he's supposed to stay neutral." Although Melinda wondered how much longer that was possible, given Auggie's grandstanding. "Auggie's getting a big head about this, though. If he thinks he can ..."

"Are you serious?" Diane gasped. "I just flipped to the inside, and here's that detailed drawing of Auggie's plans! It takes up almost a third of the page!"

"Well, he complained when Jerry told him to have professional designs drawn up. I guess he decided to get his money's worth and let the paper run it. Dare I ask what the rest of the article says?"

In short, it was classic Auggie. Dozens of customers had already told him they loved his brilliant idea. His inspired vision would carry the community forward. And this expansion would cement the co-op's place as Prosper's "cornerstone of commerce."

"That's our role!" Diane shouted. "Prosper Hardware's been around longer than the co-op, not to mention owned by the same family for over a hundred years! Well, he has some nerve!"

Melinda was still in the stifling car, paralyzed by annoyance and shock, with sweat dripping down her face. This was a disaster in the making, but she couldn't deal with it just now. She interrupted her mom's rant, told her to call Miriam, then made her escape by hanging up.

Hobo was waiting by the garage, and thumped his tail in greeting. "I don't know what we're going to do," she whispered. "Everyone's already on edge. This is only going to make things worse."

Drumming up a little publicity was one thing; Auggie appointing himself king of Prosper was another. She should have known something like this was in the works. He'd been strangely quiet about his plans lately, his morning chatter focused on Doc's progress and his own determination to nab first prize in the men's pie contest at the Fourth of July festival. The coffee hour's temperature had finally settled to a simmer. But tomorrow, tempers were sure to boil over.

Frank had done his best to keep things civil, and respect Auggie's right to expand his business. Jerry tried to stay on the fence, just where the mayor was supposed to sit. George was normally easygoing. But he had his breaking point, like everyone else, and this was probably it. And Bill? Well, he'd probably come in late on purpose, then fill his mug and scurry to the safety of the woodshop.

She had to keep it together, Melinda reminded herself as she wound her way through the maze of trucks on her way to the back stoop. The yard was noisy and busy, the opposite of the peace she needed to gather her thoughts. A table saw screeched and wailed behind the house, and the top of the picnic table was stacked with lengths of boards ... far more than she expected.

"I know, it's bad news." Hank appeared at her elbow. He was a burly man, suntanned and wearing a faded ball cap, but his eyes were kind. "The more we scrape, the more pieces we find that have to be replaced."

Hank pointed at the west side of the house,

which always took the brunt of the wind and the wet weather. Even to Melinda's unexperienced eye, it looked awful.

She could see the patches of rot, and the warped boards. Why-oh-why hadn't Horace and Wilbur taken care of this sooner? But of course, they were thrifty. When they'd last worked on the house, thirty-some years ago, they'd painted the bottom half themselves to save money. One coat, fingers crossed, and as little expense as possible. Melinda rarely found any reason to be angry at Horace, but she had one now.

Hank tried hard to stay positive. "It's much better on the east and the south, even the north side."

"How much?" She could barely get the words out. Hobo leaned against the leg of her jeans in sympathy. "How much more is it going to cost?"

Hank stared at the ground.

"Just tell me." She swallowed hard. "Tell me how bad it is."

He did, and she started to cry. Even the cash she'd saved on the chicken house's roof wouldn't fill the gap.

"We'll be as economical as we can," Hank

promised. "Won't waste a board. And we'll stay on until it's done, and done right."

Melinda dropped to the picnic table's closest bench, and her purse and lunch tote fell to the ground. Hobo hurried over to give everything an evaluating sniff, but she hardly noticed. "How much longer do you think it will take?"

"Well, we'll be here far into next week, now."

"The roofing crew wants to start Tuesday." She dropped her head into her hands. "I can't put them off."

Hank rubbed the graying stubble on his chin. "Huh, yeah. Well, the more the merrier, I guess."

"You'll all be here at the same time! How is that going to work?"

"We'll figure it out. Now, we can't share our scaffolds, that's an insurance thing. But maybe they can stage on one side, and we'll be on the other."

Melinda was suddenly grateful for the dry weather. If it rained, even one or two days, this whole house of cards would collapse. She threw her arms up in frustration. "I've had it, with everything! Nothing's going right!"

Hank frowned, then shrugged. "Oh, it's not so bad. Brian and Jeff almost got in a fight at lunch over the last of the chips, but ..."

"That's not what I mean! I'm talking about everything else."

Not just the house repairs, but Auggie's bad behavior, the tensions in town, Josh's dilemma ... She was suddenly too tired to make it the rest of the way to the back porch.

Three more sweaty guys had strolled over and now stood around her, watching her meltdown with looks that ranged from embarrassment to sympathy. At least, that's what she managed to make out through a fresh round of tears. Stormy made a beeline for Melinda's lap and planted himself there, but even his purr wasn't enough to make her feel better.

"What's going on?" one of the guys asked.

"She's upset about the wedding, maybe." Melinda thought that was Brian, but wasn't sure. "Hey," he said to her, "when are you getting married again?"

That was more than she could take.

"I'm. Not. Getting. Married!" The guys all stared at her, and she started to cry harder out of sheer embarrassment. Her noisy distress brought Pepper to the pasture fence, and he began to bray. "I may never get married, OK? It's not my wedding."

"Then I wouldn't be so worried." Jeff shrugged and looked around. "We'll get this job patched up, but if for some reason it's not done, just take the pictures over there by the garden. Honestly, everyone will probably get so drunk they'll never remember what the house looks like."

"Photos would be better out front, there by that maple tree." Hank had his own ideas. "It's too bad the lilacs are done blooming. That would have been the best place. When's the wedding again?"

She took a deep breath. "Four weeks."

Phil snorted. "So what's the problem? We'll be long gone by then. Hey, I know: Have that donkey be the ring bearer. Trust me, it'll be all anyone talks about." Pepper was still singing his song, and the guys started to laugh.

"I don't know what's so funny!" Her face was red, but she didn't care. "If you guys think you have all the answers, I want you to go out and find us a portable dance floor. We desperately need one."

That shut them up.

"See? Not so easy, is it?"

"Well, look at it this way." Jeff popped his gum. "It's not your show. So you won't end up like my sister's friend. Her dude didn't even show up."

"How long had they been together?" Phil wanted to know.

"Three years. She pestered him over and over to get hitched, so he finally said he would. Ball and chain, I tell ya. Threats don't work. That's what I keep telling my girlfriend."

Brian came back from his truck with a jumbo roll of paper towels. He joined Melinda on the bench and awkwardly patted her arm with one paint-splattered hand. "It's going to be fine." He tipped the roll her way, and she ripped off a section and nodded her thanks. "This house will look great when we're done."

"I wish the house was my only worry. I mean, beyond the wedding."

The guys seemed ready to listen. Good thing she wasn't paying them by the hour. She couldn't talk about Josh. But she could talk about Auggie.

"Never liked him." Phil crossed his arms. "Sure, his grain rates are good, my dad's gone with him for years. But he'd better watch himself. Asking for handouts, from folks around here? It's not going to fly."

Brian grimaced. "He wants to put people food in there, next to the horse meds? Gross."

It wasn't easy, but Melinda tried to laugh. Stormy was still in her lap, and still content. Maybe she should try to relax, like him. And maybe, she decided as she looked around at the guys, she had more friends than she realized.

"I'll let you get back to work." She gently set Stormy aside and picked up her things. When she tried to hand the paper towels to Hank, he shook his head.

"Just keep them, we have more. I'll add them to your tab." Then he laughed. "Oh, come on, I wouldn't do that." He waved her toward the house. "Go in and cool down. We'll finish up for the day and get out of your hair."

Melinda had missed two calls. One was from Miriam, and the other from Jerry. Nancy, Vicki and Esther had all texted their outrage about Auggie's publicity stunt. There was nothing from Josh but, well, she'd expected that.

Hazel bounded into the kitchen, eager for attention. Grace, however, remained perched on the back of the couch. Her ears were flat against her fluffy head as she glared out the picture window, watching those strangers make a mess of her lawn. The fact that Hobo circled among them, happy and eager to help, seemed to only fuel her genteel outrage.

"Change is no fun, huh?" Melinda sighed as she gave Grace a gentle pat. "I guess all we can do is roll with it."

15

Not long after the painters went home for the night, tall clouds formed to the west. By sunset, they had multiplied and turned heavy and dark. Any rain was welcome, as long as it didn't last long enough to keep the painters away tomorrow.

But the wind soon picked up, and the constant rumble of thunder made Melinda toss and turn, unable to sleep.

The threat of severe weather wasn't the only thing that kept her awake. Auggie's article had been posted to the newspaper's website late in the evening, and reading it made Melinda's blood boil.

Miriam promised to be at the store before Melinda arrived, ostensibly to get a jump on inventory, but really to help referee whatever would go down during coffee group. Melinda tried to figure out how she and Miriam could keep things civil, but gave up. She finally fell into a troubled sleep as the rain drummed against the house and the thunder echoed over the fields.

All the sudden, she opened her eyes. The room's nightlight flickered once, then twice, and the house was plunged into a silent darkness. Melinda fished the flashlight out of the nightstand's drawer, then went downstairs to investigate with Hobo leading the way. The rain had slowed to a soft pitter-patter, at least. But her yard light was out, and every switch in the house was dead.

She checked her phone, and sighed. The rural electric company's website showed the break in the grid was a few miles away; it estimated the power would be back on in a few hours. There wasn't anything to do but try to go back to sleep.

It wouldn't do any good to open the windows, as the air was just as humid and still as it had been before the storms rolled through. Horace's old air conditioner would have to work double-time to catch up and, given its considerable age, that wasn't a risk she was willing to take.

She woke with a start just after four, when everything suddenly snapped back to life.

Maybe things aren't as bad as I think, she told herself as she tried, for the third time that night, to get some decent rest. *Don't they say things always look better in the morning?*

Well, everything looked the same as before, and she was grateful for that. Only a few small branches littered the yard, and the painters' scaffolding hadn't budged in the storm. The sheep were already gathered at the pasture fence, watching for her to come out and offer breakfast.

Pepper hadn't even waited, and was busy snacking on the refreshed grass. Even the chickens were unruffled, so the storm mustn't have been too severe. Melinda was exhausted, but her mood had improved by the time she and Hobo started toward the house.

Then the roofing company called. While Melinda's rural neighborhood had been mostly spared, some parts of the county received significant wind damage. The crew was already swamped with calls for emergency repairs, and their regular jobs would have to be pushed back. It was only going to be a few days. But of course, if they got more severe weather ...

She had to count her blessings, she

reminded herself as she started for town. At least, maybe both crews now wouldn't be at her farm at the same time. And the worst of the storm had passed her by.

Too bad another one was sure to arrive inside Prosper Hardware that morning. Miriam met her at the back door, her forehead creased with worry. "Did you have it bad last night?"

"No, we were very lucky." Melinda followed her aunt through Bill's woodshop, where in-progress projects waited on the work tables. She wished she could spend the day back there, away from everyone's nosy questions and pointed opinions. "The power was only out for a few hours."

They were at the door that opened into the store, and Melinda paused before turning the knob. "I didn't see Auggie's truck out front, and he likes to be the first one here. Do you think there's any hope he won't show?"

Miriam sighed. "I doubt it. And it's just as well. We need to get this over with. Frank's so upset, he's been trying to be quietly supportive and keep his opinions to himself. But yesterday was the last straw."

"Where is Frank, anyway?"

"At city hall. Jerry wanted to talk this through first. And I think Jerry didn't want to walk into this alone."

Melinda understood, but wondered if Auggie would take that as a show of solidarity against his plans. Miriam straightened the displays by the register while Melinda started the coffee. That was Auggie's job, of course, but it gave her something to do. If last night hadn't been so tough, she might have thought to bring in cookies. Sugar could smooth things over, even a little.

George soon shuffled in the front door. "Well, Miriam, what are you doing here at this early hour?"

"If you've seen the paper, I think you know. I'm afraid we're going to need your help to keep things civil."

He sighed as he filled his mug. "I'll do my best. Truth is, Auggie's too big for his britches. It'll be good to see Frank take him down a notch or two." He stared at Melinda, then Miriam. "That's what Frank's going to do, right?"

"We don't know what will happen." Melinda came out of the grocery aisle with a package of sandwich cookies, ripped it open, and held it out to George. "Here, take a few."

Frank and Jerry soon arrived, and Melinda felt better when they took their usual chairs in the circle. Mornings at Prosper Hardware were never dull. No matter how divisive their opinions, the guys always found a way to mend fences. Maybe Miriam was right; the sooner this was all out in the open, the better.

Everyone tensed up when Auggie's truck appeared out front. "Well, here he comes," Jerry muttered.

Auggie's grin was as big as usual, maybe a bit more. And, unlike Melinda, he'd had the foresight to bring treats. "Look what I have!" He held up a box of donuts from one of Swanton's convenience stores. "Had an errand to run this morning, thought I'd pick some up on the way."

"Well, that's a lie." Frank's voice was low, but so cold it sliced through the unstable atmosphere in the room. "It's only just now seven."

"Are you saying I made it up?" Auggie's grin vanished in a flash. "I got the donuts to prove it, don't I?"

"I'm just pointing out that you say a lot of stuff that's not quite right." Frank crossed his arms when George tried to pass him the donuts. "And not just around town, or here at the store in the mornings. Even though there's plenty of that. Apparently, you say all kinds of nonsense to the paper's editor, too."

Melinda couldn't imagine this was the opening Frank and Jerry discussed, but it was too late now.

"Let's get this over with, then." Auggie turned his back on Frank while he filled his mug. "You're obviously upset about that lovely feature Sharon wrote regarding the co-op's expansion."

Miriam made an angry sound in her throat, but Melinda gave her a cautious look. *We have to let them work this out.*

"Proposed expansion," Frank corrected Auggie. "The council hasn't approved it yet."

"I'm fully aware you guys haven't voted." The donuts had landed on the sideboard, and Auggie helped himself to one before taking his usual seat.

"Are you trying to tell me the majority is against me? Because from what I'm hearing, that's not necessarily true. Besides, it's newsworthy, regardless of how you might feel about it."

He glanced over to where Melinda leaned against the counter, the dust cloth still in her hand. "Have to keep people informed, right? I can't remember who said it, but there's a saying: there's no such thing as bad publicity."

How dare he try to get her to take his side, against her family! When she said nothing, he shrugged and went on. "I mean, people have to know about it, so they can voice their support for the project. Make calls, talk it up, show up at the public hearing."

Jerry finally broke the hostile silence. "I'm trying my best to stay out of this, but he has a right to do that. And while the council will decide, they were elected to serve the will of the people."

Frank's face turned red. "Whose side are you on?"

"No one's." Auggie interjected before Jerry could speak. "Or at least, he better not be. Look, I have a right to expand my business. If I want to diversify, that's my call."

"I don't care about the gas." Frank sighed. "We need that. But the stuff inside the store, carrying groceries and whatnot? That's direct competition to this."

He pointed around him. "This town's too

tiny for that nonsense. We all have to stay in our lane if we're going to survive."

Melinda gripped her dust cloth tighter. She was angry at Auggie for trying to drag her into the debate, but it wasn't just that. She knew how thin the profit margin was at Prosper Hardware. So did Auggie. It wouldn't take much for her family's business to get into serious financial trouble.

Josh's agonizing decision was never far from her mind these days. But now, she saw it from another angle. She kept telling herself she needed to stay here and run Prosper Hardware someday, that she couldn't let her family down. But what if the store's future wasn't the sure thing she wanted it to be? Could that change her feelings about Josh's offer? Should it?

Auggie considered Frank's comment for a moment. "I see your point. I want this town to thrive, same as you. But maybe you should stop worrying about what I want to do, and think about what you should do. Owning a business means you find ways to adapt."

"And what, exactly, do you suggest I add?" Frank looked around the store. "We already carry a little bit of everything." Then he gave a tight-lipped grin. "I suppose we could start carrying more pet food. Those specialty brands are popular, and there's a high markup on them."

Now it was Auggie's turn to burn. Prosper Hardware only offered a few mainstream dog and cat brands, while the co-op did a roaring business on the high-end varieties people otherwise had to drive to Waterloo or Mason City to get.

"There, how does that feel?" Frank raised an eyebrow. "Those are some of your bestsellers, am I right?"

George had been waiting for a chance to speak, and the icy silence that followed Frank's question seemed to be as good a time as any.

"Auggie, there are quite a few people who support your plan, but there's many that don't. From what I hear, the naysayers are upset about those tax breaks. Could you do without them? I mean, it might go a long way toward smoothing things over."

"And why should I do that?" Auggie snapped. "This is a big project that's going to benefit everyone around here. Other towns offer incentives."

"Bigger towns, you mean." Jerry pointed at him. "We don't have the money for it."

"And who's problem is that?" It was clear Auggie blamed Jerry, even though the council handled the town's meager budget. "The co-op is a big part of what draws people into Prosper. I'm a leader in this community, I think you'd better ..."

Jerry was suddenly on his feet. "That may be, but I am *the* leader! I'm mayor of this town, whether you like it or not. Some days, I don't like it, either. But I am, and it's my job to steer this community as best as I can."

"Which includes supporting local businesses trying to do the right thing!"

"Is that what you call it? How about, stepping on the toes of other businesses? Grandstanding in the paper, crowing about how great you are? I don't know if that's being a leader. I think that's just looking out for yourself!"

Frank stood up. Melinda knew he was upset, but it was the wrong move to make. Even in his rage, Auggie could count. It was now two against one, and that would only throw gasoline on the fire.

"You don't run this town!" Frank shouted.

"You've pulled some stunts over the years, man, but this is going too far!"

Auggie jerked off his cap and threw it on the floor. "Vote against me, if you want, but don't assume the rest of the council will."

He stepped over to Frank and stuck a finger in his face. "All this talk about doing the right thing! You'd better take your own advice. It's a conflict of interest for you to even weigh in on this plan."

"What?"

"As you've said yourself, it could hurt your business. You'd better abstain when it comes time to vote!"

"Oh I should, huh? And if I don't ..."

"Enough!" Miriam stepped between Auggie and Frank. She was nearly in tears. "I've had enough of this nonsense! You're like two boys fighting on the playground at recess." She pointed toward the stairs and lowered her voice. "We are going up to the office. And we are going to work this out like civilized people."

Both men just stared at her.

"I'm serious." Miriam turned to Frank. "Upstairs, now!" And then she glared at Auggie. "My parents taught you everything you know about running a business. Is this how you repay our family?"

Auggie opened his mouth to say something, but Miriam didn't want to hear it.

"Go!"

Frank was already halfway to the stairs. Miriam took a deep breath, and noticed the clock on the wall. "Look at the time! We have fifteen minutes to get this place presentable. George, you and Jerry do the dishes today. Melinda, water the flowers and do your usual."

"Should I come with you?" Jerry asked.

"No, you'd better not. Actually, you should get out of here as soon as you can. If you're still around when we come back, the fight's likely to break out again."

Melinda couldn't make out all of the words being shouted above her head, but the anger, hurt and outrage was impossible to miss. This time, however, most of the commentary came from Aunt Miriam. Melinda hoped her aunt could convince Auggie and Frank to at least be civil in public, but the fight was far from over. She just hoped that, whenever the issue was finally resolved, their friendship hadn't been torn so badly that it couldn't be mended.

George came up to the counter. "I put the coffee cups back in the cabinet. I don't know if they're right where Auggie keeps them, but ..."

"He'll get over it if they aren't." Melinda sighed and rubbed her face. It was going to be a very, very long day. "Thanks, George."

Jerry folded the chairs and put them back against the wall, and Melinda insisted he take the donuts with him. "City hall's the closest thing to neutral territory we have these days."

"Well, OK. I'm so sorry, I don't know what more I could have done. Auggie was way out of line."

"We were afraid this would happen. But maybe since they got their grievances out, they'll find a way to make peace."

More shouts echoed down the stairs, and Jerry gave a rueful laugh. "I doubt it. Well, I'll be across the street for a few hours, if you need me. And I'll probably be eating these donuts, one after the other."

16

Miriam worked fast. She had Frank and Auggie calmed down, or at least willing to promise civility in public, before the store opened.

But the men's work wasn't done. Frank was sent home with instructions to spend the day painting the kitchen in their new house, rather than golfing with his friends. And Auggie was ordered to donate twelve bags of mulch to Miriam's not-yet-finished flower beds. She expected delivery by the end of the afternoon.

Public reaction to Auggie's story slanted heavily to the negative. A few customers seemed impressed by his ability to land on the front page of the newspaper, but most residents took the coverage as a sign Auggie was out of control and needed to be knocked down a peg or two. More than a few told Melinda that if Auggie wanted to be in the news, that's just what he'd get.

The Swanton paper welcomed letters to the editor, and apparently some were being crafted that took a strong stance against his requested tax breaks.

Melinda smiled and nodded through it all, too exhausted to make conversation after so few hours of sleep. It was a relief when the clock struck four, and she could pull off her apron and leave the gossip behind. Besides, there were plenty of things at the farm that needed her attention.

Her strawberries were going gangbusters now, and she'd been slicing and bagging and freezing most nights after supper. There was more sauce to can, and jam to make, and she hoped to have most of it done before Jen's crew arrived Saturday to run through details for the wedding.

Angie, with Mabel's assistance, was perfecting the coconut cake recipe, and Jessie had met the challenge of creating a menu that was both farm-friendly and summer-proof. No mayonnaise, no fussy garnishes, nothing that needed to be piping-hot or ice-cold.

Adelaide would bring some inspired ideas for the bouquets, and Vicki and Jen had worked wonders on everything else given the short timeline and small budget.

The biggest obstacle still in their path wasn't something, but someone: the mother of the bride.

Jen was Bridget's only daughter, so this was her one chance to plan a wedding. She'd hoped for a church service, a formal dinner and the whole works. Even though Jen's initial choices hadn't promised the fairytale her mom preferred, Bridget had eventually come around.

But a low-key wedding at the farm? This change in plans was a hard sell. And if the wedding was going to go smoothly, Saturday was the ladies' best chance to close the deal.

Melinda's biggest wedding task was to have her renovations done on time. But the finish line was still a ways off, and she wasn't sure when she'd be able to cross it.

"Well, they'll get to see 'before and after' today," she told Hazel and Grace on Saturday morning. A dozen more bags of strawberries waited for their trip to the basement freezer, but Melinda still had a pile of bowls to wash. "Grace, really, can't you do that in the other room? You're underfoot!"

Grace was sprawled out on the rug in front

of the sink, her fluffy belly turned toward the cool air blasting from the baseboard's vent. Hazel, at least, was out of the way, her attention focused on the birds flitting past the south-facing kitchen windows.

Melinda glanced at the clock, and double-timed her efforts to get the house presentable for guests. "Hank and the guys are making progress. I just wish it was progressing a little faster."

The north and west sides of the house were finished, and she was thrilled with the results. But the other half was still bare of paint and showing its age, along with a scattering of fresh-beige replacement boards. Even so, the painting wasn't the worst of her problems.

The roofers had been delayed yet again by their slate of emergency projects, and she'd even considered punting her place in line and waiting until after the wedding.

An old roof on the farmhouse for Jen's special day would be better than a half-finished new one, and Melinda couldn't imagine hosting such a special event with sections of scaffolding climbing the walls of her house. But such a move would drop her to the bottom of the contractor's list, and she'd be lucky to have the new roof on before cold weather arrived.

Melinda almost had the counter cleared off when she heard Hobo come through the back porch. He burst through the second doggie door and hustled to his water bowl, leaving dirty footprints across the kitchen linoleum. An offensive odor Melinda couldn't quite name wafted up from his muddy feet and, by the disgust on their furry faces, Hazel and Grace smelled it, too.

"Why do you have to be out exploring just before company arrives? It's such a nice day, I think you can spend it outside. At least, until the ladies leave." She retrieved Hobo's towel from the back porch and got to work. "I still need a shower, myself. And I guess I'll have to leave the sourdough starter out, it has to stay warm."

Melinda was confident the dishes submitted for the Fulton Friendship Circle's cookbook were road-tested and had at least one good cook's seal of approval. Except the sourdough bread recipe that came in at the last minute.

It had been in their family for generations, according to the daughter of a former township resident, but was unfortunately sketchy on the details. No one had attempted it in years. Melinda wasn't about to leave this one to chance, especially since she had no experience with sourdough, and had a little chemistry experiment going on the counter.

She sighed with relief when Vicki's SUV turned up the lane. Getting Hobo clean had left Melinda twice as dirty, but she knew her friend would be eager to finish prepping for the soon-to-arrive guests.

"Am I glad to see you!" Melinda waved Vicki inside. "I got the kitchen cleaned up, but I'm still a mess."

"Oh, leave it to me." Vicki's brown locks were perfectly in place, and her top and capris were stylish yet comfortable. "I'll get the table set and tidy up a bit."

She set her plastic tote on the kitchen floor and reached over to greet Hazel, who cautiously sniffed her hand. Grace had already vanished upstairs.

"Jessie is about five minutes behind me." Vicki pulled a length of lavender netting from her tote. "What do you think? Humidity-proof, inexpensive, drapes nicely. We'll swag this along the ceiling line of the tent. Throw up some light strings and, ta-da!"

"That's going to be so pretty. And you're using it on the tables, too?"

"Sure am. Just gathered lengths to wrap around the mason-jar centerpieces." Vicki held up a sample. "And battery-operated candles, too. All we need is someone knocking a real one into the grass." She glanced at the clock above the sink. "Run upstairs and get ready."

When Melinda came down twenty minutes later, the dining table was set with some of the white melamine plates Jen purchased in bulk online. They were cheap, shatterproof, and sturdy enough to stand up to the fantastic spread Jessie had in the works. Plastic cups and silverware, and paper napkins, rounded out the table.

Her house suddenly smelled so good, Melinda's stomach started to rumble. Jessie had obviously arrived. As had Angie, and the two women were setting out the food on the kitchen counters.

There was a pasta-and-vegetable salad, dressed with a vinaigrette. Skewers of cherry tomatoes, basil and mozzarella balls. Two slow cookers steamed with barbecued chicken and beef, and a third held Angie's calico bean recipe. Other picnic fare rounded out the meal, including a veggie tray and potato chips. Two kinds of seasoned popcorn would be tied inside small bags with name tags for easy table favors. And there, on the far end of the counter, was a sampling of coconut cupcakes as well as some chocolate ones.

"Doesn't it look great?" Angie popped into the dining room to check out the tableware. "When I think about how much time and money we spent on our wedding, it makes me sick. Really, we could have done something like this and been just as happy."

Melinda kept an eye on the lane as she put away the last of her now-clean dishes. "I just hope Jen's mom agrees."

"I can still make changes to the menu," Jessie said as she gave the calico beans a stir. "But Jen's driving this bus, so I intend to back up the bride."

Adelaide soon arrived, and Melinda helped her carry in three vases of flowers from her car. Phlox were always reliable this time of year, as were lilies. Some of the irises might still be blooming, and there were a few other varieties in Adelaide's heirloom garden that could round out the bouquets.

Although Jen's colors were lavender and purple, she was open to whatever was available. With that in mind, Adelaide had mixed in a few blooms in shades of pink, red and yellow.

Mabel was also on today's guest list, but her biggest contribution to the gathering had nothing to do with her baking skills. She knew the Schermann family well, having lived just down the road nearly all her life, and Melinda wanted her around just in case things took an awkward turn. Edith was coming along, so that was one more voice of reason in Jen's corner.

While Jen and her matron of honor, Emily, sported shorts and tees, Bridget either didn't get the memo or had chosen to ignore it. Her dress slacks and summer-pretty blouse weren't exactly suited to the farm, and Melinda just hoped her heeled sandals didn't find one of Hobo's lawn deposits. Edith wore her usual polyester pants and knit top. Her tennis shoes said that, despite her cane, she wasn't going to sit it out when the other ladies did their walk-through of the grounds.

Once everyone was there, Melinda began to relax. This was supposed to be fun, after all;

and she was proud of how her friends pulled together to make Jen's wedding-day dreams come true.

Bridget, to her credit, set her reservations aside and sincerely complimented Vicki's work on the centerpieces. "I've seen photos, of course, but these are really lovely. You've done a wonderful job."

"I'm so glad you approve." Vicki smiled and reached for her binder. "How about we go outside and look around while Jessie and Angie put the last touches on the food? We need to decide on a location for the tent, among other things."

Melinda felt a swell of pride when the group went down the back steps. Her lawn could use a little more rain, but the rest of her yard was as charming as ever. And Anna's perennial bed, while much smaller than Adelaide's, was bursting with color. Adelaide raised an eyebrow as they walked past, and Melinda knew what she was thinking.

"We'll put some of Anna's flowers in Jen's bouquet," she whispered to Adelaide as they trailed after Vicki, who was shepherding everyone toward the front lawn. I can't guarantee what will be blooming in a few weeks, but we'll make it work."

Vicki halted the group in the shade of the maple tree, which was lovely in its summer canopy, and gave a big smile as she motioned to the expanse of grass in front of the house.

"Ladies, this is option one for the tent. We were lucky to get the rental, it's what makes all this possible. It'll be a bit cozy, but I have a plan to make it work." Melinda had no doubt that was true.

"Well, I think this is a lovely spot." Edith leaned on her cane and studied the yard of her childhood home. "I think there's room, and the trees will offer a bit of shade."

"This works for me." Jen took a deep breath, as if she dreaded what was to come but saw no way around it. "Well, Mom, any thoughts?"

Bridget pursed her lips. "I suppose this could work." She sounded less than enthused, however.

Jen frowned. "If there's an objection, please state it now. Melinda's been kind enough to let us get married out here. We need to figure this out."

"It's the house." The words tumbled out as Bridget turned toward Melinda. "Are you certain it'll be finished in time? Because it looks ..."

"Awful." Edith gave her daughter-in-law a stern look. "Yes, I'll say it. But did you notice the back when we pulled up? This place will be like new when the painters are done. Melinda, it's astounding what they've accomplished so far."

She sighed and tightened her grip on her cane. "I'd been telling Horace for years that this needed to happen, but he kept putting it off. He and Wilbur were more concerned about the barn than ..."

Mabel stepped forward. "What matters is that it'll soon be taken care of."

"Absolutely," Melinda promised. "They should wrap up next week."

Jen knew the roof was next, but given how this was going, Melinda decided not to bring that up right now. And there was always the chance her choice of steel panels rather than traditional shingles might not meet with Edith's approval. Best to wait until it was done, and couldn't be undone.

Besides, Edith was ready to move on. "So, what are our other options for the tent? How about the north side? Lots of shade there."

And Edith, who knew this farm like the back of her weathered hand, started off around the corner of the house.

"We haven't fully considered that option." Vicki clutched her binder close as she hurried to catch up to Edith, who was rather swift for someone in her eighties. "Option A is the front, of course, and Option B ..."

Thankfully, the north yard was deemed too small for the tent. But it was a discussion that took Vicki and Mabel several minutes of tap-dancing to resolve to Edith's satisfaction.

"And here is our best option," Vicki said brightly as they came around to the west side of the house. "This lovely expanse of lawn between the garage and the garden is the very-best place for the tent."

Bridget frowned. "What about the clothesline?"

"I can take it down," Melinda answered quickly. "Just for a few days. Vicki is right; we have plenty of room out here."

Emily pointed behind the chicken coop, where a critter roamed the patch of wild black raspberries. "What is that thing?"

"Oh, that's my woodchuck." Melinda answered casually, as if she'd just noted the presence of Sunny or Stormy. "Don't worry, they don't bite."

"Unless you try to steal their lunch." Edith chuckled. "Oh, he's kinda cute."

The fruits were tiny but delicious; if only Melinda had them all to herself. Between the birds and the woodchucks and who-knew-what-else, she had to be crafty to get even a cupful now and then.

Bridget said nothing, but her face said it all.

Jen turned her back on the woodchuck and shifted her feet, as if trying to block the scene from her mom's view. "Oh, Melinda, that reminds me. I'm so glad you were OK after those yellow jackets swarmed you. Dave said that ..."

"Yellow jackets?" Bridget clutched her throat and glanced around nervously.

"I was down at the creek," Melinda said quickly. Jen caught on, thank goodness, and didn't give away Melinda's lie. "It wasn't a big deal, really, just a few. Anyway, Vicki, you were telling us why this is the perfect spot for the tent."

The unfamiliar cars and commotion had initially driven Pepper and the sheep to the back corner of the pasture, but this strange parade was too interesting to miss out on entirely. As Vicki pushed for the ladies to endorse Option B, he and the girls returned and gathered just behind the barn. When Pepper realized Melinda wasn't coming over to say hello, he started to bray. That was the ewes' cue to join in.

Vicki talked louder and louder. Finally, she gave up.

"I like Pepper," Jen said quietly. "But do you think he'll behave during the ceremony?"

"He's fond of company." Mabel tried to find something positive to say. "But we can always lock him in the barn once the guests start to arrive."

Jen was relieved, but Vicki saw it was time to change the subject. And few subjects were more popular than food. "Let's go in, shall we? Wait until you see what Jessie's cooked up. And Angie's coconut cupcakes are divine."

The wonderful spread earned raves from all the guests, including Bridget. Vicki talked everyone into endorsing the back yard for the tent's location, then the ladies made quick work of the rest of the details.

Adelaide's flowers were given the green light, and Jen loved the idea of having a few blooms from her great-grandmother's beds. The tent would be delivered the afternoon before, and the tables and chairs that morning. Since the ceremony wasn't until five, there would be ample time to get everything in place. The Olsons, Melinda's neighbors, would lend their generators to help power the party until the last dance ended around nine.

Photos would be taken next to the garden, or in front of the house by the maple tree. Dave would handle the playlist, and Vicki had finally lucked into renting a small, portable dance floor. Jen and Andrew had purchased an arbor trellis to serve as the backdrop for their vows, and would install it in their garden after the wedding.

Everything was coming together at last. Melinda was thrilled for Jen, but as she sat there at the table, taking part in the laughter and chatter echoing through her farmhouse, there was a bit of sadness, too. She tried not to think about the wedding she'd planned with Craig, and how it all fell apart before she made it down the aisle. Now there was Josh, and she loved him so much, but …

Mabel nudged her, and Melinda accepted a coconut confection from the tray. "As many of you know," she said as she handed the plate to Emily, "this is a Schermann family recipe."

Edith took a bite of her cupcake, and closed her eyes in bliss. "It's perfect," she announced. "Mother rarely made this cake, as coconut was hard to come by except for special occasions, but it's even better than I remember."

"We added a little almond extract," Angie explained. "Most wedding cakes have it."

Jen had happy tears in her eyes. "I can't thank all of you enough. Here I was afraid this wedding wouldn't happen. This isn't what Andrew and I intended, but it's going to be even better!"

Bridget had turned quiet, and Melinda wasn't sure if that was a good thing. Finally, when there was a lull in the conversation, she raised a hand. "Well, I don't know what you'll think about this," she told her daughter, "but I have an idea."

Jen raised her chin, ready for whatever arrow would come her way.

"Honey, listen. Everything is very nice." She gestured at the table. "It's one thing to have the reception in a tent, but the ceremony? Wouldn't you rather have it inside?"

Jen was too stunned to speak.

Edith never was.

"Oh, please." Edith threw down her paper napkin. "Stop this nonsense. It's not like she's getting married in a barn, for God's sake."

"I was simply going to suggest the ceremony take place right here, in the house."

Jaws dropped around the table. Melinda's heart raced as she looked from one room to the next, calculating. Over sixty people were coming to this wedding. There was no way they'd fit in here, even shoulder to shoulder.

"Just hear me out." Bridget leaned her elbows on the table. "I'm not talking everybody. Just immediate family." She turned to Edith. "You were married here, right in front of the fireplace. And now, it's Jen's turn. She's the last of the Schermann brides to get married at this farm. It would be a nod to tradition, like the cake."

Jen jumped out of her chair. "That's it! I don't want one more word out of you."

Bridget was about to speak again, and Jen's face burned with anger.

"What did I just say?" she shouted at her mom. "You don't listen, do you? Andrew and I would never let the rest of our guests hang around outside while a select few are allowed to attend the ceremony. Do we need to get a velvet rope? Maybe a bouncer to keep the riffraff out?"

Bridget tried another tactic. "The ceremony is what matters most to you and Andrew, right? And the party is what matters most to your guests. I say, everybody gets what they want."

"No, Mom, that's just you getting what you want." Jen crossed her arms. "And it's not going to happen."

Edith glared at her daughter-in-law from across the table. "You've said enough. And you've done enough to ruin what has been, until now, a very lovely afternoon." She narrowed her eyes, and Bridget went pale. "I won't subject Melinda and her lovely friends to any more of this nonsense. Just remember, we have a forty-minute drive to get home. I expect it's going to feel much longer than that."

Jen turned to Melinda. "We would never impose on you like that. I can't believe she even ..."

A strange noise echoed from the kitchen. A sharp, popping sound. Then another. And an unearthly yowl of surprise and disgust.

Angie ran to the doorway. Just then, a blur of calico fluff streaked across the floor and past the table, and vanished into the living room. Melinda didn't know which way to go first.

"It's the sourdough!" Angie gasped. "Oh, Melinda, it's everywhere!"

Sure enough, blobs of sticky, fermented dough now clung to the counter and the floor.

Jessie peeked in for a look. "Good thing we covered up the food before we sat down to eat. Was that Grace who just flew past us?"

It was. Jen found her crouched behind Melinda's reading chair, wedged into the safe space between the bookcase and the adjoining wall. The poor girl must have been right under the starter when it exploded, as tufts of dough flecked her long coat.

"Here, baby." Jen tried to coax Grace out of the corner. "Oh, you poor thing. Why don't you come out, and ..."

Melinda knew that look in Grace's eyes. She was about to say something, but it was too late. Jen yelped and rocked back on her heels, her right hand clasped around her left.

"How bad did she get you?"

"Not too bad. It's just a scratch."

Mabel had already fetched the first aid kit from the bathroom cabinet. "And here the day was going so well. Or at least, marginally well, up until the last few minutes." She handed Melinda the antiseptic spray and a bandage. "Between the critters, wild and domestic, and the yellow jackets and who-knows-what-else, I hope Josh can make it to the wedding. I hope we don't need his medical expertise, but who knows what might happen?"

17

"Just keep the carrot in your hand," Josh told Aiden. "Hold it by the end. There, like that."

Aiden giggled when Pepper dropped his snout over the fence and gently took the treat. "He likes it! I think he's smiling."

Melinda certainly was. The sight of Josh holding up his son so they could give Pepper a snack was one she could get used to seeing. It was Josh's weekend to have Aiden, since Father's Day was tomorrow, and they'd come out to the farm after breakfast to play with the animals before Bart's auction started at ten.

The Lutheran church was hosting the lunch stand, so they would certainly hang around long enough to sample the ladies' legendary beefburgers and homemade pies. Josh wasn't sure how long he and Aiden might stay, as the tables of housewares and the calls of the auctioneer might not prove very interesting for a little boy, but Melinda didn't mind. She planned to spend most of the day there, as it was a chance to visit with her neighbors, but it was more important for Josh to have as much time with his son as possible.

And, he might actually get it, as Karen and Thomas had insisted he not take any calls this weekend. It would be several weeks yet before Doc was back at work, and all the veterinarians were doing their best to take breaks.

As soon as Josh put Aiden down, Hobo ran out from behind the machine shed.

"Come on, Hobo. Let's play fetch." The little boy picked up a small stick and threw it as hard as he could. It only sailed a few feet, but Hobo gamely hurried after it. Aiden then ran off toward the garden, saying he wanted to see the strawberries. Hobo was at his heels, and Stormy and Sunny joined the procession when it passed their shady napping spot on the west side of the garage.

"He really loves it out here." Josh put an arm around Melinda. "It's the same when we go to my parents' farm. He can't get enough of the animals and the chance to run around and explore."

"He's a country boy at heart, then." She

stole a quick kiss. "Just like his dad, I'd say."

An unfamiliar truck came down the road, a cloud of gravel dust following behind. It was soon followed by a car, and then another.

"Quite the traffic jam for this neighborhood," Josh said. All the vehicles slowed at the next intersection, and every one of them turned west. More cars and trucks were coming up from the south. "Looks like Bart will have a good turnout for his sale."

"I hope he gets a decent profit today." Melinda took Josh's hand and they began a slow stroll across the lawn. "He and Marge had a lot of antiques, I guess. But the house is in rough shape, I don't know if anyone's foolish enough to pounce on it."

"Oh, maybe 'foolish' isn't the right word." Josh winked. "Someone might have a vision for it. You never know what could happen."

Melinda almost teased Josh about whether he had a secret plan to fix Bart's place up for himself, but didn't. While they tried not to talk about the decision that loomed before him, it still cast a shadow over so many of their conversations. The future, and the new uncertainty of their relationship, seemed to meet Melinda at every turn.

And it wasn't just Josh that had her concerned. The public hearing on Auggie's plan had been Monday night, and the frustration and hard feelings it stirred up continued to reverberate through Prosper. The chambers were packed and, while Jerry did his best to keep the room civilized, several heated arguments broke out among the residents.

Just as Melinda suspected, there was still overwhelming support for the gas pumps. Nearly everyone who spoke was furious about the tax breaks and kickbacks, however, so much so that Auggie's proposal to renovate the inside of the store barely received a mention.

The council members sat through the two-hour meeting in near-silence, trying their best to appear neutral. Their only action was to move their discussion and a potential vote to their mid-July meeting, instead of the one at the end of the month. Frank later told Melinda the city's leaders hoped the delay might give people a chance to calm down, but she wondered if the council members' personal positions on the project were starting to shift, one way or another.

Auggie, who sat in the back of the room and simply listened to everyone else's comments, made good on his promise to stay quiet during the meeting. As requested by Miriam, he had also stopped bringing the topic up during coffee hour. But the tension remained, and Melinda often breathed a sigh of relief when the guys left.

Things just weren't the way they used to be. But it was a beautiful summer morning, Josh and Aiden were here, and all the neighbors were gathering at Bart's; she shouldn't waste it worrying about the future.

"Melinda!" Aiden called from the strawberry patch. "There's so many of them! Can I pick some?"

"Well, Dad?" Melinda raised an eyebrow at Josh. "What do you think?"

He let go of her hand, and started for the back porch. "I think fresh strawberries sound perfect on a day like today. They'll tide us over until lunch. Let me go in and find a bowl."

* * *

The Wildwoods' long lane had ditches on either side, and was too narrow to provide any parking for the sale. Instead, a large chunk of the unused front pasture had been mowed, and employees of the auction company now directed attendees to park in marked-off rows. Melinda and Josh drove separately, and not just because he and Aiden were likely to leave early. She didn't need to buy anything, but driving Lizzie meant she was prepared if she couldn't bear to go home empty-handed.

While the house was in sad shape, Melinda was pleasantly surprised by how nice the yard looked. Bart never bothered to mow more than a wide path around the house, barn and the closest shed, leaving the rest of the property as a weedy, wild tumble of vegetation. But all that had been cut down for the sale, and the area that would have been the front lawn now boasted more than a dozen metal tables lined with housewares and knick-knacks, and two rows of heirloom furniture.

With the grass cut to a navigable height, the property's numerous trees were really able to shine. Their mature canopies also provided welcome shade for the onlookers, and a cluster of oaks east of the driveway provided a cooler spot for the food stand's tables.

Josh, who'd parked in the previous row, was waiting with Aiden when Melinda decamped from Lizzie's cab. "They've really cleaned things up for the sale. But I see what you mean about the house. It looks worse during the day. That one time I was here, it was dark, and ..."

Aiden was all ears, so Josh stopped talking. He'd come over with Ed one blustery night when Bart twisted his ankle in the ice and snow. Marge thankfully hadn't wandered out into the cold, but she was incoherent and confused. After that incident, their adult children began their push to get Marge and Bart to leave farm life behind.

The sale wouldn't start for half an hour yet, but the yard was already full of onlookers. The weather was perfect for a farm sale, and the solid odds of finding a bargain among the boxes and crates were matched by this rare opportunity to get an up-close look at the township's oldest home.

Housewares would kick off the sale, and the property would go up for bids at one. The Wildwoods' stash of antique furniture would be offered last, in a bid to keep a good crowd around for the rest of the sale.

Mabel and Ed were on their way back from the lunch stand, oversized cinnamon rolls in hand. "I have to say, I'm impressed by how they shaped this place up." Ed paused to dig into his roll with a plastic fork. "Mmm. I wish there were more sales, so I could get one of these more often."

"Someone has worked wonders with this place in the last week." Mabel gestured around the yard, which sat up on a small rise. "And that view!"

John and Linda Olson soon joined the group. "I can't believe I'm saying this, but it's pretty up here," John admitted. "You know, if someone was really ambitious, they could knock down the house and start over. But it'd be a ton of work."

Ed sighed. "That's for sure. I hear there's too much that needs upgrading. The sewer line, the well, the list goes on and on."

"I hope someone buys it, though," Linda said. "I'd hate for the land to no-sale. If nothing else, for Bart's pride. He's a tough cookie, but this has to be hard for him. I'm glad Marge isn't here."

Given her condition, the family had decided not to tell Marge about the sale until it was over. Bart had reluctantly agreed to keep things quiet. Melinda spotted him over by the barn, talking and laughing with a group of older men. If he was upset, he certainly didn't show it. But then, Bart wasn't known for wearing his emotions on his sleeve. Unless, of course, he was angry.

Their group of neighbors expanded again when Will and Helen Emmerson arrived, along with Clarence and Eleanor Murphy. They were soon joined by Angie's husband, Nathan, and their two young daughters.

Little Blake was at Grandma and Grandpa's, Nathan explained, since Angie was working the lunch stand, and Emma and Allison were enough for him to manage on his own the rest of the day. Nathan soon drew Josh into the conversation, and Aiden quickly made friends with the girls.

When Mabel suggested she and Melinda give the housewares a look, Josh encouraged her to go. "We'll get along just fine."

"Look how well Josh fits in with our little group," Mabel said as they started across the lawn. She seemed as proud as if Josh were her own son.

"I thought he would." Melinda smiled. "But then, he's used to dealing with every personality imaginable."

Adelaide met up with them at the first table, which was packed with yet-unknown treasures. She reached for a porcelain cat figurine with distinctive calico markings, and placed it in Melinda's hands. "Now, who does this look like?"

"I didn't get a number yet. I told myself if I don't have a number, I can't bid. Which means I can't drag home something I don't need."

Adelaide laughed. "Oh, nonsense. Bid cards are free, no harm in signing up. But if you quickly succumb to temptation, you can borrow mine."

In the next row, Melinda found another gem: Harriet Van Buren, who lived north of the blacktop. While she was now in her eighties, Harriet still piloted her old Cadillac over to Melinda's when she wanted to buy fresh eggs. Melinda hadn't seen the distinctive car among the vehicles in the front pasture, and Harriet said she'd gratefully accepted a ride from a neighbor.

"Marge was quite the collector." Harriet sifted through a stack of heirloom doilies. "Of course, Bart's family owned this place for decades before he and Marge moved in. Many of the antiques surely came with the house."

Melinda and her neighbors wandered the makeshift aisles for several more minutes, and Melinda was soon lost in her thoughts. There was a story behind every vase, every old book, every lamp or chair. But most of those tales, she was sure, had been lost long ago. This house had been here since the 1870s, which meant it existed for forty years before Horace's grandfather built her house. The two years she'd lived in this township, by comparison, were just the blink of an eye.

Sometimes it seemed like she'd been here forever, but in a good way. Especially now, when she planned to visit Minneapolis next week to see Susan and Cassie. They'd known each other since their early twenties, and had worked together at several marketing and media firms over the years. Melinda counted them among her closest friends, but she hadn't seen enough of them since she'd moved back.

She was determined to make it happen this time, and not just because she longed to see her old friends. There was a circus to attend, and she didn't want to miss it.

Claire Smithfield, a formidable woman who'd been a mentor to all of them early in their careers, was retiring from the wildly successful marketing firm she'd built from the ground up. She was holding a lavish reception at her home, and word was she'd invited nearly two hundred people to witness her victory lap. It shouldn't matter, really, but Melinda had been wracking her brain since her invitation arrived: Whatever was she going to wear?

Adelaide came back around the table and lowered her voice. "Other side, fourth box from the left: Hawk Hollow creamery bottle."

Melinda glanced around, relieved no one else was within earshot. "Do you think you can get it? I was thrilled to find mine in the basement. Thank goodness the Schermanns never threw anything away."

"Well, word of our little ghost town has spread, thanks to the cemetery restoration and the cookbook project." Adelaide considered her odds. "But I don't know if the true value of Hawk Hollow has hit the local antiques market yet. Maybe I'll get lucky."

The house's kitchen door was propped open, and curious visitors roamed in and out. Adelaide raised an eyebrow. "You know, I've never been inside. Care to take a peek? The sale won't start for a few more minutes."

Melinda was ready to go. "Absolutely. This could be our last chance to look around."

Two men were coming out just as Adelaide and Melinda were going in. "Well, what do you think?" Adelaide asked.

"It's terrible." The older man shook his head. "More of a project than I'd ever want to take on."

The younger one glanced over his shoulder. "If you're interested, you'd better find out who the ghosts are first. Dad's not a believer; but I can assure you, they come with the house. I really need some pie."

"Oh, dear." Adelaide sighed as the men wandered off toward the lunch stand. "If everyone else has the same reaction, I'd say Bart's going to be disappointed."

The kitchen shined with sudden cleanliness, but the linoleum was cracked and faded, and several cabinet doors drooped with broken hinges. There was an ancient brown stain on the yellowed plaster above their heads, and a piece of trim was missing from the doorway into the next room.

"Did you see those windows?" one woman whispered to her husband as they passed by.

"Rope and pulley. All the ones I checked had a broken cord or a cracked pane. How could anyone stand to live here?"

"That fireplace hasn't worked in years," her husband muttered. "Who knows what's up in that flue?"

Melinda didn't know if the house was haunted. But standing in what had been the Wildwoods' living room, with its lingering cigarette smoke and grime-marred wallpaper, she was overwhelmed with feelings of hopelessness and despair.

Adelaide crossed her arms, as if warding off a chill. "When we bought our house, it'd been vacant for a year or so. It needed a total overhaul. But it had a happy vibe, like it was saying, 'come on in.'"

Melinda studied the bare floorboards, which were so scratched and scuffed she couldn't tell what their original color had been. "What do you think this house says?"

"Be out before dark," Adelaide whispered.

The rest of the downstairs contained an even-smaller room that had been the Wildwoods' bedroom, and a cobbled-together bathroom. The side porch's door was so off-kilter that it barely opened, and outside it

were rotten floorboards and a roof so cracked
that the sunlight streamed through.

Only one person at a time could navigate
the steep, narrow stairs. Many visitors
wouldn't attempt the climb, but Adelaide and
Melinda were determined to see the rest of the
house.

"Hold tight to the rail," Adelaide said over
her shoulder. "Oh, dear, maybe not; it's loose."

More crumbling plaster, more peeling
wallpaper. Another ugly water stain on the
ceiling in what must have been a bedroom,
although the roofline was so low the space
would barely pass for an attic these days.
Melinda peeked through one open door, and
shook her head. "Not much else to see, except
more decay."

They made their way to the first bedroom's
lone window, and stared out its grimy panes at
what had once been a generously sized
garden.

Melinda studied the wild tangle of weeds,
and thought of how the Schermanns always
took such pride in their own plot. "Horace was
stunned when I told him the Wildwoods were
trying to list this place with a realtor."

"Does he know anything about its history?"

"When he was a boy, during the Great Depression, the sweetest old couple lived here, John and Lottie Leary. They were poor, and the house was a little rundown even then, but it was always scrubbed clean. Good neighbors, he said. The kind everyone wants to have."

"Makes me wonder who our new neighbors are going to be." Adelaide frowned as she studied the spider's web of cracks creeping over the plaster. "Who's crazy enough to take this on?"

* * *

Melinda took a deep breath once they were outside again. It would be hot this afternoon, but the air was still fresh and carried the sweet smell of the recently cut hayfield behind the barn. Most of the onlookers were gathered around the first table of household items, where the auctioneer collected bids on a vacuum that had to be as old as Melinda.

She caught up with Josh and Aiden by the garage. While in sorry shape, it was still better than the house.

"Word is the property will go super-cheap, if at all," Josh reported. "Will overheard the auctioneer and his assistant. It'll no-sale if they can't meet the family's minimum bid. Which isn't much."

Bart wasn't the nicest of people, but it made Melinda's heart hurt to think of him standing there, trying to hang on to his pride, when the auctioneer's calls rolled to a stop and no one raised a hand.

"What happens then?"

"Don't know. They'll have to come up with a Plan B, I guess."

"Plan C, actually. This is Plan B. Plan A was that realtor I told you about. He didn't last even an hour out here. Did you get over to the barn?"

There were some interesting vintage tools set out on tables inside, Josh said. A grouping of old farm implements out back held a few rarities that might drum up some cash from the collectors in the crowd.

"And there's a truck!" Aiden pointed to the side of the driveway.

"Oh, yes." Josh ruffled his son's brown hair. "It's from the 1940s, I guess. Been sitting under that oak for maybe half that long, though. It doesn't run, but for someone looking for a restoration project, that won't stop them."

She raised an eyebrow. "Oh, really?"

Josh laughed. "Yeah, like I have time for that. Let's get over to where the action is."

The small housewares were sold by the box. Melinda used Adelaide's bid card, and got the cat figurine plus a bunch of other stuff for only three dollars. She hadn't taken the time to paw through the carton earlier, but it offered a set of measuring cups, a small outdoor thermometer carrying the name of the co-op in Swanton, and what appeared to be an antique perfume bottle, along with several other items.

"Looks like you hit the jackpot." Josh held up a small toy truck, and passed it to Aiden. The little boy was thrilled, and carefully placed it in his pocket. "How about I take everything out to Lizzie before we get some lunch?"

"Thanks. Mabel warned this could be addictive, and she's right. We'll meet you over by the food stand."

Aiden took her hand, and they made their way through the crowd to wait in the shade. Adelaide grinned as she passed by with a box of goodies that had the Hawk Hollow Creamery bottle tucked inside.

As they waited for Josh, Melinda spotted Bart and his son talking with a small group of men. Both of them were laughing and joking, but as soon as the others moved on, their postures changed.

Lenny said something to Bart, who crossed his arms and took a small step back. Melinda couldn't hear Bart's response, but Lenny's reaction told her all she needed to know. Bart pointed an accusing finger at his son, who threw up his hands and shook his head. What happened next was something Melinda never expected to see: Bart's chin wobbled, he wiped his face with the back of his hand, and his gray stubble was soon dotted with tears.

"Why is that man crying?" Aiden gripped her hand tighter. "Is he sad?"

"I think so." She knelt down next to him. "That's Bart. He's my neighbor. Or rather, he was until last week. He can't live here anymore. That's what's going on here today: they are going to sell Bart's house."

Aiden took it all in for a moment. "It's sad when people move away," he whispered. "When my daddy moved away, he cried, too."

Melinda swallowed the sob that formed in her throat. Her eyes blurred with tears, and she turned away from the people passing by on the way to the lunch stand. "I'm so sorry," she finally told Aiden. She didn't know what else to say. "I bet you cried, too, huh?"

Aiden nodded. "He said he would come visit me, all the time, and that he was going to miss me. But he had a new job, and he had to move away."

"Your daddy loves you very much. It must have been really hard for him to leave."

She saw Josh coming through the crowd, and her heart felt like it might break in two. How could he stay here? This opportunity was too good to turn down, and nothing half as close to Elkton was likely to ever come his way.

Melinda looked down at the little boy who still held her hand. No matter how much Josh loved his current practice, no matter how much he loved her, there was so much more at stake.

But then Aiden looked up at her, and gave a little smile. "I miss Daddy sometimes. But I get to visit him, and see Charlie. And now I can come to your house and see Hobo, too. And Pepper."

"How's it going?" Josh kept his voice light,

but he looked worried. "Are we ready for lunch?"

"Let's eat." Melinda smiled at Aiden. "I'm hungry. Aren't you?"

"What happened?" Josh whispered as they got in line. "You're so ..."

She plastered on a smile and waved to one of the ladies from the church. "I'll tell you later."

They found seats at one of the metal tables with Nathan and the girls, and Melinda tried her best to participate in the chatter and laughter circling around them. As good as the food was, she could barely taste her lunch. Once Aiden was busy with his half slice of cherry pie, Josh bumped her with his elbow.

"Let's clear our trash, huh?" He stacked their paper plates together, and nodded toward the barrel set away from the tables. "Aiden, will you be good for a few minutes?"

He grinned, his mouth so full of pie he couldn't speak.

Nathan handed over some plastic cups. "Thanks. Saves the ladies from cleaning up."

Once they were away from the others, Josh leaned in. "Something happened while I was gone. Please, tell me what it was."

She did. His pained expression almost brought her tears back. Josh tossed the trash in the barrel and put his hands over his face. "That was a terrible day. And something I never want to go through again."

Melinda wondered if, or when, Aiden might find out about his dad's job offer. And if Josh decided to stay here, would he ever have to have a similar heart-wrenching conversation?

I know I could have moved back closer to you, but ...

"You were honest with him, explained it as clearly as you could." She managed to shrug her shoulders, as if all of this was long in the past. But it wasn't. Not anymore. "He seems to have adjusted pretty well, all things considered. But that's just it, honey. You have a chance to do things differently, to go back. How can you not?"

Josh raised his chin. "Do you think I should take Kathy up on her offer?"

People were staring at them. She walked toward the treeline at the edge of the yard. Josh followed, and they turned their backs to the crowd.

"You know I can't bear the thought of losing you. But Aiden is your son, he's your world."

"He's a huge part of it, yes." Josh touched her cheek. "But so are you. So is my whole new life here." He sighed. "I knew what I was doing when I bought the Swanton practice. Believe me, I agonized over it, over how this would affect Aiden. I made my decision, and I made peace with the consequences."

"I know, but a chance like this isn't going to come around again. Don't you think it's important to ..."

Josh gave her a level stare. "Are you trying to say I'm a bad father if I don't move back?"

Her mouth dropped open. "No, I ..."

"Well, I hope not." The hurt in his eyes made her look away. "This is my decision. You know I'm leaning toward staying, but ..."

"Then why do I feel like you want me to tell you what to do?" She almost threw up her hands, just like Lenny had, but didn't. It would be so obvious to everyone they were arguing. "You don't say it in so many words, but I feel it."

Josh looked down. Melinda waited for him to deny it, but he didn't. She put a hand on his arm.

"I'm sorry. I'm sorry to get upset like this. But Aiden's face, when he told me, just broke my heart. And this has been a very emotional day, anyway. Bart's a bit of pain, sure, but he's still my neighbor. He's trying to put on a brave face, but this must be devastating for him."

"Change is hard." Josh put an arm around her shoulders. "Doesn't matter what kind of change it is." He straightened up and took a deep breath. "Let's not talk about this anymore today, OK? Besides, I think Aiden's got about an hour before he's going to crash. Let's get some pie for ourselves, and then I should probably take him home for a nap."

Angie's banana-cream pie was outstanding. Melinda decided she must be feeling a little bit better, since she could actually taste it. But it now seemed like the sun was too hot, the air too humid, and the farm yard too crowded with strangers. She just wanted to go home and lie down herself, in the coolness of her own farmhouse, away from all this uncertainty.

Aiden gave her a big hug before he left, his little hands still sticky with cherry pie filling even though Josh had tried his best to wipe them clean. Josh did the same, and Melinda found it really hard to let him go. "I'm sorry." She didn't know what else to say.

"Me, too," he whispered. "I'll call you later."

She found Adelaide in the crowd, and was pleasantly surprised to see Mason was now there. "Couldn't miss out on the big moment," Adelaide's husband said. "Decided it was worth setting my own home improvement projects aside long enough to get over here and see what happens."

"It may not be much, I'm afraid." Melinda relayed what Josh had heard.

Bart stood at the far edge of the crowd, his face once again a blank mask with no hint of the turmoil going on inside. His son looked worried, and his daughter seemed to be on the verge of tears.

Adelaide studied the sea of faces. "So many people here that I don't know. Makes you wonder what the deal is. Is someone brave enough to tackle that house?"

"Maybe if the price is right." Mason shook his head. "I can't imagine what it's going to cost. I love old houses, too, but is it even worth saving?"

Promptly at one, the auctioneer announced it was time to sell the property, and reminded everyone the farm would change hands "as is, where is, with no concessions from the sellers." He'd chatted up every piece of furniture, every box of knick-knacks as if they were too wonderful to miss out on, but he knew better than to bother with the house and outbuildings.

His first suggestion was higher than Melinda expected. No one raised a hand, or called out. He rambled on, dropped the offer, then did it again. Nothing. Bart squared his shoulders, as if he expected the worst.

"Oh, I hope it doesn't no-sale." Adelaide pushed her palms together. "Poor Bart. How terrible to feel like your home has no value left, nothing at all."

"What about the farmer who owns the fields around it?" Melinda asked. "Could he turn it into crops, or pasture?"

"Maybe. But they'd have to clean it up, tear everything down. That costs money. And time."

The suggested bid dropped again. And then, a hand went up on the other side of the crowd. A grin spread across the auctioneer's face. "Well now, that's more like it! Come on, folks, if you're even a little bit interested, now's the time to speak up. It's a diamond in the rough, and you'll get it for a song."

No one else moved and, after several more tries, his ramble ground to a halt. "Sold! Bidder thirty-eight." The crowd erupted in claps and cheers, even a few whistles. Bart looked relieved. And to Melinda, that was all that mattered.

"We paid more for our last car," Mason said to his wife. "And it wasn't even new. For a second there, this place was looking pretty good. It'd be a huge rehab, but ..."

Adelaide rolled her eyes. "Absolutely not."

Mabel soon appeared out of the crowd, and Melinda grabbed her arm. "Oh, aren't you relieved it's over? I'm so glad for Bart's sake that it sold. Now, we just need to figure out who bought it."

Mabel raised an eyebrow but said nothing. Or rather, her big grin said it all.

"No!" Adelaide couldn't believe it. "Are you serious? Ed's always saying how bad his knees are, how would he ever ..."

"Oh, we're not going to flip it." Mabel laughed. "It's a little sad, of course, that no one's going to live here again. Or should I say, no people are going to live here."

Ed soon caught up with his wife, and they told their neighbors about the idea they'd hatched a month ago: Before the year was out, the Wildwoods' farm would transform into the Watson Wildlife Refuge.

Mabel's family had lived in the township since its pioneer days, and both she and Ed were interested in local history and land stewardship. One of Clarence and Eleanor's grandsons worked in conservation, and he'd helped the Bauers figure out how to create a haven for wildlife on these two acres.

"If no one else wanted it, we knew it would be devastating for Bart and Marge," Ed explained. "And all this talk about Hawk Hollow's had us wanting to create some sort of legacy for Mabel's family. Besides, this place is already a favorite of the deer and racoons and everything else. We talked to our tax guy and really, it's not going to be that expensive if we do it right. Who knows? Maybe we'll get some eagles setting up a nest or two in here."

Family members were already on board to clear off what was left of the outbuildings. The barn could be salvaged for its wood, and the Bauers planned to donate the house to the Prosper Fire Department. The organization would use it for a training exercise that would benefit several local agencies.

"You're going to burn it down?" Melinda was stunned. But she had to admit, it was a wonderful plan.

"We'll let the experts handle it, but yes." Mabel looked over her shoulder at the house. "I hate to see something so old be demolished, especially when we're trying to preserve the township's history. But given its condition, this the best option. Sometime before the snows hit, we're going to have the biggest bonfire you've ever seen."

The auctioneer had moved on to the rows of antique furniture, and the house was already forgotten by most of the crowd. As Ed and Mabel wandered off to talk to Bart and his family, Melinda and Adelaide tried to take it all in.

"I never would have expected this." Adelaide shook her head. "But really, this is the best thing that could happen."

Then she laughed. "You know what's the most shocking part? That Ed and Mabel were able to keep this a secret for so long."

18

Melinda took a swig of champagne, and nearly coughed when the bubbles tickled the inside her nose. Cassie and Susan laughed. But it was the good kind, from friends who know you best and support you when you aren't on top of your game. Because even in her comfortable flats, Melinda felt way out of her league at this well-heeled party.

"I've forgotten about that part," she admitted. "Of course, if I'd remember to sip, and not gulp, that would help, too." Her cocktail dress still fit, at least, and she hoped its classic lines hid the fact it was three years old. But really, why did she care what any of these people thought? Melinda pondered that as she took another drink.

Uncomfortable in her dress sandals, Susan shifted her weight from one foot to the other. "My feet are killing me. I don't care who's here, I really wish we weren't."

The "gathering room," as the engraved invitations had called it, of Claire Smithfield's mansion could hold the whole footprint of Melinda's farmhouse. White-jacketed waiters glided among the guests, their silver trays stocked with appetizers from one of the Twin Cities' of-the-moment bistros and, of course, more champagne.

Outside, beyond a line of seemingly endless French doors, the swimming pool's turquoise-tinted water glinted in the late-afternoon sun.

"We're breathing rarified air in here." Susan singled out a woman not ten feet away. "CEO of her own firm. And that one? National award winner for marketing. At least, until she had her first kid and quit the biz. And at nine o'clock, we have the Woman of the Year for a Minnesota public-relations organization."

Cassie checked her dark curls hadn't escaped their chignon. "Twenty years ago, even ten, I would have given my right arm to get invited to something like this. Not anymore. It's one big schmooze-fest."

She reached for an appetizer as a waiter passed by. "Trouble is, I don't care to schmooze with anyone here. I'm still shocked I was invited."

"Well, that small company you landed at is really making waves," Melinda reminded her. "And Susan, you're at one of the most-respected firms in the city. Now, as a hardware store clerk, I really don't know why I'm here."

"Because you needed a good excuse to visit us." Susan smiled. "It's been way too long."

"We're all here for the same reason." Cassie lowered her voice as another group of designer-clad women glided past. "Each of us, at some moment in our past, collaborated with Claire in one way or another. She wanted every single one of us here to revel in her crowning achievement. Which is walking away from it all to retire in Florida."

Susan spotted an empty table on the side of the room, and the ladies pounced on it. It took a few more minutes, but Melinda decided she was getting the hang of this. The champagne, but not the socializing.

A few faces looked familiar, but she'd yet to run across someone she was certain she knew. Maybe that was because so many of the older women had apparently spent years, and lots of money, morphing into caricatures of their younger selves. Foreheads were strangely wrinkle-free, lips were a little-too plump.

Melinda couldn't wait to slip away from here, escape from this distorted snapshot of her old life, and go to Cassie's to change into comfortable clothes. Because the ladies' next stop would be Amadori's, their favorite old hangout, for an Italian meal packed with carbs and cheap wine.

Cassie rested her chin in her hand. "When's this speech supposed to happen?"

"Five sharp." Susan sighed. "But I promised Sam I'd hang out until five-thirty. I'm the only one from our firm that's here, so I need to wave the flag in case someone wants to chat about a future project."

"I used to love networking." Melinda shifted restlessly in her chair. "But now, my conversational skills are focused on keeping the peace at coffee hour at the store."

"And how is Auggie these days?" Susan wanted to know. "Is he learning to play nice with the other kids in the sandbox?"

"Hardly. And we're still several weeks out from when the council will take his plan up again."

Letters to the editor were running anti-Auggie by a ratio of three-to-one, thanks to the tax breaks he demanded from the city. And while the council overall had heeded Jerry's plea to keep their opinions quiet for now, Jake had penned a long-winded op-ed praising Auggie's business plan.

All the tension made Melinda wonder if Auggie's plan had enough support to pass. And if Uncle Frank, as much as he didn't want to bow to Auggie's demands, should abstain when it came time to vote.

"I'd love to see Auggie working this room." Cassie took another sip of her drink. "He'd take these society ladies down a peg or two. He certainly has some interesting ideas about how to drum up publicity for his cause."

Susan crossed her arms. "At least he has a cause he believes in. I suspect many of our fellow guests lost their drive years ago. They're just biding their time until they make partner, or can follow Claire out the door." She groaned. "Former coworkers Amanda and Tiffany at the swan ice sculpture, coming this way."

"Big smiles, ladies," Cassie whispered. "Maybe this won't be so bad."

"Oh, it's so exciting to see all of you!" Tiffany trilled. "Isn't this a lovely party? I've worked with Claire several times over the years. She's been a wonderful mentor."

"I want to be her someday." Amanda sighed with envy. "Look at this house! Did you know, her firm has over a hundred employees now? And that's not counting all the smaller companies they partner with all around the Midwest."

Tiffany gestured toward a man toward the front of the room. "She's on husband number three, you know. But isn't he a dream?" Melinda had to admit, the guy was handsome. But he also looked like he'd rather be anywhere but here.

Amanda pointed out all three of Claire's now-grown children had attended Ivy League schools. One was a doctor, another a lawyer, and the youngest was an engineer. "That's the only sad thing. None of them went into marketing, so she doesn't have a legacy."

"But we are her legacy," Tiffany gushed. "Everyone she motivated and inspired over her career. I owe everything to her."

Next came the inevitable questions about what everyone was doing now. Cassie went first, and Amanda and Tiffany tried to seem interested in her updates. Susan got a warmer reception, simply because she was at one of the highest-profile firms in the city. Shock and fake smiles greeted Melinda's news, just as she expected.

Tiffany blinked. "Well, that's … interesting."

"But you do all the marketing for the store, right?" Amanda tried to find a common thread. "That must be so rewarding."

"It is." Melinda took another swallow of champagne, and said no more. She didn't feel like playing this game any longer. The room was getting warmer, she was sure of it. Too many people packed into the space. And too much hot air.

In the awkward silence, Cassie suddenly stood up. "I hear the strawberry tarts are incredible. Why don't we go check them out? And Amanda, I'm so glad we ran into each other. My firm has this new project I want to tell you about."

As Cassie drew them away, Susan let out an irritated sigh. "Fakes, both of them. Don't pay any attention to what they say, or how they look." She widened her eyes, mocking the women's superficial expressions. "I bet you're happier than half the people in this room, Claire included."

"Well, we're about to find out. She's taking the mike."

Cassie soon returned with three plates. Melinda's tart had little flavor despite its rich hue, which was obviously obtained by a great deal of food coloring. Suddenly, she craved a handful of strawberries from her own patch.

Hobo was probably out there right now, napping in the cool dirt as he waited for Ed and Mabel to arrive so he could help them do chores. He had a bad habit of smashing some of the fruit, but she didn't mind. The patch was so large, she could hardly keep up with its bounty. Besides, the season would be over in a few weeks.

It was hard to focus on Claire's speech, which was full of grand gestures and carefully crafted praise for her biggest enablers and most-prestigious clients. And Melinda noticed how, under all that precisely applied makeup, Claire looked, well … tired.

Melinda suddenly felt the same, and not just physically. She'd loved her old career. It was challenging, creative, and had given her friends like Susan and Cassie. But it was now in her past, and she didn't feel like reliving it for much longer.

Once Claire received her standing ovation and the guests returned to their networking, Melinda started around the table. "I'm going out by the pool."

"It's beastly hot out there." Cassie craned her neck to take in the small number of attendees who'd escaped to the terrace. "Are you OK?"

"I'm fine. Won't be long. After all, Amadori's awaits us."

Melinda swiped a fresh glass of champagne on her way out. Cassie was driving, so she might as well. She scanned the dozen-or-so faces in small clusters around the pool and sighed with relief. No one looked familiar, even if she deducted points for forehead lines and crow's feet, wider midsections and less-toned arms.

Or actually, added points, she told herself. Getting old was far better than the alternative. And every line, every wrinkle on these women's faces had surely been earned. Melinda knew hers had.

She found a patch of shade under a patio umbrella and took a deep breath. It wasn't just this party, and these faces, that felt unfamiliar. Everywhere she went in this city seemed the same way. She'd left a little early to give herself time to drive through her old neighborhood, and felt lucky to find a parking space in front of her vintage apartment building.

Melinda had sat there for a few minutes, the air conditioner on full blast, and stared up at her former home. Who lived there now? What was their life like? And marveled at how, just two years later, she could barely remember how her own life had been.

"Um, Melinda? Is it really you?"

A male voice startled her out of her reverie, and she turned around. Unlike so many faces at this party, she would know him anywhere.

Her ex, Craig Simpson.

Not just her ex. The man she'd almost married.

There were a few strands of gray in his sandy-brown hair, but the eyes were the same. Those blue eyes she'd fallen in love with, right away. Way too soon. And they'd blinded her to the truth that she and Craig weren't as right for each other as they wanted to be.

"Hey." She wasn't sure what else to say, wouldn't have been able to get the words out if she had.

"I wasn't sure, at first. I mean, I saw you walk by." He gestured at the row of glass doors.

So he'd followed her out here. That made her a little bit happy. Which made her sad, at the same time. She looked around them, desperate to make conversation. "I didn't know you knew Claire. She never worked in broadcasting, that I remember."

Craig covered sports for a television station in the Twin Cities. Not the same one he'd been at when they met but, well, she kept tabs on him online. Just a little.

"Oh, no, you're right." Craig laughed. "I'm quite the outlier here, this isn't my crowd. Kind of like you, these days," he added softly.

So, he'd been doing the same. "You moved back home." It wasn't a question.

"I did, yes. It wasn't planned, but Uncle Frank had a heart attack, not long after I was laid off here. They needed help, so ..."

She filled him in on her life, and Craig smiled.

"Sounds like you ended up where you needed to be." His observation hung in the humid air between them, and Melinda felt a wave of relief. Yes, she had.

"My wife knows Claire." Craig stuffed his hands in his pockets. "Pretty well, actually. Cynthia works at her firm. She's a senior account manager." His voice filled with pride. "So I guess I'm among the plus-ones here."

Melinda took a swallow of champagne. "Cynthia must have worked hard to get to where she is. If she's climbed that high, there's nothing but good things in her future, for sure."

Craig took a few more steps in her direction, his posture suddenly relaxed. Melinda took a deep breath and returned his smile. They'd already cracked the ice; no reason they couldn't hang around for a few minutes, catching up. She had no interest in what was going on inside, and Craig surely didn't, either.

Things were good, he said. He had what he'd always wanted. A thriving career. A house in the suburbs. And a wife. They'd only been married ten months, so no kids yet, but …

As he rambled to a close, a silence settled between them.

"I'm sorry," she whispered, before she even realized what she was saying.

Craig stared at her, surprised.

"I'm sorry." She said it louder this time. "We've both done well for ourselves, in our own ways. I felt I was doing the right thing, when I ended it. I'm sorry it was so hard on you. It was hard on me, too."

Craig glanced back toward the house, then stared at tinted concrete under his feet.

"You're sorry." He bit off the ends of his words. "Well, good, because ... look, it obviously wasn't going to work out, so yeah, you did the right thing." There was an acid in his tone that made Melinda's heart speed up. "Even so, you blindsided me with that! It didn't have to be that way, you could have ..."

"Blindsided you?"

People were starting to stare. She lowered her voice. "How can you say that? We were fighting, all the time. The wedding decisions, the house we were buying." She shook her head. "We had problems. Serious problems. You knew that, as well as I did. You had to!"

"Oh, really? I thought we were going to work them out, not just ..." He flung out one hand. "Not run away from them, give up."

"I didn't give up on us!" Melinda's face burned hot. "I tried, several times, to talk to you about it, about everything! Just because I was the one that put a stop to it, doesn't mean it was all my fault!"

"So you saved the day, then?" Craig was shouting now. "Saved us both from, what? A good life together? No, that's not it. I think you were scared. Scared to make a real commitment, for just once!"

The champagne glass slipped from her fingers and shattered on the concrete. Everyone on the terrace was watching, everyone was pointing, but she didn't care.

"That's not true. I loved you!" Her voice wavered with so many emotions, she couldn't recognize them all. "You know that I did. But it was never going to work."

"You don't know that! Dammit, Melinda, I loved you so much. I didn't care about the reception, the rings, the house. None of that. We could have eloped. All I wanted was you."

Melinda was too upset at first to notice the handful of women who'd appeared behind Craig. But one of them, she now saw, was terribly pale. And furious. Even with her own emotions careening out of control, it only took Melinda a second to figure out who it was.

Craig swallowed hard, raised his chin, then turned to face his wife.

Cynthia said nothing at first. Then she pointed at her husband.

"You will not embarrass me like this. Out front, in ten minutes. Be there, or I'm leaving without you."

Her gaze flicked briefly over Melinda before she turned away. Melinda was nothing to her, just some unstable stranger at an elegant party who didn't really belong there in the first place. And Melinda was nothing to Craig, hadn't been for a few years. That was how it should be. What Melinda, in the end, had decided she'd needed.

Not wanted, but needed.

Craig hadn't moved. He just stood there, his eyes full of tears and hurt.

"I'm sorry," she told him again, and she started to cry.

Someone grabbed her arm. It was Susan. "Let's go. Cassie has your purse."

Susan had her halfway to the garden's side gate before Melinda realized what was happening. Her tears, which had come from pain, now sprang from relief. Her friends were there, and they'd take care of her, just as they always had.

She glanced around her once, but Craig was

already gone. Susan cursed as she flung up the gate's latch. "I thought that was him, but I couldn't be sure. He passed by while we were fending off Tiffany and Amanda, and ... good, there's Cassie."

The passenger door popped open, and Cassie grabbed Melinda's hand. "Honey, just get in. We're out of here."

Melinda buckled her seatbelt and closed her eyes. Just as she was about to lose herself in old, painful memories, another thought popped into her mind. "Do you know what this reminds me of?"

"I have no idea." Susan answered drily from the backseat. "A cheesy romance novel?"

"Well, maybe." Melinda wiped her eyes with the back of her hand. "Do you remember the day after I was laid off, when I went to clear out my desk? I took the bus downtown, but you two came to pick me up. Susan, you helped me out with my box. And Cassie, you were at the curb with the getaway car."

Cassie giggled. "Oh, you're right!"

"And we went to Amadori's for lunch." Susan picked up the memory. "And you didn't know what you were going to do, or what the future would hold."

"History is repeating itself." Cassie turned at the next stoplight and headed toward home. "But you're in a much better place this time. Even so, I think we'd better take a cab downtown."

* * *

Susan opened the pizza box and gave its contents an appreciative sniff.

"Mmm. This is going to be good." She took two slices, then gestured at Melinda and Cassie. "Eat up. It's not Amadori's but, well, it's Italian."

"I'm really glad we decided to stay here and order in." Cassie deposited a bottle of cheap white wine on her kitchen island's counter. Her kids were spending the night with their dad, so the friends had the place to themselves. "I don't know about you two, but I'm exhausted. That party was far more interesting than I thought it would be."

Susan gave Melinda a frown of sympathy. "How are you holding up?"

"I'm OK, I guess. But maybe I'm still in shock from seeing Craig again." Melinda took a bite and chewed slowly, tried to savor the unexpected. There were few pizzerias near

Prosper, and none of them were as good as the friends' old standby here in the Twin Cities. The wine was cold and crisp, but even that wasn't enough to erase the memory of Craig's wretched face.

That was bad enough, but the things he said. And then, there was his wife. Melinda put her head in her hands.

"You know," Cassie said gently, "if you still have some feelings for him, even a little bit, it's not that unusual."

"That's just it." Melinda sighed. "I would have expected to feel something, but there was just … nothing. I mean, up until when we started shouting at each other."

It was as if some part of her hadn't even recognized him. Craig hadn't changed much in looks, other than getting a bit older, but she could say the same for herself. It was more like their love, what they'd had together, now felt like it belonged to someone else. Someone she no longer was.

She tried to explain that to Susan and Cassie, and they understood. "Sometimes Jim comes to pick up the kids, and I think, 'who are you?'" Cassie stared at her left ring finger, which was bare. "It all feels so surreal."

"But it's not just that." Melinda adjusted her ponytail. "Some of the things he said, they were so hurtful. Especially because they're true."

Her friends gasped in disbelief, but she held up a hand.

"No, I mean it. I tend to question everything, too much. Things get rocky, and I feel the need to bolt." She started to cry. "Why can't I just ... good things come into my life, good people. Good men," she corrected herself, "and I get so busy putting up walls, just in case it all goes bad, that I push them away."

"Why do I think this isn't about Craig anymore?" Cassie put down her fork. "Honey, tell us what is really going on."

Susan leaned over the island. "What happened with Josh? Because something has definitely happened."

For weeks, Melinda had kept her promise to not discuss Josh's dilemma. But here, with two of her best friends in a place that was worlds away from her regular life, she couldn't carry the burden any longer.

"Oh, no!" Susan was on the verge of tears herself. "What are you going to do?"

"I don't know." Melinda wiped her face with a paper towel. "I just don't know. At the auction, when Aiden said what he said, it just hit me all at once how hard this has been for him. When I told Josh, I didn't mean to imply he's a bad father."

"Well, I'm sure he's not." Cassie set her mouth in a firm line. "But it was really unfair of him to toss it back in your face like that."

"Makes me think you really hit a nerve," Susan added. "Parental guilt is huge, even in situations less important than this one. Josh has to be worried about Aiden, and how all this has affected him. He can't help it."

"He loves Aiden, so much. That's really his only possible reason for moving back, I know. But it's a big one. Bigger than what we feel for each other."

"And you won't go with him?" Cassie asked gently.

Melinda shook her head, the tears coming again. "No. Believe me, I've thought about it, worked through all the scenarios. It's not impossible, but ..."

"But it feels like it," Susan finished the thought. "Because Prosper is home again, after all those years away. I'm sure Brookdale is a nice little town, but it's not where you belong."

"Any more than you belong here." Cassie gestured around them. "As much as I wish you still did." She thought for a moment.

"I know how you feel about Prosper, the store, your farm, your family. But do you think Josh is your true home? I mean ... wherever he is, is that where you most want to be?"

Melinda let that sink in for a moment.

Yes. Yes, that was true. She wanted to be with Josh. And, as much as she sometimes didn't want to admit it, she needed to be with Josh.

But how could she give up everything else for him? She just couldn't.

"I want things the way I want them," she finally said. "I want Josh. I want to stay in Prosper." She shook her head. "But Aiden needs his dad. How is Josh going to feel as the years go by, and he misses out on so much? What if he resents me for it?"

Susan frowned. "I can't imagine he'd do that."

"You don't know. And what's that like for Aiden, having his dad so far away? His life is never going to be the same."

Cassie cut into the pan of brownies cooling on the counter. "Well, sadly, this is an area I have expertise in. Aiden's life has already been irrevocably changed, and that happened before you ever came into the picture. For better or worse, he's already settled into this new routine. Josh's moving back would make him happy, of course. But it's never that simple."

"He told you how much he enjoys visiting his dad's new home, and seeing Charlie." Susan gave Melinda's arm a squeeze. "He likes you, and your farm. It's not perfect, sure, but it's a good place to start."

Cassie settled back in her seat with a sigh. "You know, if I could have done anything different, I would have divorced Jim sooner. I thought it was best for the kids if we stayed together, put on this brave front." She shook her head. "All I did was drag out the inevitable. You love Josh, and he loves you. And it sounds to me like he really wants to stay."

"I think he does, too. But I can't tell him what to do."

"Then don't," Susan said. "What you can do, what he needs you to do, is to tell him it's OK for him to stay. Reassure him he's doing the right thing."

Cassie thought this over as she took another bite of pizza. "You were talking about running away from things. Why not, just this one time, you run toward something? Or in this case, someone?"

Melinda blinked away fresh tears. "I don't want to lose him."

"Well, then, that's settled," Cassie said brightly. "Tell him you want him to stay. Beg, if you need to."

Susan and Melinda stared at her in disbelief. *Beg?*

"OK, maybe don't do that. Something a little less dramatic should do the trick."

Melinda knew her friends were right. And maybe, with their encouragement, anything was possible.

19

Melinda tried to focus on her clipboard despite the howls and meows echoing off the community center's high ceilings.

"The Carlsons. Here you are." She felt as relieved as the woman in front of her looked, with a rocking carrier in each hand and another at her feet. All three cats were wild with fear and anger.

"Do we have Muffin, Jenny and ..."

Melinda peeked inside the tote on the floor and saw a strapping, gray-and-white tomcat who was missing part of one ear. "That must be Scruffy."

"He's my big tough guy." The woman smiled. "But he won't have to be after today. He's going to have a better life."

Melinda pointed with her pen. "You can set them over there, below the windows, and then fill out this paperwork." As much as she wanted to chat with the woman and learn more about three of that day's patients, the check-in queue stretched to the front door and there was only one other volunteer to help.

The woman looked around and gave a nod of approval. "Always loved this building. Glad to see it's getting a new life, and the history's still intact. And all this natural light, too. Not like when I brought Max, Mollie and Maggie in last fall, over at city hall."

Her gaze zeroed in on the two exam tables at the back of the room. "How are you going to fix all these kitties today with just two vets? I hear Doc's doing well, but he's not back in the game yet."

"Oh, we'll find a way to get it done." Melinda's tone was perky, and she spoke loud enough so some of the other pet owners would hear. It was all Karen and Josh could do to make the rounds at both practices, so they were off the community-clinic schedule. Thank goodness for Iris Anderson, a Charles City veterinarian, who'd joined the program in the spring.

And someone else had just arrived, all business and ready to go.

Thomas McFadden doffed his faded ball cap to several people waiting in line and basked in their greetings and encouragement. "Hello, everyone! I'm all set to snip." It was almost as if he expected a round of applause to break out in his honor.

Melinda was still sometimes caught off guard by how many area residents remembered Doc's predecessor, but at least they remembered him fondly. He and Karen were from different generations and far-apart mindsets, but they'd reached some sort of professional truce and his skills had certainly been needed.

"Your table is ready." Melinda pointed out one corner. "Sorry, we're stretched thin, so there isn't a tech to assist you the whole time. Let me know what you need, though, and I can fetch supplies."

"Oh, that's fine." Thomas' eyes twinkled. "I brought my own assistant." He motioned to an elderly woman behind him. "Honey, there you are! I want you to meet everyone before we scrub in."

There wasn't time to socialize, but just in time, Melinda stopped herself from rolling her eyes. Nancy, who was also checking in patients, gave Melinda a wide-eyed look that said, *we'll never get started at this rate.*

Once his wife was busy chatting with those waiting in line, Thomas sidled up to Melinda. "So, are we really seeing number five hundred today?"

"Yep." Melinda handed a farmer his paperwork, and moved on to the next person in line. "Sometime this afternoon he, or she, will be on the table. Sharon's coming over from the paper. We decided it was the perfect photo op to promote the clinics."

Thomas leaned in. "You know, it would be a hoot if the special one ended up on my surgery table. Iris is a gem, I've known her for years but, well, she's not from around here."

Melinda wanted to point out he'd left Prosper several years ago, and Mason City was twice as far away as Charles City. And besides, she didn't expect to have the time to choregraph which vet got which cat. She was more concerned about whether the milestone patient would hold still long enough for a photo. Of course, they could sedate the kitty first, but that wouldn't be as good.

"We'll see what we can do." Melinda smiled and shook Thomas' wife's hand. "How about you get ready? We'll get started in half an hour."

Norma breezed past with a box of syringes. "Tell Miriam again how much I appreciate her taking the counter today. And Bev and Gertrude helping us, too."

"It takes a village. We're lucky our town has supported this program like they have."

Melinda could only shuffle the deck of regular volunteers so many ways. It was a great relief when Bev offered to help for part of the day. And when Melinda dropped a load of cat food off at Gertrude Millard's last week, the caregiver of Prosper's stray colony had been kind enough to volunteer.

Nancy and Melinda finally cleared the line of incoming patients, and the community center quickly evolved into a temporary veterinary hospital. The last of the latecomers had just been settled in a back room when Nancy ran to one of the windows and gasped. She motioned for Melinda to join her. "Did you know about this?"

Doc's truck had just pulled into a parking space, and he was carefully exiting the passenger side, crutches and all, with his wife's help.

"He told Karen he wanted to join the Cuddle Crew, if he felt up to it," Melinda said.

"I guess he does." Auggie, George and their buddies were already settled in the main room's quietest corner, ready to hold the still-sleepy cats wrapped in blankets until they came around from the anesthetic.

Melinda's phone beeped. It was a text from Miriam.

Doc came in, got his surgery kit. I couldn't talk him out of it. Sorry, I tried.

Her mouth fell open. Had Doc lost his mind? He was healing, sure, but there was no way he'd be able to stand at a surgical suite for hours on end.

Doc expertly maneuvered his crutches across the hardwood floor. He looked tired, and his usually lean frame had a little more padding from extra helpings of Anne's cooking, but his grin stretched ear to ear. His arrival elicited an enthusiastic, if surprised, welcome from the clinic's volunteers. Iris smiled and waved to Doc, then started on her first patient of the day.

The look of shock on Thomas's face, Melinda decided, was priceless. If only he would stop gawking and start working.

They needed another set of hands. But another distraction? Absolutely not.

"Oh, this was a last-minute thing." Doc answered Norma's question with a casual shrug. "But I'm tired of sitting at home, and I'm glad the clinics have continued despite all the craziness. Just figured I'd stop in and help."

Anne grabbed Melinda's arm. "I tried to talk him out of this nonsense. More like, we yelled about it for almost an hour this morning. He threatened to drive himself over here if I wouldn't, can you believe it? He wouldn't listen to Miriam, either."

"You were right to bring him, then. When he gets an idea, he's as stubborn as Auggie."

Doc claimed this was a last-minute decision, but being out of commission for a month had given him plenty of time to come up with a plan. He insisted he could work sitting down, and knew there were a few lower-height folding tables in the center's storage closet.

Anne sighed when she saw George wheeling an ergonomic, padded chair out from the back office. "He's already got his buddies doing his bidding, so I think we've lost the battle. I'll stay around and make sure he has what he needs. And that he doesn't overdo it."

Melinda had to get back to Prosper Hardware, but would return early in the afternoon for the milestone moment. She'd given Sharon a rough time estimate for that operation, but wondered if it would come sooner rather than later.

And not only because there were now three veterinarians present. She couldn't be sure, but she may have just seen a look of challenge pass between Thomas and Doc. "Call me if this gets really out of hand," she told Nancy. "No one is to rush through surgeries to beat anyone else. This isn't a pissing match."

"Or a stitching match." Nancy winked. "I don't think we'll have to worry about that. While you and Anne were getting Doc's table ready, Iris told them both that very thing. And that her tech is keeping an eye on them."

Fran had her arms crossed as she stood at attention next to Iris' workstation. Her laser-like focus went from Doc to Thomas, and back again. When Thomas started to smirk, she sent him a glare that would crack ice.

"That would be enough to make anyone mind," Nancy told Melinda. "For the umpteenth time, I'm so glad Iris volunteered for our little cause."

Bev later reported that having Doc and Thomas in the same room made for an interesting lunch break.

"Trash talk, I'd call it," she told Melinda that afternoon. "You'd think they were two young guns, facing off on a basketball court or some such nonsense. But if I had to guess, they're secretly excited to work together again, if only for the day." She glanced around the bustling community center. "We're getting close, just a few more to go. We'll have our milestone surgery within the hour, with maybe ten more kitties after that."

"Good." Melinda glanced at the large round clock on the wall. "So Sharon won't have to wait long for her photo."

Even though she had her arms full of towels, Bev waited.

"What is it? Is the Cuddle Crew out of cookies again?"

"No, thank goodness. Although I think everyone's a little tired of Auggie bragging about his project." Bev lowered her voice. "Nancy was wondering if you want to pick out our star attraction yourself. See, we have quite a range of talent back in the waiting room." She smothered a smile as Fran passed by.

"They're all upset, as you know. But some are more photogenic than others."

"Great idea. No matter who we choose, it might be tough to get the shot we want." They started down the hallway. "Let's see who's the most cooperative."

All was silent behind the first closed door, as those patients were on the road to recovery and waiting for their rides home. The second room, however, erupted with howls of indignation when Melinda slowly opened the door.

Bev was right. The line of remaining patients offered quite the casting call.

"See, now I might pick him." Bev pointed out a brown tabby scowling in the back of his cage. "He's as common as they come, but that's a good thing. It'd show that any cat, no matter how average they might be, deserves this chance."

"I like that idea." Melinda tiptoed closer and peered in. The tom sprang forward and lashed out through the cage door's bars, his claws on full display. "Or, maybe not." She checked the strip of masking tape on the top of the carrier. "This is Bandit. Very fitting. Doc's already injured, I don't think he needs a trip back to the emergency room."

"So you're going to let him do it, then?" Bev nodded her approval. "With Karen and Josh out, I heartily agree."

"He's been such a supporter of the program, we never could have gotten this far without him." Melinda moved down the row. "Karen was still new when we started this. If Doc hadn't thrown his support behind it, talked it up to the farmers while he was on his rounds, we wouldn't be where we are today."

A calico cowered under the blanket covering the next crate. She was beautiful, but probably too terrified to hold still for a publicity stunt. The black cat next door seemed more relaxed than the rest, but Bev pointed out he might not show up well in the photo.

The big ginger boy on the end, though, looked like he might cooperate. If they bribed him with treats.

"Classic." Bev made her endorsement. "Oh, and he has white feet and a little patch under his chin!" She checked the tag. "This is Leo. I'll go tell Nancy, and we'll line these babies up to get him in the sweet spot."

Sharon arrived soon after, and Melinda

answered her questions about the program and their future plans while Nancy gave Doc the good news. When Melinda wandered past his table, he was all smiles.

"So I get to do the honors, huh? McFadden's going to be sore."

"He'll get over it." Melinda shrugged. "But really, he's been a great help. How are you holding up?"

Doc shook his head. "It's funny, my leg feels pretty good. But my hands are cramping a bit." He flexed his fingers and laughed. "Guess the physical therapist and I need to get on that. Feels good to be back, though, even for just a few hours."

"Well, I was shocked to see you pull up this morning. But we'll all be glad to have you back in the saddle soon." She tipped her head toward Auggie and George. "Coffee hour hasn't been the same since you've been out."

"I hear it's been tense, even though George says he's trying to keep the peace." Doc thought for a moment. "You know, I talked to Josh last night. He has a lot going on."

Melinda sighed. "It's been crazy. He's bouncing all over the place, trying to get it all done."

Doc looked at the floor, then back at Melinda. "He told me. About the offer."

"Oh." Her stomach dropped, and she didn't know what else to say. If Josh confided in Doc, maybe he was giving this idea some serious thought. After all, that was why he'd asked Melinda not to say anything: why needlessly worry their friends if he still might turn it down?

"I'm glad, I guess, that he felt he could come to you." She kept the tears back, but barely. "It's been really hard for him, trying to keep it quiet while he decides what to do."

Doc busied himself wiping down his table for the next patient. "I'm trying to stay out of it, what's going on between you and Josh. Really, I am. But I'll just say this: When the right person comes along, nothing else matters. He'll stay if you ask him to. I have no doubt about that."

Melinda wasn't sure if she should laugh or cry. "You sound like Susan and Cassie."

"They're wise, your friends. Anne said the same, you know." He sat up straight and flexed his fingers. "Well, here comes the next one. How's my hair look? Will I need to comb it before the photo op?"

"Looks fine to me." She smiled. "Thanks. A million times over."

It wasn't long before the big moment arrived. Norma brought Leo out of the waiting area, and he started to shift around in his carrier. "I hope we don't have to sedate him first," she told Melinda. "Should we make a run for it and see what happens?"

The two vets who were the backbone of the program couldn't be there, but Leo had plenty of onlookers for his time in the spotlight. Melinda soothed Thomas' ruffled feathers by asking him to get in the photo with Doc, Iris and the vet technicians. It helped that Doc couldn't stand and hold Leo in his arms, as Leo seemed most comfortable getting as flat to the table as possible.

Doc worked his magic, and soothed Leo with gentle hands, kind words and the stash of treats Melinda brought along. Sharon snapped three quick shots before Leo announced with a yowl that his two minutes of fame were up.

"Good job." Melinda reached toward Leo, and was rewarded with a nip on her finger. "Well, OK, not so good. Norma is going to help you nap, and when you wake up your life is going to be so much better."

The hustle and bustle started up again. Eight more cats were in line after Leo, and it wouldn't be long before the earlier patients' owners would begin arriving to retrieve their furry friends.

Like the rest of the volunteers, Auggie had observed the spectacle from the far side of the room. After Leo was taken away to be prepped for surgery, he ambled over to Doc and Melinda. "Well, I bet this feels good. Five hundred and counting!"

"It really does." Melinda smiled from ear to ear. "And we'll keep going."

"A little publicity never hurt." Auggie smirked. "And we all know the local paper's the best way to get the word out around here."

True. But if the avalanche of letters to the editor was any indicator of the general public's reaction to Auggie's plan, he could be in trouble. Melinda was still choosing her words carefully when Doc spoke up. "Oh, sure," he said gently. "But of course, one always has to think about the potential backlash, as well."

Auggie stuffed his hands in his pockets and didn't answer at first.

"Well, I'm sure glad you're on the mend," he finally told Doc, and Melinda knew he meant it. No matter the fate of Auggie's grand plan, that wouldn't change. They had been friends for too long. Melinda just hoped Uncle Frank and Auggie could find a way to reconcile when this was all over.

Norma was on her way back with a now-groggy Leo in her arms. "It's lucky you felt well enough to come by today," Auggie told Doc. "Just in time for the big moment. Isn't that great how it happened to work out?"

Doc chuckled as he readied his surgical supplies. "Oh, it wasn't an accident. I've been working toward this as soon as I found out number five hundred would be on the table today."

The surprise on Auggie's face made Doc laugh even harder. "Come on, man. You're not the only one who understands the value of a little publicity. What better way to spread the word that I intend to be back behind the clinic's counter in two weeks?"

* * *

The elementary school's grounds were filling in with families and couples awaiting the start of Prosper's Fourth of July fireworks show. Blankets, camp chairs and coolers were everywhere, and the mood was as bright as the full moon hanging in the clear sky.

"It's a great night for fireworks." Josh pulled a can of pop from Melinda's little ice chest. "The perfect end to what's been a near-perfect day."

Melinda stifled a yawn and hitched her chair closer to Josh's as another couple spread a blanket next to them. This was the highlight of the day's festivities, and space was at a premium. "Oh, I remember when I was young enough to do that," she whispered to Josh. "Sit on the hard ground for more than a few minutes. No more. In fact, I wish these chairs had a little more back support in them."

"Get up for a bit, stretch if you want. I'll keep watch over our spot."

"I'll be all right, thanks. I got plenty of exercise today at the store."

The Fourth of July festival drew a couple-thousand visitors to the little town, and it was always Prosper Hardware's busiest day of the year.

A pancake breakfast at one of the churches always kicked off the day, followed by the parade. After that came food tents and kids' activities in the park, as well as softball games over at the school. This year, Vicki added a slate of old-fashioned competitions in the afternoon, the sort of events she'd wanted to offer on Founders Day but ran out of time to get organized for that inaugural celebration.

The nostalgic games included watermelon-seed spitting, a husband-calling contest and a cow-chip toss. Doc, who rode in the back of his own truck while his son drove it in the parade, had used some of his downtime to call up clients and get Vicki the game pieces she needed.

The men's pie contest had drawn big crowds again this year. Auggie, possibly smarting from some of the criticism of his expansion plan, seemed to have doubled his efforts to beat the competition. His work paid off, and the judges awarded his triple-berry pie first place.

The gift card and apron weren't especially valuable, but Auggie didn't seem to mind: it was the bragging rights he wanted most.

The only thing that would have pleased Auggie more was securing the popular vote as well. But the public gave that honor to a man from Eagle River for his mocha-cream creation.

The crush of visitors began to ease by evening, as several other communities, including Swanton, had fireworks displays as well. Josh had brought Charlie with him to Melinda's farm, and not just so the dogs could hang out together.

It was peaceful in the country on the Fourth of July, and Charlie and Hobo could lounge inside Melinda's farmhouse without having to fear any bangs or flashes going off outside.

But the peace at her farm wasn't going to last long. Jen's wedding was less than a week away, and the chaos would start in earnest on Friday.

Controlled chaos, she reminded herself as she took some oatmeal cookies from the cooler. The roofers finished just yesterday, and Melinda was over the moon about the results. The steel panels were forest green with flecks of gray, a few shades darker than the old shingles, which made the freshly painted clapboards look even whiter and brighter.

The roofing crew's final task had been to mount her iron weathervane on the south peak, and Uncle Frank's handiwork was now proudly on display.

Everything was done, and it looked amazing. Well, not everything. Melinda just had to mow the lawn, and weed the flowerbeds, and pick up stray twigs, and ...

All of that could wait until tomorrow. She and Josh hadn't seen much of each other lately, and she'd been looking forward to tonight. And maybe dreading it, too. They needed to talk; she had so much to say.

Or really, not much.

Don't go. It was as simple as that.

She'd put it off for days, hoped maybe he'd broach the subject again so she wouldn't have to. But it couldn't wait. Between Jen's wedding, and the council taking up Auggie's plans at next week's meeting, her life was sure to get even crazier in the near future. It was better to know exactly where she stood. Susan and Cassie's advice, and the unexpected nudge from Doc, had given Melinda the courage to speak up.

All she had to do was throw it all out there, lay her heart on the line, and hope for the best.

Easier said than done. But she had to do it.

As often happened when they were out in public, a few revelers stopped by Josh's chair to pick up free veterinary advice. Melinda turned her attention to the growing crowd, and spotted Nancy and Richard a few rows over.

They had arrived late, and were looking for a bare patch to park their camp chairs. But even loaded down with gear, they still found a way to hold hands. Melinda sighed, and took a bigger bite of her cookie. Nancy was so happy, so content. What would it be like, how good would it feel, to know exactly where she stood with Josh?

It was dark now, and bobbing flashlights at the far end of the grass hinted the fireworks crew was moving into position. A cheer of anticipation rose up from the field. "Let's go!" a man shouted in the next row. "Let's get this started!"

It would be more than an hour until they were back at the farm, and alone. Suddenly, it was more than Melinda could stand. As soon as the advice seekers moved on, she touched Josh's arm.

"What is it?" He smiled. "Do you want me to get you something? I think there's more pop in the cooler."

"No, I'm good. Or at least, I can be." She

took a deep breath. "What I really want is ... well, I want you to give me something, I guess."

"Anything." That smile again, the one that always made her day and melted her heart. She was lucky, and she knew it.

"Anything?" She grasped his hand. "I hope you know what you're getting yourself into with a statement like that."

A boom echoed across the sky. The first firework bloomed above their heads, a shower of red and yellow that had the crowd whistling and cheering.

This was either going to be very romantic, she decided, or at least the noise and the dark would buffer their impending argument from the eyes and ears of everyone around them.

"I want you to stay." As soon as she said it, Melinda knew for certain she'd never wanted anything so much in all her life. "Please stay. Don't go. Don't leave."

Beg if you have to, Cassie had jokingly said. Well, Melinda couldn't quite bring herself to do that, but this was her chance to play the only card she had.

"I love you. You know that. I know I told you to make your own decision, that it was all up to you. But I can't bear the thought of losing you."

Josh looked away for a moment, then turned back. In the next burst of sparks raining down from above, she saw tears on his cheeks.

"I feel terrible about this." Melinda wiped away her own. "I mean, about Aidan. I'm being selfish, and needy, and all of those things I try so hard not to be."

And then, there in the dark, she felt a smile spread across her face. "But my whole life has changed because of you, because of what we have. I don't know what I'd do without you. What do I have to do, what do I have to say, to keep you here with me?"

She felt vulnerable, exposed, her heart barely beating as she waited for what seemed like forever. Whoops and cheers echoed all around them, and the glittering lights in the sky made her head spin.

Josh squeezed her hand, his face shadowed by the dark, and he said something. It was hard to make out, though, under the next sonic boom.

She could hardly breathe.

"What? I didn't ..."

Oh, if he was going to leave, if he was going to smash her heart into pieces, he needed to just get this over with.

Josh, however, had something else in mind. He leaned over the arm of his chair and took her face in his hands. "I've been wanting to tell you, been trying to find the right moment. But everything's been so busy, with Doc out and the holiday." And then he smiled again. "I can't go, Melinda. I love you, so much. I can't imagine loving anyone else."

Her heart felt like it might burst from happiness and relief. "Are you sure?"

"Yes," he said, as another explosion lit up the sky. "Yes!" he shouted over the noise. "Did you hear me that time?"

"Yes!"

They were yelling now, but not for the reasons she'd feared they would. Her spirits soared like the fireworks spreading above them, as if she herself was filled with color and light. And hope for the future.

And then she kissed him, right there in front of hundreds of people, and kissed him again. Everything, and everyone else, just melted away. No one seemed to notice. Or maybe she was too happy to care if they did.

"We'll work this out," Josh promised her under the roar of the crowd. "All that matters is we're together." Then he let out a whoop and pulled her so close, so quickly, that her camp chair started to fold in on itself.

"Doctor Vogel," she gasped, laughing so hard she could barely get the words out. "Be careful, or you might have a human patient to attend to. Oh!"

Over she went, and she landed in the plush grass at his feet. She still grasped his hand and, with one quick pull, Josh was down on the ground next to her.

"Hey! Weren't you just saying we're too old for this stuff?" But Josh was in no hurry to get up.

"Well, I'm not going to be down here by myself." She glanced over her shoulder and groaned. "Look, the brace snapped! Good thing I have a spare chair at home."

Then she touched his cheek. "But you're one of a kind."

Josh pulled her in for a long kiss as the booms echoed around them and the sky again filled with a rainbow of light. The crowd was on its feet now, cheering on the crew as they launched into the show's grand finale.

When they finally broke apart, Josh propped himself up on one elbow. "I'll call Kathy tomorrow, let her know to start looking for someone else. It's a great offer, but I can't leave. Not my practice, not my friends. And certainly, more than anyone or anything else, I can't leave you."

"No, you can't." Melinda pulled Josh close. In a few minutes, the fireworks would be over and it would be time to head home. But she didn't want to waste a moment. "Because I'm holding your hand, and I'm not going to let go."

20

Other than the patriotic decorations still displayed in some of the windows, any obvious reminders of the Fourth of July celebration had already left town by the time Melinda arrived the next morning.

Jerry was a member of the Swanton Jaycees, and the organization's members worked diligently during and after the festival to clear away the trash.

Even Auggie was right where he was supposed to be. His truck was already parked along Prosper Hardware's curb and, as she drove past the front windows, she spotted him as the sideboard, filling the coffeepot. And this morning, Doc was expected back at coffee group for the first time in more than a month.

Yes, Prosper had returned to normal. But when Melinda had opened her eyes that morning, and rolled over to enjoy the sight of a still-sleeping Josh, she felt entirely different.

He would stay, and that changed everything.

Other than Doc, none of the guys knew what Josh had been wrestling with for several weeks. And so, there was no need for any announcement to the coffee group. Melinda decided she liked that, very much. Being back in Prosper sometimes felt like living in a fish bowl; she was grateful for any shred of privacy she could find.

Auggie had the chairs in the customary circle, with one added back in for Doc. Melinda spotted Frank's car at the corner, and Doc's truck had just pulled up out front.

"We should have a red carpet or something," Auggie called to Melinda as she came up the main aisle. "The guest of honor has arrived."

"And so has Anne." Frank hovered by the front door, waiting to help his friend get settled. "Doc's not cleared to drive quite yet."

"Do you think she'll stay?" Auggie's tone was cheerful, but Melinda could tell he wasn't crazy about the idea. After all, tradition was tradition.

Melinda set her purse and lunch tote on the counter. "I doubt it. I bet she's going to go home to a quiet house, make herself a cup of tea, and soak in the solitude."

Jerry and George were right behind Doc, and the guys cheered him on as he carefully settled into his chair. George relieved him of his crutches and leaned them against the wall, and Melinda brought him a mug.

"Room service, even." He beamed, then pointed to the tote bag at his feet. "Anne sent cookies, as a thank you for taking me off her hands for a little while."

Frank was quick to pounce on the treats. "These are neat. Patriotic sprinkles and all."

"They're from the superstore," Doc explained. "But they're still good. We had family over last night, but Anne's been too busy looking after me to do much baking."

"I didn't know you were so high maintenance." George was eager for a treat when the cellophane package was passed his way.

"Well, normally, I'm not. But with a busted leg, I've had to lean on her more for things."

"Must be nice, huh?" Jerry filled his mug. "Just lounge around, relax, be catered to like that."

Doc groaned. "It's terrible. I've been climbing the walls. McFadden and Karen have been swamped, trying to keep up, and I've been stuck at home, watching television. I don't know what we would have done if Josh wasn't here to pick up the slack."

He shot Melinda a quick, questioning glance the other guys were too busy enjoying their cookies to notice. She gave a slight nod and smiled, and Doc winked.

"Hey!" Auggie pointed at her. "I heard you and Josh had your own fireworks last night."

"Oh, really." She glared at him and continued to clean the counter. "And who told you that?"

Auggie was notoriously nosy, and she'd had to talk to him more than once about blabbing her business around town. Ed had been likewise chastised for reporting to Auggie when Josh's truck was at her place in the late and early hours. Seriously, there was no way Auggie would have any idea what happened once Melinda and Josh finally got through the traffic and made it back to the farm.

But the more she tried not to blush, the warmer her cheeks felt. Doc and Jerry smirked. Frank tried to hide behind his coffee mug.

"No one had to say anything." Auggie

giggled like a schoolboy. "Why, there you two were, rolling around at the fireworks like a couple of high-school kids."

Jerry turned in his chair. "Just because it was dark, doesn't mean people didn't notice."

Oh, so that was it. Her laugh was as much about relief as anything else. "I'm glad everyone thinks it was so romantic." It certainly was, later on, but she wasn't about to tell them about that. "So, does anyone know exactly how we ended up on the ground?"

That stumped them all. She explained about her camp chair, which closer inspection this morning showed was truly wrecked beyond repair, and the men laughed harder. At least this time, it wasn't at her expense.

"That is why Mary and I stick to the old-school lawn chairs, with the webbing," George said. "Sturdy as can be."

Frank gestured toward Doc with his cup. "So, when are you back on duty?"

"Late next week. Just office work, a few hours a day. Then in-clinic appointments only for at least a while. I've promised the doctors I'll take it easy."

"What about McFadden?" Jerry frowned. "How are you going to break the news to him that he's retiring for the second time?"

Doc sighed. "Slowly. We need his help for several weeks yet, until I'm back at full speed. And I want to give Karen a chance to catch her breath. I know, I know; two roosters in the same coop isn't the best idea. But he doesn't have much else to do, anyway, so we'll find a way to get along. We always did, truth be told."

"Cooperation is really important." Auggie nodded sagely. "In business, and in the community, too. People have to help each other, find a way to get along."

Jerry and Frank exchanged a wary glance. The council meeting was next Monday and, while the agenda wouldn't be finalized until Friday, everyone knew what would be the biggest item on the list. George looked like he wanted to steer the conversation to safer ground, but his mouth was full of cookie. Melinda saw she needed to change the subject, and fast.

"I hear Emmet's opening the barbershop next week. That'll be exciting."

George was quick to chime in. "I'll say. I don't have much hair left these days, but I'll be glad to not have to go to Swanton for a trim.

Does anyone know for sure when the lady stylist is going to start? Mary's been asking."

"Not for a month or so," Jerry said. "Emmett and Patricia will have their hands full just getting settled. They closed the other shop right before the holiday. I think everything's being moved here tomorrow."

"I'm glad for them," Auggie said. "We need more commerce in this town, not less." He crossed his arms and stared at Frank. "I just wish people were as excited about my plans to improve things around here."

"Hey, don't start." Jerry waved him off, but Auggie was already on a roll.

"And why not? I have just as much of a right to grow my business as Emmett does."

Doc stayed quiet, and Melinda knew why. He'd told Karen that, in all the decades Prosper Veterinary Services had been in this town, no one had ever asked for kickbacks when the office was remodeled or new equipment was purchased. But he wouldn't speak publicly against his old friend, especially when Auggie had started that fundraiser to help with his medical bills.

"We don't need a fuss, not this morning," George said quietly. "Save it for the meeting."

"Oh, I intend to." Auggie didn't say more, which was just as unsettling as if he'd launched into another tirade. Frank stared at the floor.

Jerry turned his back on Auggie and gave Melinda a big smile. "How are those wedding plans coming along? Saturday's the big day."

"It's amazing what we've been able to accomplish in two months. Uncle Frank, I've been meaning to tell you: the weathervane is perfect up there above the kitchen. Really, the whole place looks like new."

"I wondered how it's been going." Doc was pleased. "A fresh start for that old place. Has Horace seen any photos of it yet?"

She shook her head. "I haven't had time to get up to see him. It's been too long. But he'll be at the wedding, of course. I can't wait to see his reaction!"

Jen didn't have to worry about sharing her special day with Horace and Maggie, other than counting them among her guests. In fact, any talk about marriage had apparently been set aside for good.

Melinda had been careful to not ask Horace, as she knew he would bring it up if he ever wanted to talk about it. But Kevin confirmed a few days ago that there would be no wedding bells in the elderly lovebirds' future.

And they were, indeed, still in love. They pecked at each other, of course, just as they did when they were young. But their visits were otherwise happy ones, and they talked on the phone as much as they ever did. Wilbur's continued decline was also a major factor in their decision. The care he received at Scenic Vista was wonderful, and at a fraction of the cost of the dementia unit at Maggie's retirement village.

Sometimes, romantic love couldn't conquer all. Or maybe, it didn't have to, because things were good just as they were. Melinda thought of Josh, and she couldn't keep the smile off her face as she counted the cash register's drawer. Yes, things with Josh were very good.

"What's the forecast for this weekend?" Frank leaned out of his chair and peered toward the west. "It's supposed to storm this afternoon, but I hope the clear weather is back in time for the big day."

Auggie eagerly took the bait. "Ninety-percent chance later today, maybe some hail. Hot and sunny for the weekend."

Jerry steered the conversation toward how the Chicago Cubs were faring these days, and Melinda breathed a sigh of relief as the clock's hands reached eight. She dreaded Monday's council meeting, and whatever fallout it would bring. But at least, in a few more days, this endless tension might have a chance to evaporate.

* * *

Miriam came in just before eleven. "So, how did it go this morning? I didn't dare ask Frank. His face told me he wouldn't want to talk about it."

"We tried to keep things civil, and sort-of succeeded." Melinda sighed as she organized the last of the patriotic-themed inventory on a small shelf by the register. There were just a few packages of paper plates, and a scattering of hand-held flags and tri-colored bandanas. At seventy-percent off, she expected thrifty customers to snap them up before the day was done. "I just wish Auggie would tone down the bragging; or better yet, scale back his plans. Even if the council greenlights everything, he's damaging his reputation with his attitude."

"I'd like to check that attitude." Miriam

frowned as she pulled on her apron. "The democratic process must play itself out but, I have to say, I hope the council hands him his ego back on a platter."

Miriam looked around at her family's store, and shook her head. "Competition is one thing; competition from a longtime friend and former employee is another. But this? This goes far beyond that. And yes, I'm taking it personally, in case you hadn't noticed."

Melinda's mood began to dim despite her elation over Josh's decision to stay. By the time she went across the street on her lunch break, her emotions were nearly as heavy as the moisture-soaked air draped over the town. Her hairline was coated in sweat by the time she entered the library.

Nancy looked up from her post at the circulation desk. "It's a beast out there, isn't it? I'm trying to stay in, if I can."

Melinda slipped her two books into the drop-off bin. "Thank goodness it wasn't this humid yesterday. Even so, I think it's safe to say the crowds in the Methodist church's community room were drawn inside by all that fabulous pie, not just the air conditioning. How much did we raise?"

"About twelve-hundred dollars." Nancy beamed. "More than last year. We'll be able to upgrade the rest of the computers."

Melinda looked through the cased opening into city hall, and saw Jerry was still at his desk. "Doesn't he usually peel out of here before lunch? I guess he's catching up after the holiday."

Nancy shook her head. "He's worried about Monday's meeting, and what might happen. You know he hates confrontation. I keep telling him, we have to let things play out."

"Miriam said the same thing, just now. But it's hard." Melinda checked out her next read, which was waiting for her on the "hold" shelf, then wandered next door.

Jerry looked up, the creases around his tired eyes even more noticeable than they'd been that morning. "Hey. I have a decision to make. Want to help?"

"Am I allowed to? I'm not an elected official, you know."

"Well, count yourself blessed and give me a hand, anyway."

He reached into a side drawer and pulled out a ring of paint samples. Melinda stifled a groan. They'd never gotten around to that online survey of potential colors for the water tower. With everything else going on, couldn't he let this go, at least for now?

"That's exactly my point," Jerry responded when she asked.

He tapped the ring on the table, and a rainbow of cool, muted colors fanned across the desk.

"I'm going to bring it up at Monday's meeting, show the council some suggested colors. The room's going to be packed. It won't make the big problem go away, but it will give people around here something else to talk about."

Or fight about, Melinda thought but didn't say. And she couldn't believe five men would want to spend more than five seconds debating different shades of blue and green.

"Now, which do you like? Just point out the ones that jump out at you, don't overthink it."

So she did.

"Done!" He reached for a sticky note. "Now, if I could just ..."

"Wait a minute!" Melinda was laughing now. "How did I become the city's decorator? That's it? Those are the ones you're going to show them?"

"Well, I'll give it some more thought, but yeah. I'll show them maybe a dozen. But I'll recommend they study those three the closest." Jerry dropped his head into his hands. "I wish everything could be this simple. Nothing's black and white around here."

* * *

Melinda's melancholy deepened through the afternoon into what could probably be called despair. What could Prosper Hardware do to counteract Auggie if his plan went through?

She saw price wars on mundane products, like cereal, in her future. Years of battling Auggie at every turn. Countless coffee hours filled with awkward silences, rather than the fun gatherings that used to give her mornings a jolt of optimism. Opinionated customers trying to draw her into conversations that pitted one business against the other.

It all made her stomach churn. Prosper had always been a town where everyone worked together, not against each other. Didn't Auggie see what he was doing? This wasn't just about dollars and cents, it was about community spirit and common sense. As the afternoon ticked by, Melinda's despair turned to irritation. And then, she was just plain mad.

By the time she punched out at four, the sun had disappeared and a line of heavy clouds was approaching from the west. As she cruised down Main, her fingers tapped the steering wheel while her mind mapped out what she was about to do.

Once she bumped over the railroad crossing, she flipped on her blinker and turned into the co-op's parking lot.

She wasn't exactly sure what she was going to say. But today, she'd decided, was her chance to say something. Before it was too late.

Tomorrow was already Thursday. She was off Friday because of the wedding, and the deadline for the council agenda was at noon. Even if Auggie could see her side of things, it would take him a day or two to find the courage to change his proposal. As for admitting he'd gone about all this the wrong way? Well, she couldn't even hope that would happen.

The lot was nearly full, and a gust of hot wind scattered the gravel as she hurried toward the entrance. A small swarm of elderly regulars huddled around the coffee pot, drinking the scalding-hot brew despite the sweltering afternoon. They weren't the most flexible of men, physically or emotionally. How did Auggie think they'd react to losing their sacred space?

Melinda wandered through a few aisles, pretended to study the wares as she tried to gather her thoughts. A glance toward Auggie's office showed he wasn't inside. Between the honesty of his regulars and the eagle eyes of Dan, his assistant, his door was literally always open.

If only his mind wasn't so closed.

Dan was behind the counter. Melinda raised her eyebrows at him, and he pointed to the stairwell. The air conditioning in the store barely made it that far, and she was sweating again before she reached the first turn. By the time she made it to the second-floor landing, the temperature had jumped another ten degrees and her irritation flared again.

"Why can't he move his weather lab downstairs?" She panted as she continued to climb.

"The instruments work just as well lower down. But no, he's the king of this castle, and he has to be up in the tower where he can survey his kingdom."

The alcove's door was open to the relative coolness of the concrete hallway, and the roar of a fan echoed from inside. Auggie looked up when she finally staggered into the little room, but he didn't seem surprised to see her.

Had he expected this visit? That thought made her even angrier, as it meant he was trying to stay a step ahead of her. Auggie had always been her friend. Heavy-handed with his knowledge and advice, but still ...

"Good gravy," she gasped as she dropped into the only other chair. "It's so hot up here. And what are you going to do when you get too old to climb those stairs?"

"I'm a tough old bird. Fans in the summer, space heater in the winter. I manage."

Pebbles and Mr. Checkers hadn't been downstairs by the counter, greeting their loyal subjects, and now she saw why.

Mr. Checkers was on the top shelf of the cat tree, pretending to be asleep. His lady friend was sprawled out on the wide shelf in front of the bank of windows, watching the dark clouds roll in. Melinda was amazed by their calm demeanors, as Grace and Hazel turned into fraidy-cats the moment the air pressure dropped in advance of a storm.

How long had it taken her to climb all those stairs? Because the sky was noticeably blacker now, and tinged with a shade of green that made Melinda uneasy. Or maybe it was just her errand.

"So ..." She looked around as she tried to catch her breath. "How's Chaplin?"

Auggie flinched slightly at this unexpected turn in the conversation. Good, she'd surprised him. "Oh, he's great. You know he's loving the indoor-home life. Jane wasn't sure at first, we hadn't had a cat before but, well, he's charmed her like everyone else." This was all said as he continued to stare at his laptop screen, flipping through weather-station reports.

Now, he turned in his wooden office chair and smiled.

"I can't thank you enough for helping me bring Chaplin around. I mean, we would have worked it out eventually," he added quickly. "He just ... gave me a turn, that's all. So familiar, you know." There was caution in his eyes. "Of course, no one needs to know about all that."

"And they won't." She stared back at him. "I gave my word, remember?"

He nodded. "And I believe it."

"I'm not sure if I can believe the same about you."

Melinda knew this wasn't the best way to start this conversation, but there was no easy answer. She was too tired, and too frustrated after Auggie's performance this morning. And while she was elated with the new understanding she had with Josh, those weeks of worry had also taken their toll.

She shouldn't take it all out on Auggie. But maybe, just maybe, he deserved it.

His face, however, said he didn't agree. "Oh, really? And what's that supposed to mean?"

Melinda crossed her arms. "Grandma and Grandpa taught you how to run a business. You learned a lot from them, and learned well. They were so proud when you started working here, and everyone knew the last owner would sell out to you when he retired."

"Oh, come on. This isn't about your grandparents! It's about ..."

She held up a hand, and he went quiet.

"Let me finish. They didn't just teach you the nuts and bolts." It was sort of a joke, and maybe a bad one, but they were both too angry right now to even acknowledge it. "You also learned how to be a good community partner. How to work with other businesses in town, not against them."

"You're right." Auggie raised his chin. "But your grandparents also taught me to think for myself. Look for opportunities on the horizon, and be ready for them when they arrived."

He glanced out the tall windows, where the view was more ominous by the minute. "Speaking of which, shouldn't you be getting for home? The weather service just issued a severe thunderstorm watch. And besides, I've heard this spiel before, from Frank and Miriam. I know they're upset about my plans, and I have to say I can't blame them, but I need to do what I need to do."

Mr. Checkers came down from his perch and jumped into Melinda's lap. She absentmindedly stroked his buff-and-white coat. "That may be, but you need to hear it from me, too. Because some day, I'm going to be in charge of Prosper Hardware, and I'll be your competitor. I'm just as worried about the future of that store as they are." She shook her head. "More so, in fact."

He took that in for a moment, then sighed. "I get it, but ..."

"Yeah, I bet you do." She glared at him. "And you should. Because you know how thin the profit margin is on our store. People in this town have no idea, but you do. Is the cash flow on your expansion plan so enormous that it's worth putting another business out of business?"

"The gas is going to be a moneymaker for me, big-time. And it's going to change this community, for the better." Then he turned away, and busied himself scratching Pebbles under her chin.

"The extra merchandise, well, it could help me a little bit."

Suddenly, Melinda saw a light at the end of the tunnel. "But what if the council won't give you the tax credits? What happens then? You know people are against those."

He sighed. "Well, that's going to be a problem. Remodeling is expensive, and this place hasn't been updated in years. I'll need every dime of that money to break even."

Melinda knew Auggie was proud, that he hated to admit when he'd been wrong. But this? It was dangerous. Not just for the co-op's bottom line, but for the community, too. If Auggie took on too much risk, and it didn't pan out, was there a chance his entire business could be in jeopardy?

Prosper Feed Co. drew customers from miles around, brought them into town to shop. The last thing this little community needed was another empty storefront.

"Please don't put your company at risk just because you're stubborn." To her surprise, Auggie didn't even try to defend himself on that point. "Why not just put in the gas pumps, which is what you were going to do from the start?"

"Because it's too late!" Auggie was now as nervous as he was defensive. "It's all anyone's talked about for weeks. You should hear the things people are saying to me about the tax credits."

Melinda didn't have to ask. She'd heard plenty in the past several weeks.

"If even half of them show up Monday, there's no way the council's going to give me the rebates I need. But, what am I supposed to do? Call Jerry and tell him to pull my plan from the agenda? I'd never live it down."

Melinda thought for a moment. Auggie

might be in turmoil, but she knew exactly what she needed to do.

This was the part she was so good at. Or had been, back in her marketing days. And maybe, she could be again. Not just to help her family's business, but to help a friend save face.

Right now, she wasn't sure he deserved it. But she needed to take her own advice: Everyone in this town should help each other, support each other.

She reached around Mr. Checkers for her purse, which was at her feet, and pulled out a small notebook.

"No, don't drop the plan. Just amend it. Keep the gas pumps and the canopy. Everyone wants that. Ditch the store expansion and the money grab, stick to what you know people are rooting for. Scale this back, and there's no way the council will turn you down. Better yet, you won't have to put your business at risk just to save face."

Auggie sighed. "That's the safest way to go, I know. But I'm still going to get a ton of crap for it."

Melinda laughed. "Actually, no. That's where I come in."

She proposed they work together to craft a press release that acknowledged the city's resources were already stretched thin. After careful consideration, Auggie had revised his plan to serve the best interests of the town, and to be a good neighbor to the other businesses that call Prosper home.

There was just enough time to get the update in tomorrow afternoon's paper, and Nancy would post it online as well.

By the time the revised agenda came out Friday, it would already be old news. By Monday, Auggie could expect residents taking the podium to thank him for putting their community first.

"Are people really going to fall for that?" Auggie was taken aback, but she could almost see the gears turning in his mind. "This is all I have to do to get myself off the hook?"

"Absolutely. Well, and be gracious and humble at the meeting. That'll be very important."

She wrote faster now, as the ideas flowed. "Oh, and here's the best part. This gives us another chance to tell everyone how wonderful it will be to have gas available in Prosper again. And the new canopy will let them fill up in comfort. We also get to remind everyone how long you've run this co-op, and how it's been a vital member of the community for a hundred years."

"We?" Behind those thick-rimmed glasses, Melinda thought she saw tears in Auggie's eyes. "You'll really help me with this?"

"Yes." She ripped off the page and handed it to him. "Now, if you're OK with that, I'll brush it up when I get home. You can look it over in the morning, at the store."

Auggie finally nodded. And then he smiled, and he didn't have to say a word. This was the way out he'd been searching for. But he'd been too proud, and too afraid, to take it on his own.

"You know, I think we could add something here. We have a big sale coming up next week. Let's tell everyone about it. And on Monday morning, there'll be free coffee, lemonade and donuts for the first fifty customers in the door."

Melinda laughed. "The meeting's Monday night. That sounds like bribery to me."

"You got that right." Auggie raised an eyebrow. "Give them free stuff, and people will be quick to forget I changed my mind."

21

The garden gate's iron hinges creaked in the hot, humid air. "Come on in." Adelaide waved Melinda through. "We'll have the pick of the crop for tomorrow."

Melinda studied the bursts of color, the delicate petals and the healthy stalks of her neighbor's heirloom flower garden. Butterflies and bees flitted from perch to perch. "Jen couldn't have done better with the best florist in Mason City. How are you even going to choose?"

Adelaide beamed. "Oh, I'll wander out here in the morning and see what strikes my fancy." She reached down to pick up Panther, who'd followed them from the house at that slow ramble cats preferred, and had just now arrived. "What do you think? Are you going to help me select the bouquets?"

"Sunny and Stormy prefer to roll in the dirt, rather than help me harvest vegetables." Even though the sun had dipped near the horizon, the sweat still ran down Melinda's neck.

"It'll be interesting to see how they handle the wedding. They've been hiding in the barn since the crew came to set up the tent."

That "crew" consisted of Ada, Kevin, Dave, a handful of other Schermann relatives and some of Jen and Andrew's friends. The couple wanted to assist, but were told to relax before tomorrow's ceremony.

Vicki was at the farm this evening, clipboard in hand, keeping everyone on task. Which allowed Melinda to slip away to the Beauforts' for a few quiet moments before the big celebration.

"How much is left to do tonight?" Adelaide brushed a careful hand through the lilies as she evaluated their blooms.

"Once the tent is up, they'll string the lights. I hope that's all until morning. Kevin and Dave got the mowers out and did the lawn this afternoon. Thank goodness, as I hadn't gotten to it yet."

"So, there'll be the aroma of fresh-cut grass for the ceremony, too." Adelaide shook her head in awe. "Everything is coming together. I almost can't believe ..."

"Don't jinx it." Melinda brushed away a mosquito. "We have twenty-four more hours to get through." Then she gave a wistful sigh. "At the same time, you know it's going to go too fast. All this planning and anticipation, and then it'll be over."

"That's always how it goes." Adelaide still held Panther, and she flipped her gray braid over her shoulder so he would stop trying to chew on it. "Change is always going on, all around us. Nothing stays the same for long. Something ends, and something else begins."

Melinda looked east over the lush, green fields, which nearly shimmered in the humidity. She couldn't see her own farm from here, but the thick treeline of the Wildwoods' acreage was clearly visible. "I have to keep reminding myself that Bart's moved out. I mean, I'm glad for his sake, it's for the best. I can't believe I'm saying this, but I might actually miss the old grouch."

Adelaide's smile was a little bit sad as she reached for the garden gate, which had been latched against the curious noses of the Beauforts' two dogs. "I know. It seems strange that no one lives there anymore. Other than the wild critters, of course."

As they started back toward the house, Panther finally demanded his freedom and Adelaide let him have it.

"There's other neighborhood news." She paused on the open back porch to survey her selection of plastic buckets, the cleanest of which would transport wedding flowers tomorrow. "Lauren's found an apartment in Swanton. She's moving out at the end of August."

"Oh, good for her! So she's going to stay around, obviously."

"She likes her nursing job, has made a few friends her own age." Adelaide raised an eyebrow. "No boyfriend, not yet. She's not wanting to rush into anything, which I think is smart. Of course, I try not to mother her too much." Adelaide sighed. "We've gotten used to having her here. I think there's going to be a little bit of empty-nest syndrome when she spreads her wings."

"But the little experiment was certainly a success." Melinda reached for a bucket that looked wedding-worthy, and set it to the side. "You helped her make a fresh start. When do you think the place will be officially open for guests?"

"Oh, give us a year, at least." Adelaide tipped her head toward the house's clapboard siding. "Mason has so many projects in the works. But then, we're retired. No reason we can't just keep this little slice of heaven to ourselves a while longer. By the way, I was relieved when I read Auggie's little write-up in the paper. Prosper needs gas, but Prosper Hardware doesn't need that kind of competition."

Melinda leaned against the porch railing. "He broke the news at coffee hour yesterday morning. Everyone was so relieved, they quickly forgot about how long he'd dragged his feet, trying to get the city to pay for some of his renovations."

"All that stuff about wanting to be a good neighbor." Adelaide laughed. "Auggie's full of vinegar sometimes, but he's a savvy old bird."

Melinda only nodded. "Oh, yeah, he's full of surprises." Auggie wanted everyone to think he'd come to this conclusion on his own, and she'd agreed. It was simpler that way, and the sooner he mended fences in the community, the better.

With his grand scheme now whittled down to only the gas pumps and the canopy, his proposal was sure to get the council's unanimous approval. Construction could start in a few weeks, he'd told his friends yesterday at the store, and the project would be completed sometime in the fall.

Melinda's phone buzzed in her back pocket. It was Vicki.

"What?" Melinda put a hand over her other ear. The Beauforts' elderly rooster was rather disorganized, and often crowed at sunset as well as sunrise. "What did you say?"

Adelaide leaned in, worry deepening the gentle lines on her forehead.

"Oh, great. I'll head home right now."

* * *

"When did this happen?" Melinda was barely out of the car before Kevin and Dave caught up to her by the garage. Hobo danced at their feet, too excited about having company to realize something was amiss.

"Just fifteen minutes ago," Dave said. "You know, the thing seemed to be running a little noisy, but then, it's probably as old as I am. We were mapping out the stakes for the tent, and it just made this funky growl, and that was that."

Melinda stared at the now-silent air conditioner behind the house, then put her hands over her face. She should have replaced it sooner, or at least had it serviced at the start of the summer. But then, she'd been so busy with Jen's wedding, and distracted by Auggie's demands and Josh's job offer.

And now, a houseful of guests would be here in the morning, including a bride-to-be. And her farmhouse would be as hot as an oven.

"I kicked it," Kevin added, a helpful tone in his voice. "Kicked it twice, actually, thought it might help. Uncle Horace did that sometimes, said it needed a shove now and then to keep everything screwed together. Mom went in and turned the thermostat off, let it sit a bit, then flipped it back on. But nothing."

Vicki was on her way across the manicured lawn, her clipboard still firmly in her grasp. "Good, you're back. Anyone in particular you want to call? It's after hours, but someone will pick up."

Melinda knew that was true. She also knew there'd be a hefty emergency service charge to get a repairman out here in the morning. It was too late to expect someone yet tonight, and all the repair shops had to be swamped. With this heat wave dragging on, units all over the county were surely drawing their last breaths of freon-fueled air.

"It's not the end of the world." Kevin struggled for something positive to say. "It's not like it's winter and the furnace is out. I mean, the wedding's outside."

"But we'll be staging from inside the house. That's command central." Vicki checked her list. "The ladies are arriving by eleven. Lunch at noon. Final try-on of the dresses at one." She pointed her pen at Melinda. "Nancy's a sewing pro, she'll come out in case there are any last-minute alterations. Hair and makeup at three. Pictures at four, before everyone melts in the heat."

"What time do I need to be here, again?" Dave stifled a yawn.

Vicki checked the schedule. "Groom before two, rest of the guys by three. And remember, Jen ditched the ties."

Dave turned to Kevin. "You all have me to thank for that."

"I brought mine, just in case." Kevin and Ada would spend the night, rather than head home to Mason City. Jack, Kevin's boyfriend, would pick up Horace before the wedding. "I thought that was the safe thing to do. Your mom's not happy about the ties, and you know how she likes to get her way."

"What are we going to do about the air conditioner?" Melinda wailed. "If we don't get it back on, you guys won't be the only ones dressing down. The whole wedding party will end up in shorts and tank tops, and Bridget will really lose it then."

The thought of Jen sweating through her lovely ivory dress in front of noisy fan was enough to bring tears to Melinda's eyes. Jen had been a trooper through this whole process. And, on top of all the wedding stress, she and Andrew had spent the last several days moving into Edith's former home. They were already anxious and tired. It was very important that tomorrow be memorable ... but only in a good way.

After all, Jen was the last Schermann bride at this farm. Melinda wasn't family, but it was on her shoulders to make this work. Hers, and Vicki's.

She looked at her friend, who raised her chin, adjusted her designer shades against the setting sun, and considered their options.

"We had a wonderful guy install our system. He came up from Waterloo, though." Vicki thought some more. "Doesn't George always go on about how great his handyman is?"

"Yes." Melinda tried to remember the name, but couldn't. "But he's almost as old as George and Mary. And I don't think this is quite up his alley."

"I can't fix it myself," Dave admitted. "But my buddy Travis is a genius. He can do just about anything."

"Does he do air conditioners?" Vicki wanted to know.

"Well, hmm. He's a mechanic, so ..."

"We need someone reliable, and fast, and willing to come out on a Saturday morning." Vicki sighed. "Who could it be?"

Melinda suddenly had an answer. Or at least, one that would get them close. "I know who I'm going to call. He can't do it himself, but he knows just about everyone for miles around. Better yet, he owes me a favor."

Auggie answered on the second ring. He worked his contacts and, within the hour, Melinda had an iron-clad promise from an Elm Springs repairman to be at her farm at seven the next morning.

"Well, it's all going to work out." Ada lifted the pitcher of lemonade from the picnic table and filled three glasses. She handed the first one to Melinda. "Careful, that glass is sweating so bad, you might drop it."

Everyone else had left for the night, and it was just too warm inside the house. Even the screened-in front porch was stifling.

Kevin gave Melinda a grin. "All this needs is a little vodka. Do you have any, by chance?"

"No, sorry. Besides, I need to keep a clear head. Who knows what else might transpire between now and five tomorrow evening?"

"What might transpire while we perspire." Kevin's glasses had slid down his nose, and he pushed them back up. "And I think you mean nine tomorrow night, when it all wraps up."

The tent was now perched on the back lawn, and its white canvas glowed in the dark. After much debate, the crew decided to raise the side panels and anchor them to the frame for the night.

Melinda's farm was home to countless critters, most of them wild as could be, and it was better to let them roam in and out than risk damaging the tent. After all, Jen and Andrew really needed their deposit back.

Ada stretched out her legs and looked around. "It's a beautiful summer night. I remember when we were kids, we thought it was great fun to pitch a little tent and sleep outside."

"Horace used to camp on the lawn?" Melinda couldn't imagine it.

"Oh, no." Ada laughed. "I'm talking about us young ones. By the time we came along, times had changed and our parents weren't as strict as they used to be."

She pointed over at the house, so quiet in the dark. "Ever notice how the windows are spaced out, just so? All old houses are that way, cross-ventilation in every room."

Melinda instantly knew it was true. As she mentally walked through her home, she saw the symmetry everywhere. Her heart swelled with gratitude for where life had brought her. Back home, back to her family. And to this wonderful farm, and to Ada and Kevin and Horace and the rest of the Schermanns.

And to Josh. Other than the fireworks show, they hadn't had a real date in weeks. Along with Andrew and Jen's wedding, tomorrow evening would be a wonderful way to celebrate their own future.

"Well, we better get off to bed." Ada reluctantly rose from the picnic table. "Tomorrow will be here before we know it."

Hobo came out from under it long enough to get some goodnight pets. But then he lowered himself back into the cool dirt underneath.

"Hobo has the right idea." Kevin yawned. "But I don't think my back will let me bunk out here with him. Exactly how many fans do you have?"

* * *

Auggie's buddy more than kept his word. Melinda had just finished in the barn when she heard a truck rumble down the gravel, and it was barely past six.

A stranger's arrival, and at such an early hour, sent Sunny and Stormy scurrying to a safe place as soon as they finished their breakfast. Pansy and the rest of the hens had taken one look at the monstrous white thing roosting on the lawn, and decided their run wasn't where they wanted to be. But the sheep and Pepper remained at the pasture fence, all eyes and ears, while the air conditioner had its checkup.

The good news was it could be repaired, and Melinda wouldn't have to spring for a new unit. Not yet, anyway. The not-so-good news? Due to the unit's age, Joe didn't have the part handy. A Mason City supplier had one in stock, and luckily they were open on Saturday mornings.

By the time he fetched the part and worked his magic, it would be lunch time before Melinda's old farmhouse was back in the modern era.

"I hear there's a wedding today." Joe hitched up his work jeans for the umpteenth time and studied the tent. Melinda wondered how many animals had inspected it overnight, but she didn't care. It was still standing, and that's what mattered.

"Horace and Wilbur's great niece, huh? That's great she and her guy were able to buy Edith's house. And I'm glad Horace's lady friend's going to make it to the party." Joe latched his toolbox and started back toward his truck, Hobo at his heels. "Wasn't that a fine thing when they met up again, after all those years?"

Melinda trailed behind, impressed by Joe's wealth of knowledge. But then, it probably reflected every bit of relevant gossip Auggie had at his disposal. "Yes. Yes, it was."

"My mother's over at Scenic Vista," Joe explained. "I bump into Horace from time to time. He and my grandpa were good friends in high school. Well, I'll head home for breakfast and then run over and get that part. The place opens at nine."

"Run over" was a ninety-minute round trip. That didn't include the time it would take at the parts store, or how long Joe would need to make his repairs.

"I can't tell you how much I appreciate it. Just let me know what your hourly rate is. This is going to take up a good chunk of your day."

Joe guffawed. "Hourly rate? Are you from the city, or something?" Then he nodded. "Oh, yeah, you are. Horace told me all about you, back when. The price is just as I quoted, no more. I'm honored to make sure the Schermann clan doesn't melt before the ceremony. Besides, if I hang around the house this morning, my wife will insist I mow the lawn." He winked. "By afternoon, it'll be way too hot for that."

Melinda was so relieved, she thought she

might cry. "Joe, you're a lifesaver. I'll have strawberry muffins coming out of the oven by the time you get back."

She took a deep breath as Joe's truck disappeared down the lane in a plume of gravel dust. He was right, it was going to be a scorcher. But the sky was clear, no chance of rain. The tent was in place; the chairs and tables were coming in a few hours, along with enough Schermann relatives to set them up.

All Melinda had to do was feed her helpers snacks and lunch, clear space in her dining room for the girls to have their hair and makeup done, do her best to keep Vicki and Bridget from throttling each other, and then host a party for sixty-some guests on her lawn.

Piece of cake. Coconut, to be exact.

"Hobo, can you believe it?" There was a spring in her step as they started across the dew-kissed lawn toward the back porch steps. "There's supposed to be a wedding today. And we just might make it happen."

* * *

The stylist wiped her brow with the back of her hand, and turned the closest fan so it was blowing directly on Jen. "Now, what are we thinking? Loose waves would be so lovely with that V-neckline." Melinda had removed a mirror from the dining-room wall to give Jen's dress a place to air out. But even devoid of ruffles and tiers, it looked to be wilting in the heat. "Or a half-up, half down?"

"Ponytail." Jen polished off her muffin with one final bite. She was in a sleeveless button-down shirt and shorts, as were the other ladies in the bridal party.

"Oh, that would be ... simply elegant." The hairdresser widened her eyes at Bridget, who pursed her lips in irritation.

Jen hadn't cared too much about having her hair and makeup professionally done, which had been a mistake in the end. That gave Bridget an excuse to bring her stylist along, and it was clear who was in charge. Or at least, thought they were.

Jen grabbed the ponytail already in her hair, and looped it around her hand. "Wrap it into a bun. Just keep it low, please."

"I think it's a wonderful idea." Vicki was quick to jump in. "And you have those layers in the front; how about a wrap-around braid on each side? That would keep everything in place."

"I love that." Jen beamed her approval before her mom could say a word. "Let's do it. At the last minute, of course, or it won't stay fresh."

Vicki's sandals clicked across the linoleum as she came into the kitchen, where Melinda and Mabel were eavesdropping while pouring glasses of iced tea.

"Vicki one, Bridget zero." She filched an ice cube from a freezer tray, and swiped it across her forehead. "I will triumph today, ladies," she whispered. "Jen is going to have the day of her dreams. For almost two months, I've listened to that woman henpeck her, and I've had enough."

"Just promise me there won't be a fist fight." Melinda reached again for the fly swatter. Between every window screen being pressed into service, and the back door constantly opening and closing, there were a few uninvited guests at this pre-wedding gathering.

"Oh, I'll be sweet as pie." Vicki gave Melinda a thumbs-up for her direct hit, then reached for the swatter and delivered a satisfying death blow to another fly on the table. "Ada, is there anything I can help with?"

"We're just about done." Ada shuffled in the back door and dropped into the closest chair. "Goodness, it's almost better outside. I don't know how we ever managed out here before air-conditioning."

Cold sandwiches and salads waited in the refrigerator for lunch, and Melinda planned to feed the outside helpers at the picnic table. The fewer people in the house, the better. Every surface was sticky with humidity, despite all the open windows trying to catch what little breeze was available. Melinda was sure if she put her hand on the wood trim, she'd leave a print in the varnish.

There had been a rush of customers at the parts store, which put Joe behind schedule. But he was back and, with any luck, they'd have air conditioning again within the hour.

"It's all coming together." Mabel reached for a stack of paper plates. "Let's get these people fed. We need to let the last of our helpers leave by two, so they can clean up and be back in time."

Edith had just arrived, escorted by Andrew. After a quick kiss from his bride-to-be, he went out to help with the preparations. As the sandwiches were passed around, talk turned to less-tense topics than the wedding. And soon, laughter echoed over the roar of the fans placed by the open windows.

Edith and Ada were squeezed in at the head of the table, and the sisters were soon chatting as merrily as Jen and her friends. Melinda looked around the room, tried to soak in the moment, and knew Anna was smiling down upon them all.

As lunch came to a close, she went into the living room and came back with a wrapped package. "Jen, I might as well give this to you now."

"Oh, you didn't have to! Letting me get married here was more than enough of a gift."

Mabel beamed from ear to ear, her eyes alight with excitement and pride. "I think you need to open it right away."

Jen pulled away the tape. "The cookbook!" She clutched it close, then held it up for everyone to see. "From the Fulton Friendship Circle, Great-Grandma Anna's club."

"An expanded edition." Edith took the book and carefully opened its cover. "My, how wonderful! You got it done, just in time."

"And Jen, yours is the very-first copy. There's a carton of them in the back room, so you can hand those out to close family today. We'll start sending out the rest next week."

Ada soon returned from the kitchen, a box in her arms. "I know it's customary to open gifts the next day, and to have the groom join in the fun. But mine can't wait, either."

"Might as well." Jen began to undo the wrapping paper. "We're not exactly on-script with this wedding, the way it is." She looked into the box, then put a hand over her mouth. "Oh, Ada, are you sure? It's your favorite piece!"

"And now it's yours. And not just for the wedding." The other women gasped over the cut-glass cake stand, which was rimmed with a flower-petal design. "Mom only used it for special occasions. I don't know about the rest of you, but I'd say today counts."

"It'll show off your coconut cake perfectly," Mabel said. "Cupcakes are practical for the guests, but this will be front-and-center when you and Andrew cut your pieces at the reception."

"It's going to be perfect." Jen's eyes filled with tears. "Everything is going to be just perfect. And here I thought this wouldn't even happen, at least not for months and months."

She wiped at her face with the back of her hand. "Good thing I haven't put on my makeup yet."

The kitchen door creaked open, and Dave motioned to Melinda. "You're needed outside."

She followed him into the back porch. "Is Joe almost done?"

"Yep, he said ten minutes and you can close up the house and crank that baby back on." But Dave looked nervous.

"Oh, no. What is it now?"

"Well, it's the tent." Dave pointed out to the back yard, where Vicki's crew was shuffling chairs and lifting tables back and forth. "I can't believe I'm saying this, but ... it's too small."

Vicki met them by the picnic table, her face flushed from more than the heat.

"I don't know what we are going to do!" She thumbed through her clipboard, pulled out a drawing, and thrust it into Melinda's hands. "I mapped it out, for goodness' sake!"

"Is this not the tent you ordered?"

"It is," Vicki admitted. "I just measured to be sure. Not that it would matter now, it's too late; and it was the only one we could find that was even close to what we needed. We knew it would be tight, Jen and I talked it over. But we didn't account for how hot it is today. Now that all the tables and chairs are here, and we set them up, it's … it's a complete disaster!"

Melinda felt sick to her stomach. Vicki had worked so hard on this project. She was smart and resourceful, but she wasn't a professional wedding planner. And they'd been lucky to even get this tent.

"Let's go see." She gently took a now-crying Vicki by the arm. "There has to be something we can do."

They ducked under the canopy, and it was clear Vicki was right.

No matter how they arranged everything, it was just too cramped. The tent could accommodate everything for the reception, but there wasn't adequate space to set up the pergola for the vows, or allow the wedding party to join Jen and Andrew up front as they said them. As for the portable dance floor, which was still in pieces against the back of the garage? Forget it.

It was simply too hot, and would be too rude, to ask some of the guests to sit outside the tent. It also wasn't fair to ask the guys to arrange some of the tables on the lawn before the ceremony, then have to haul them back in for the reception. The helpers were already grimy and hot, and needed to go home as soon as possible.

Melinda rubbed her forehead, which was dripping with sweat, and tried to come up with an easy solution. But she couldn't find one. "There's no way everyone would fit in the house, even standing-room only. And it's just too hot out here; none of the trees have enough shade to keep everyone out of the sun."

Dave had disappeared around the corner of the garage with Kevin and Andrew. They soon returned, but Dave quickly made a beeline for the back door.

"Well, here's our Plan B." Kevin rubbed his hands together. "Or F, or whatever we're up to at this point. I think we can put the dance floor between the garage and the house, it's not very big. We'll string the lights on the side of the garage and in this tree. It'll cool off later, and we can take advantage of the breeze."

"That'll work." Melinda was relieved. "Might even be better than before."

Vicki wadded up the drawing Melinda had given back to her, and stuffed it in her tote. "We're going off script here, but I don't know what else we can do. Now, about the staging for the ceremony ..."

Andrew and Kevin exchanged a wary look.

"We have an idea for that," Andrew finally said. "It's not just our best option, but probably our only." He took a step back. "But I'm not officially family for, oh, a few more hours. Kevin, maybe you should do the honors."

So he did. Vicki gasped and dropped her clipboard.

Melinda's mouth fell open. And then, she ran for the house.

22

Melinda burst into the kitchen just in time to hear Bridget's glass of iced tea slip from her hand and shatter on the hardwood floor.

"*What?* Are you out of your mind?"

"Mom! Just listen, for once." Dave raised his voice over the commotion that had erupted in the dining room. "It's brilliant, actually. You said how great it is that Jen's getting married out here. The last Schermann bride ..."

"My daughter is not getting married in a barn!"

Mabel came into the kitchen, where Melinda was frozen to the linoleum. "Where's your broom and dustpan? I'll sweep up. Dave's a brave one. But he's right. We're running out of time to do much else."

Melinda grabbed a few kitchen towels and followed Mabel into the next room.

"I certainly will get married in a barn, if I have to!" Jen shouted at her mother. "Or the machine shed, or in the ditch. I really don't care where."

Bridget tried another tactic. "We can move the tables."

"No one is standing around outside in this heat. I won't allow it, and neither will Andrew. Dave's right, the haymow will work. Horace and Wilbur put those stairs in not twenty years ago, and the handrails, too."

"Not everyone can do the steps! Your grandmother ..."

"Is sitting right here." Edith's tone was low and cold. "I'm not an invalid. I'll manage it, I brought my cane. Horace can make it, too, with a little help. Maggie might not, but well, she's just the girlfriend."

Melinda choked back a laugh just as the kitchen door opened again. Andrew soon brushed past and positioned himself behind Jen's chair. Vicki huddled in the doorway with Melinda.

"We are getting married today, in the barn." Andrew's tone was gentle but firm, and Jen reached up and took his hand. "Melinda has been kind enough to let us say our vows here at the farm, and we are not going to make her sorry she decided to help us."

No one said anything. In the silence, Melinda could feel the power dynamic in the room shift. Andrew and Jen weren't just in love, they were a team. And Bridget, today and in the future, was always going to be outvoted. She knew it, too.

"Fine. Whatever you want to do." Then came a big sigh of resignation that Melinda suspected, and seriously hoped, was about more than the wedding. "I guess it's a good thing we told everyone to dress casual because of the heat. Now that we're …"

"Wonderful!" Vicki clapped in a sharp, efficient manner that got the room's attention. "Let's have everyone who's not in the wedding party scoot out to the barn, and we'll get busy. There's just enough time to get set up."

The vast haymow was mostly empty, as Melinda kept only a short-term supply of straw and hay on hand this time of year. Once the floor and stairs were swept clear, Dave and Kevin brought up the pergola and staged it on one end of the loft.

A few chairs were carried up for the older attendees, but everyone else could stand through the brief ceremony. Extension cords brought up power for the sound system, some fans, and the pergola's strings of lights. Mabel helped Vicki rearrange the synthetic floral swags on the metal frame.

Melinda wished the downstairs was cleaner, but who would have expected it to host a wedding? She and Mabel cleared some items out of the path to the steps, then tidied up as best as they could. At least the doors had been open all day to mitigate some of the odor.

"Jen expected to walk down the aisle, like any bride." Mabel gently shooed Stormy out of the way with her broom. "Then she didn't have one, but now she does again! It's just in a barn, that's all."

"It's not as cool up there as it is down here, but at least everyone will be out of the sun." Melinda looked around and nodded. "That's good. Or at least, close enough."

Once the hayloft was ready, most of the volunteers hurried home to clean up. Jen and the other girls took over Melinda's upstairs bathroom, and Andrew, Dave and Kevin were content to take turns in the old shower stall in the basement.

Adelaide and Lauren soon arrived with the flowers, and chose a few more stems from Anna's perennial bed to round out the bouquets. The small dance floor didn't take long to set up, and Melinda was thrilled to see how perfectly it fit between the garage and the house.

"We'll be dancing under the stars tonight," Melinda told Mabel as they gave the yard one last look. "I have just enough time for early chores before the guests start to arrive."

After that, everything happened so fast. Many of the attendees had carpooled, which made it possible to fit their vehicles in rows in the yard and down part of the driveway. While the sheep mostly stayed in the far corners of the pasture, Pepper posted himself along the driveway's fence and hee-hawed greetings to their guests.

Hobo, much to his disappointment, found his doggie doors had been locked and he was confined to the house. But with cool air once again circling through its rooms, he soon stretched out in his bed and fell asleep, exhausted from supervising the day's activities.

Melinda cleaned up the dining room, stacked the dirty dishes in the kitchen, then made a quick pass through the rest of the downstairs. Horace, Maggie and Edith, along with a few other elderly guests, were to stay inside where it was cool until right before the ceremony. The first-floor bathroom would also be available to them, so they wouldn't have to navigate the porta-potties parked by the machine shed.

Melinda was nearly, finally done with the dishes when Josh arrived.

"How are you holding up?" He took the towel out of her hands and gave her a kiss. "I wish I could have gotten here sooner, but McFadden's on vacation and a few calls came in. Anything I can do?"

"Whatever you can manage. It's not going to be perfect, but ..."

"And it doesn't have to be." He looked out the window above the sink, and shook his head with admiration. "The yard looks amazing, it's like something out of a movie! And doing the vows in the haymow." He chuckled. "It's going to be a wedding no one will forget. Why don't you get upstairs and get ready? I'll take over from here."

Unlike the last few days of stress and trouble, the ceremony went off without a hitch. As Jen and Andrew made their promises to each other, Melinda glanced up at the haymow's sturdy beams and towering ceiling, and marveled at how the peaceful space felt so much like a church.

While the wedding party took photos by the garden and in front of the freshly painted farmhouse, Angie and Nathan arrived with the coconut cake and the cupcakes. The special dessert soon made its debut inside the tent to a round of applause from the guests and, just as Mabel predicted, it was perfectly sized for Anna's cake stand.

Jessie's picnic-style buffet was a huge hit, and Dave soon had Andrew and Jen's playlist drifting from the speakers set up around the dance floor.

There were so many memorable moments. But Melinda's favorite, by far, was the sight of Horace and Maggie slow dancing to "I'll Be Seeing You."

They were so careful that they barely moved, and literally hung on to each other while Wendy watched from the sidelines, walkers and canes at hand.

Later on, Melinda spied Horace resting in the tent and took the empty chair next to him. "That was quite the dance, a bit ago. You and Maggie have the moves."

"Oh, we were tearing it up, all right." He chuckled and loosened his tie. "I was worried she'd fall over, and she was the same way about me. You know, we used to go to this dance hall in Eagle River, back in the day. The bands would play until midnight, and we were out there with the best of them."

Melinda couldn't quite imagine Horace ever having that kind of energy, or Maggie, either. But then she remembered a photograph of them as teenagers, when they were so different than they were now.

Or maybe, not that different. When they'd danced, she'd seen the same light in their eyes as they had that summer day seventy years ago. Just like Jen and Andrew, right now. And the way Josh looked at her, and how she looked at him.

Horace and Maggie were still in love, after all this time. How could they stand to be apart?

She was about to gather her courage and ask, when Horace reached for his cane. "Well, this is a nice party, but I'm not used to all these people. What say we take a little walk?"

Melinda didn't have to ask where they were going. Horace shyly skirted a group of guests lingering by the garage, and started toward the barn. The worst of the day's heat had finally broken, and a gentle breeze at last whispered across the fields. With the sun now low in the west, everything had taken on a soft glow, and the lights around the dance floor shined bright.

Horace and Melinda walked in silence, just how she knew he liked things to be.

"It's nice out here, always has been in the evening," he finally said as they reached the pasture fence. "Mother always claimed this was her favorite part of the day."

"Mine, too." Melinda was about to lean on a fence post but took a small step back, mindful of her dress.

"I like to come out here sometimes, just to watch the sunset. Isn't it beautiful?"

At the sight of Horace, several of the ewes gave a greeting and ambled across the grass in his direction. They were too far off yet to read their ear tags, but Melinda knew Annie had to be in the lead.

Horace waved to the sheep, then turned his gaze toward the southwest. "It's too bad about Bart and Marge but, well, that time comes for everyone."

"Change is hard." Sunny had found them at the fence, and Melinda reached down to give him a pet. "If Wilbur's roommate hadn't moved out, would you have even considered going to the nursing home?"

Horace grunted. "Goodness, no. I would have stayed out here until, well, until something bad happened. I was too stubborn. Kevin and Ada had it all planned out. All this nonsense about going for a visit, that Wilbur needed me. It was all a trick to make me give it a try."

"Well, it worked. And I, for one, am glad about that."

Horace smiled then, and looked back at his former home. "My stars, but it's all shined up. I like that metal roof, too. It's different, but it suits the house just fine. I wish Mother and Father were here to see what you've done with the place."

Melinda looked up into the lavender-hued sky. "Oh, I'm sure they're aware of what's been going on around here. I don't think we could have pulled off this wedding without a little divine intervention."

Pepper had caught up to the handful of sheep, and everyone wanted a bit of attention.

Horace was more at ease around animals than he was with most people, and Melinda saw her chance to speak up.

"So, I hear you and Maggie aren't getting married, after all. Is that for certain, or just for now?"

He rubbed Annie's nose. "Oh, we'll carry on as we have. Wilbur wouldn't handle the transition well, but it's not just that. When you get to be ninety-something, you get pretty set in your ways. We love each other, always have. But you can't fix the past. Our time for that came and went, long ago."

Pepper tried to grab the flared sleeve of Melinda's dress, and she pulled her arm out of his reach. "I know what you mean. No one can have everything they want in life."

"It's true that no one's life is perfect. But sometimes, when you are really blessed, you don't have to choose." He gestured around them at the farm. And then he pointed at Josh, who was laughing with Kevin and Dave by the back steps. "Sometimes, you can have what you want. It's not one, or the other. It's both."

Then he chuckled. "You know what? I think you should ask him to marry you."

Melinda's shoulders shook with laughter. "Are you serious? We've only been dating six months."

"But you've known him longer than that. And you know he's the one. Because he is." His blue eyes glinted with wisdom. "If even an old farmer like me can see it, you know it's true."

"Well, I don't think that's going to happen anytime soon. But I promise, you'll be one of the first to know if it does."

"Oh, it will." Cane in hand, he turned back toward the house. Melinda fell in step next to him, as it was clear Horace had said what he wanted to say. "I could go for some lemonade. And then I need to kiss my girl goodbye, because Wendy said they would head home before nine."

* * *

Melinda settled into the porch swing next to Josh, and kicked off her dress sandals. "Well, that's the last guest to leave." Ada's taillights glowed in the dark, then disappeared down the lane.

"I better check the back screen door's hinges in the morning, make sure they're still attached. I don't think it's ever had that much of a workout."

The front porch was lit by only the diffused glow from the kitchen, on the other side of the house. The rest of her home sat comfortably in the dark, the old house resting after what surely had been one of its most memorable days ever.

Josh put his arm around her, and she felt the warmth of his bare arm touching hers. Like the rest of the men, he'd rolled up his shirt sleeves as soon as the ceremony was over. "It's going to be awfully quiet around here, after all the craziness." Even in the dark, she could sense his smile. "However are you going to manage?"

"Well, it helps that you're still around." She reached up and touched his cheek, then kissed him.

"Oh, really? Are you sure you aren't just stringing me along for the free labor? I mean, there's plenty of cleaning up and tearing down to do out there tomorrow morning."

"And it all can wait until then. Besides, I'll have plenty of other help, too. I think they'll be back by eight, Ada said." She yawned. "I need to get that egg casserole mixed up and in the fridge. There are muffins left, but maybe I should make a coffeecake."

"Slow down there." Josh pushed off with one bare foot, which sent the swing into gentle motion. "How about we just enjoy this beautiful view, even for a few minutes?"

And it was lovely. Out here, in the gentle gloom of a warm summer's night, she could see the blanket of stars that dotted the sky, and the glowing winks of the fireflies as they flitted across the peaceful lawn.

Hobo, who was stretched out on the cool painted boards at their feet, let out a deep, contented sigh. Grace and Hazel finally came out of hiding not fifteen minutes ago, and while Hazel had settled into her favorite corner of the couch, Grace had followed Josh and Melinda out to the porch.

She now watched the swing intently, her green eyes aglow in the half-light, and jumped up at just the right second to land in Melinda's lap.

"It's so peaceful." She stroked Grace's fur, and was rewarded with a purr. "When I first moved out here, the silence was almost deafening. But then I realized, when I slowed down and listened, it wasn't silent at all."

The crickets' chirps punctuated the cicadas' summer songs, and a frog answered from somewhere down by the road. A few soft snuffles echoed from the front pasture, where she could just make out a few of the ewes as they enjoyed a bedtime snack.

But the most wonderful sound of all came from the back side of the house, where the air conditioner cycled back to life.

"That's true." Josh pulled her closer, and she rested her head on his shoulder. "There's always something out here to see, to experience." Then he laughed.

"You know, Vicki's a pro at this wedding thing. If she didn't already do so much, I'd say she could turn it into a lucrative side hustle."

"She's already mentioned it. Even so, I think my time as a wedding planner is done."

"After what's gone down the past few days, I can certainly see why." The porch swing's chains creaked a few beats before he spoke again. "But you know," there was a teasing note in his voice, "I hear it's a much-different situation when the wedding is your own."

She smiled in the dark, but didn't say anything at first. There was so much she could say. She almost told him what Horace said just hours before. But the time didn't seem to be right, and that was fine with her. There was no need to rush things. And this moment was perfect, just as it was.

"I love you," she whispered. "You know I do."

"Good. Because I love you, too." He kissed her neck. "How about we go inside?"

Grace and Hobo bounded through as soon as Josh opened the door. When he reached back to take her hand in his, Melinda stepped over the threshold and locked out the rest of the world.

Josh pulled her into his arms and, just before his lips touched hers, a single, wonderful thought drifted through her mind.

I'm home.

What's next

The end! I was determined to wrap up this series on a happy note. Even so, it's bittersweet to know our visits to Melinda's farm have come to a close. I hope you've enjoyed reading these novels as much as I've enjoyed writing them.

But it's just goodbye for now: I'm working on plans for a new series set in the Prosper area. And while Melinda won't be the main focus, I think it's safe to say she will show up from time to time, along with several other of the "Growing Season" characters we've all come to know and love. In the meantime ...

Sign up to find out more: Go to fremontcreekpress.com, click on the "connect"

please turn the page ...

page, and add your email to the newsletter list, if you aren't already on it. As soon as I have information to share about a new series, I'll let everyone know.

Fresh recipes: As always, you'll find new dishes posted under the "extras" tab on the website. If all this talk about coconut cake has you craving a slice, you're in luck. There's also a tasty appetizer, as well as my favorite brownie recipe, to share with your family and friends.

Thanks for reading!
Melanie

Made in the USA
Monee, IL
22 April 2023

32264897R00254